CW00536841

FROM A CAT'S VIEW

AN ANTHOLOGY OF STORIES TOLD BY CATS

Edited by Robin Praytor

 **POST-TO-PRINT PUBLISHERS, LLC**
PHOENIX

Robin Praytor/Post-To-Print Publishers
Phoenix
post-to-print.com

Publisher's Note: This is a work of fiction. Names, characters, places, and incidents are a product of the authors' imaginations. Locales and public names are sometimes used for atmospheric purposes. Any resemblance to actual people, living or dead, or to businesses, companies, events, institutions, or locales is completely coincidental.

From a Cat's View/ Robin Praytor – 1st ed.
E-book: ISBN 978-0-9984685-4-9
Trade Paperback: ISBN 978-0-9984685-5-6

Time spent with cats is never wasted.
— Sigmund Freud

CONTENTS

FOREWORD

Our best lives are lived when we allow ourselves to view the world through differing perspectives. Robin Praytor and her cadre of talented authors provide a glimpse through one such perspective—that of a cat. With tales of joy, sadness, mystery, and suspense, each story will have you turning the page to see what comes next.

Reading gives us the chance to learn new things, or it can whisk us away to places where we can forget the persistent drumbeat of everyday life. *From a Cat's View* offers the reader both: It teaches us compassion for our four-legged feline friends by letting us see things from their unique perspective while entertaining us with a mixed genre of short stories and poems.

Prepare to be transported into the realm in which cats live, to have your heartstrings tugged, and above all, be ready to live your best life as you add a new view of the world to your repertoire.

Kara Piazza
President
Writing Piazza Press

DAVID CHORLTON

TWO HOURS

A moment's panic. I escaped.
I glimpsed the open door
and ran. Eight months at a new address
and never been outside. Too many
coyotes down at night
from the mountain. Where to run
after I jump onto and over
the wall, into the wide
open wash with no way
for anyone to know which direction?
Twelve years old
and never seen a quail
until now, but it's almost dusk
and too late to chase them. So what
options do I have?
The neighbors remember
what happened before. They're out
with their flashlights
trying to sweep the darkness aside.
Finally, I'm still
and crouched in a corner
with beams of light reflecting
from my eyes. They're closing in, about
to grab and deliver me
back home, to the safety
freedom doesn't know.

An artist and poet, David Chorlton was born in Austria and grew up in Manchester, close to the northern English industrial zone. In his early twenties, he went to live in Vienna and from there made many trips around Europe to enjoy and paint its landscapes and towns. Since moving with his wife to Phoenix in 1978, he has grown ever more fascinated by the desert, its wildlife, and the mountain ranges of southern Arizona. The region is a frequent subject of his poetry. To learn more about this talented author and artist, visit his website, davidchorlton.mysite.com.

Editor's note: In addition to the poem, *Two Hours*, the cover art for *From A Cat's View* and the sketches displayed throughout the anthology, are David Chorlton's creations.

THE CEMETERY CAT

Night crept into the cemetery earlier than in the rest of town, and dawn came later than usual.

Perhaps the mountains to either side snatched up the sun in late afternoon and held it ransom until long after breakfast. Or maybe Nature, lover of all things atmospheric, decided a glorified skeleton farm was too unsettling a place on which to bestow so many hours of daylight. Gothic iron fences and chipped granite angels looked best in twilight, after all, especially when the fog blew in from the river to wind around the gravestones like tulle.

Whatever the reason, geology or spookiness, cemetery nights were longer, and people avoided cemeteries at night. As if ghosts and ghoulies only worked the late shift, and the daylight would protect them from invisible echoes of the past and the dark things that hovered at the corners of their eyes.

Nonsense. It was the same superstitious thinking that made otherwise rational people toss spilt salt over their shoulder and say their prayers at night. But if they believed the nonsense protected them—and kept them from admitting they were nothing but helpless specks of carbon and water floating in an infinite void of evil that wanted to steal their souls and wear their faces like Halloween masks—so what? If a little nonsense keeps society from falling apart, more power to them.

But cats know better.

Cats can see the orbs and specters, and apparitions, and other unfathomably horrible things that humans can't see. Cats see beyond the realm of the living, past the curtain where the levers and cogs of the universe operate, and understand that they, like humans, are just specks in a void. But cat specks get fed milk and are given little bits of string to play with, so they are okay with the occasional demons or poltergeists so long as the spirits stay more or less in their place.

Which is why, in the cemetery of nearly perpetual night, there were cats to keep the ghosts and demons at bay. One cat for each grave—three-hundred forty-seven in all—some of them feral and some pampered pets who snuck off to purr at ghosts when their humans went to work.

Their leader was a sleek, black shorthair named Pawdrey Hepburn (because people are cruel like that). Pawdrey had long since graduated from chasing orbs, those irritating little bits of energy that buzzed around fresh graves. She'd outlived all the toms and queens before her. And probably even outlived the old woman who had named her Pawdrey Hepburn, though she'd not been home in years to find out and had no desire to go back.

Because of her age, and the wisdom that came with it, she'd earned the right to live out the rest of her life from a place of honor. The tall gravestone was still warm from its scant hours of sunlight and radiated heat like only a nice lap can. To Pawdrey's knowledge, its occupant, one Myron Farnborough 1900-1976, had never tried to escape to the world of the living, and that made his stone the perfect place to nap, cozy and undisturbed.

Pawdrey lounged on Myron's gravestone while the other cats dealt with ghosts that weren't so well-behaved. Her paws hung off either side, and her cheek rested in a groove worn into the granite. There she intended to stay until morning, or quite possibly until the end of time. It was just *that* good of a napping spot. Then the humans came.

The iron gate opened with a groan of protest, and three flashlight beams swept through the darkness. Dozens of glowing eyes glared back from behind headstones, and spirits rumbled beneath the freshest graves. *The nerve of people.* Probably searching for a lost cat, not even bothering to consider that maybe the cat wasn't lost at all, that maybe it had realized its purpose was more than lounging around the house or bringing gifts of dead birds to ungrateful humans.

It was probably a new "Fluffy."

Twenty of the cemetery cats were named Fluffy — the result of a severe lack of creativity in the brains of the two-legged. The Fluffies patrolled the mausoleum together. Being trapped behind walls did ugly things to a ghost's psyche, as did knowing that the human who claimed to love you had put all of two seconds into choosing your name, so the cats named Fluffy could relate to mausoleum ghosts.

Still, it was better than being called Pawdrey Hepburn.

Pawdrey lifted her head and watched the humans stumble their way through the cemetery. One of them, a scrawny little male, held a camera. A female wore headphones and carried something tantalizingly fuzzy on a stick. If Pawdrey had been a younger cat, that fuzzy thing would have been hers by now. The third walked with an arrogance, likely unearned, his hat turned backwards and his weaselly face so smug that he must have been a Siamese in his last life. That one, the one who fancied himself the leader, carried a wooden board in his hand.

Pawdrey sat up. *Oh*, hell *no*. It was a spirit board. With a sharp howl of warning, Pawdrey scattered the other cats and sent them to guard the most restless spirits, those likely to be stirred into reanimation by foolish humans and their insatiable curiosity. If only one ghost left the door to the other side open, the demons would enter. She leapt from Myron's headstone and crossed the humans' path, hissing and arching her back for maximum ferocity. For better or worse, humans were superstitious about black cats, as well. But not, it seemed, these humans.

"Nice kitty," the female said, her hand brushing the top of Pawdrey's head as they walked by.

Pawdrey narrowed her eyes. It took balls to walk into a cemetery at night and condescend to its queen ghoster. Clearly these people hadn't been neutered.

With no consideration for the ghosts sleeping underfoot, the scrawny human shouted, "There it is!"

The humans headed for Myron's grave and began setting up their equipment. Pawdrey ran after them, hissing and spitting and clawing at their ankles. Not Myron; anyone but Myron. Pawdrey wasn't about to lose her prime napping spot because of a few nosy humans who couldn't let things be.

"Rolling," said the scrawny one, pointing his camera at the smug one, whom Pawdrey was certain exemplified what some humans called a "douchebag."

"Welcome back to *Treasures of the Dead*. We're standing on the grave of coal magnate Myron Farnborough, rumored—*ow!*"

Pawdrey calmly licked the blood from her claws.

"I got it," said the female, scooping up Pawdrey with her free hand. Pawdrey fought and yowled her way back to the ground before leaping menacingly onto the headstone. "You need a band-aid, Chad?"

Chad—of course his name was Chad—checked his ankle and shook his head. "Just a little scratch." He looked at Pawdrey and took a step to one side and then continued his commentary. "We've found the grave of Myron Farnborough, a twentieth-century coal magnate, whose fortune—including what was stolen from his partner, Edgar Zane,—is said to have been buried somewhere in town. Many have searched in vain, but none have asked the man himself." On that ominous note, he knelt in front of the spirit board that he'd placed atop Myron's grave.

Pawdrey felt Myron stir as Chad muttered pseudo-Latin nonsense. Whether it was a conjuring spell or not, the intention was clear, and Myron had gone too long deprived of human contact to let it pass without a response.

Pawdrey purred as loudly as she could and rubbed her face on the gravestone to calm the agitated ghost.

"Myron Farnborough," Chad intoned, "are you present?"

The triangular planchette rattled on the spirit board.

"Dude," the cameraman whispered.

"You're not doing that, Chad?" the female asked. The microphone she held drooped as she bent forward to study the board.

"No, I'm n—hey, can someone shut that cat up?"

With the spirit growing restless, Pawdrey abandoned her purring and resorted instead to yowling at the top of her lungs. Her warbling shriek sliced through the night and rattled spines. A cry that, once upon a time, would have inspired tales of banshees and forever labeled entire stretches of forest as cursed by a mournful enchantress.

On that night, though, it was a rallying cry.

Eyes appeared from behind gravestones and between the old oaks that grew in the back of the cemetery. The cats came in droves: the nameless feral ones who guarded the unlabeled paupers' graves. The pampered Lady and Checkers and Marmalade with their rhinestone collars and jingle bells that rang out like hailstones with every step. The old, master ghosters and the newly weaned orb-catcher kittens. And all twenty of the mausoleum Fluffies. They ran *en masse*, their bodies vibrating with purrs, to congregate at the grave of Myron Farnborough and soothe his way back to eternal slumber.

The humans watched in alarm as the cats gathered.

"What are the cats doing?"

"Dude, this is weird."

"Are you *getting* this?"

Myron's ghost continued to push through the barrier between worlds. Humans are a social species, a fact that is not erased by something as insignificant as death. After so many years in the isolation of the afterlife, another human was trying to communicate with him. No number of cats could have stopped him from answering.

A ghostly hand broke through the veil between worlds, clawing up from the ground like something out of a zombie movie. The humans saw nothing. For them, spirits existed as distorted sounds and cheap visual effects on trashy television shows. It never occurred to them to look for the shimmer between air molecules, or to listen for the echo of breaths no one was taking.

But the cats ... ah, the cats could see Myron, clear as if he were flesh and blood standing before them. He was handsome,

Pawdrey thought; the human equivalent of an old tuxedo tom who'd been in one too many fights but still held his tail high with dignity. He was dressed in a good suit and a bowler hat and carried a cane topped with the silver head of a cat. Oh, yes. Getting handsomer by the minute. Pawdrey knew she'd liked him, and not just because his gravestone was the tallest and best for napping. He had once been a fan of cats.

Myron glanced around in a daze for a few moments before his eyes locked onto the three humans still trying to communicate via the spirit board.

"I'm here," he announced. "What do you want?"

"Jeez, Mike, did you spill catnip or something? What are they doing?" Chad's alarm turned to fear.

"Hello?" Myron reached out and tapped the cameraman on the shoulder.

Mike jumped like he'd gotten his tail bit by a rocking chair and swung his camera around. "Something touched me!"

"Was it a cat—"

"It wasn't a cat, Cheri! I know what a cat feels like! This was cold!"

Myron tried again, touching Chad this time, and the scene devolved further into chaos. The humans shrieked and swore as hundreds of cats howled for Myron to return to the grave, and Myron's frustration grew until, quite unaware of his deceased state, he began demanding the "ungrateful twerps" acknowledge his existence.

The humans gathered their equipment and ran. When they got home and set about editing their footage, they might have detected a flicker of light around the grave. They would undoubtedly post the video online and claim they'd made contact with Myron Farnborough, never knowing that their claim was true or that the flicker of light was not Myron Farnborough but something far more sinister.

Only Pawdrey Hepburn, too old to bother getting caught up in the panic, was calm and perceptive enough to notice the other spirits creeping out of the doorway Myron had opened.

—◻—

Pawdrey hadn't left the cemetery in years, not since her human companion was taken away in that awful van with the siren and flashing lights. The cats, and their ghosts, were supposed to stay behind the cemetery fence. But Myron ruined that, he and all the little demons he'd let out from the afterlife. They tasted like dust, the demons. Like old mothballs and dreams that never came true. But they made delightful little squeals when Pawdrey bit down on them, which made the task of hunting them far more satisfying.

Mice were good at getting into little holes where a cat's paw couldn't hope to reach. But demons could move like smoke, curling and twirling through screen doors and through the tiniest cracks in foundations, to invade the lives of humans and cause mischief. When demons found their way into a house without a pet door or an open window, the cemetery cats were forced to use other means of ingress. They mussed their fur and crept low and scared up to the door, and then meowed their most pitiful meows. The proper term for what humans call "adopting a stray cat" is "inviting a con-artist into your home." If a cat allows itself to be taken off the street and fed kibble while wearing a collar that reads, "Mr. Tinkles," you can be sure that cat has ulterior motives.

Pawdrey watched as cat after cat chased orbs and smoke into houses; the toms and queens, the feral kittens, Cleopatra and Whiskers, and all the Fluffies. And she watched when none of them came back out. Perhaps the draw of a warm lap and a ray of sunshine was too much for them. Perhaps they had never known the pain of losing a beloved human. Well, *she* wouldn't fall for the lure of soft blankets and chin *scritchies*. Not again.

She followed Myron, butting his leg as he drifted bewildered through the town. How everything must have changed since his death. The people he knew aging and dying, buildings being built and painted. Was it even recognizable? Perhaps so—it dawned on Pawdrey what he was doing. Assuming the twerps from the cemetery were telling the truth, Myron had a stolen fortune buried somewhere in town. That kind of unfinished business was catnip to ghosts. Poor Myron must have been waiting in the afterlife for years, hoping for a ritual or a wayward spell to strengthen him and give him that little nudge out of the grave.

Pawdrey regarded the ghost with pity. Cats don't have unfinished business. If they die without catching a certain mouse, then they were never meant to catch that mouse. This is one reason why no one sees the ghosts of cats. And yet Pawdrey couldn't help but recognize something in Myron's face, an eternal sadness she couldn't place, like there was something she should have done differently. A wrong she should have set right long ago.

She stopped in front of a familiar house. Myron kept walking.

It was a little house. A cottage really, white with blue trim. In contrast with the cemetery that always seemed dark, every window in the cottage drew in the sun. And there were always mice in its walls, and a nice lap, and a can of tuna.... Until there wasn't. Pawdrey didn't need to look in the windows to know the old woman wasn't there. Too many toys in the yard and too few flowers. She followed after Myron.

—▫—

It took hours of aimless wandering, but Myron finally found a tree that he seemed to recognize. There he stood, clawing at the bark with his ghostly hands, unaware that he wasn't strong enough to interact with the real world.

With an irritated twitch of her tail, Pawdrey climbed. Her joints ached and yowled; she hadn't climbed a tree since ... well, since she'd watched the flashing lights take the old woman. Maybe she should have gone back to the house after that, seen if the woman survived. She'd never found the woman's name on any of the gravestones, but that meant nothing. Humans didn't always bury their dead. Still, the woman had been good to her.

Pawdrey found a miniscule knothole in the tree, so small that no human had bothered to look inside for the past forty years. In the knot was a small glass bottle with a piece of paper rolled up inside. She looked at Myron inquisitively. His face lit up, and she pawed until the bottle came loose and tumbled to the ground. Her landing was less graceful than she'd have liked and sent jolts of pain up her back legs. These were not the problems of a young cat. Hiding her discomfort, Pawdrey picked up the bottle and gave a muffled meow. After a moment of confusion, Myron shuffled off again, following some instinct only he understood.

They stopped at a large brick building, the sign out front proclaiming it "Whispering Oaks Senior Living." Ah. It was coming together now. Myron stole from his partner, buried the fortune, and hid a note or a map in the tree. And Myron regretted it and wanted to give Edgar the money. If Myron was old when he died, Pawdrey figured Edgar Zane must have been ancient by now. She purred her compliment; how smart of Myron to know where they put old humans when they couldn't live on their own anymore.

She followed Myron up the ramp and summoned all her charm, smoothing her ragged fur, and curled her tail around her feet just so. She meowed, sweetly at first, then louder and more demanding, until the door finally opened. Pawdrey went in without waiting for an invitation and let Myron lead her to a frail-looking man in a rocker. He glanced up as Myron approached as if sensing his old partner's presence. Pawdrey jumped into his lap, her hips and knees protesting, and dropped the bottle in Edgar's hand. She gave Myron a narrowed glare, the one that made even the most disobedient kittens take notice, and he dissolved into nothingness.

About time, Pawdrey thought, and left Edgar to head back to the cemetery. With the others choosing to stay with the humans, she would be the only cat keeping the spirits at bay. It would be a lonely life, but who needed company anyway? On her way out, she passed a room and stopped in her tracks.

The door was ajar, and a woman lay in bed with tubes connecting her to gently beeping machines. She didn't smell like Pawdrey's woman; she lacked the aroma of coffee and soil and that awful perfume. But it was her. Pawdrey knew it deep in her heart.

Pawdrey poked her head into the room and meowed softly. Would she be mad that Pawdrey hadn't looked for her?

Helen stirred and turned her head. She squinted, perhaps too tired to reach for her bifocals, and a small smile crept across her face. "Well, if it isn't Pawdrey Hepburn," she whispered.

Pawdrey hesitated. Helen's spirit was already preparing to leave, and she wasn't sure she could stand to say goodbye after all the years and then finding her again. It was easier to think Helen had never missed her, and to pretend humans weren't worth her time, and that it hadn't hurt to lose one.

But no warm headstone could ever compare to a good lap.

Pawdrey ran and leapt onto the bed, enjoying a brief moment of feeling like the lithe kitten she'd been when Helen found her. She snuggled into the best lap there was. Pawdrey and Helen napped in a sunbeam. Somewhere in her heart, Pawdrey knew it was the last time, and she purred extra hard to calm Helen's spirit. The cemetery could take care of itself for a little while.

ABOUT THE AUTHOR

Jennifer Lee Rossman

"I'm that nerd who can recite the periodic table backwards, talk about dinosaurs for hours, and has a betta fish named, Fincess Leia."

Jennifer Lee Rossman is a science fiction geek from Oneonta, New York, where she cross-stitches, watches *Doctor Who*, and threatens to run over people with her wheelchair. Her work has been featured in multiple anthologies, and her time travel novella, *Anachronism*, was published in May, 2018. Her debut full-length novel, *Jack Jetstark's Intergalactic Freakshow*, is scheduled for publication by World Weaver Press in 2019.

Blogsite: http://jenniferleerossman.blogspot.com
Twitter: @JenLRossman
Facebook: @JenniferLeeRossman
For Amazon and Goodreads, search: Jennifer Lee Rossman

SPECIAL

"Ya come for Maxie?"

My mate Leo and I jerked to a stop and slipped on the ice that frosted the cracked asphalt of the alley. I spotted Alyssa first, having learned to search the darker nooks and crannies where she lurked. She'd mastered the skill of just sitting, a shadow in the shadows, scaring passersby with her menacing whisper.

"Tha's why yo' here, right? Good ol' Max?"

"Yes, Alyssa." I settled myself. Leo shifted close beside me.

A burst of frigid December wind blew through the alley and whipped up bits of ratty paper and grit. Flakes of snow swept in as well — reminders of the approaching storm. Tucked in the shadowy nook of a window, its glass long broken, Alyssa showed no signs of noticing. I felt Leo's shiver, though, and I'm sure he felt mine. We huddled closer. "We've come for Max. He can't stay here. You know that," I said.

Alyssa glared down at us; her hooded, vibrant green eyes narrowed. "I can take care o' him, if you jus' gimme the chance." She shifted position and made ready to melt into the darkness behind the window. "If someone jus' gimme a chance."

"Your mother disagrees, Alyssa. We've discussed this." I blinked a large flake from my eyelash. "The street's *your* home, not Max's."

Ever the older, wiser one, Alyssa sincerely wanted to take her sibling under her wing. Had the situation been different, she might have done a decent enough job of it, too. I felt bad denying her a chance to make something of herself and give her life meaning. But Leo, and Max's mother, Charlene, and I, felt Max was too.... That Max deserved more of a chance.

"He nothin' special," she hissed. "We all the same here. Gutter kind, survivin' bes' we can. Why he get any better?"

"You only have to look at him to see why."

I'd never much liked Alyssa. She regarded me likewise. We remained cordial during my visits with my sister, Charlene, and her children—I couldn't have any of my own and reveled in being the doting aunt. I'd made as much progress with Alyssa as I ever would. It stung; my mere presence here a reminder of the gulf between us, never to be bridged. But I had to come since Charlene couldn't come to me. This bothered Alyssa even more, as though I was responsible and came by to rub it in. Our lives turned on a matter of fate. Alyssa would never understand or find peace. Fate had shaken and stomped her with the rest of my family.

And with Max about to disappear from her life, she hated Fate even more.

"I jus' as deservin'," she hissed. "I help out, keep the family goin'. Where my chance?"

We stared at each other for a long moment. I knew then this would be my final visit to the neighborhood. "I'm sorry, Alyssa. This is just ... how things turned out." I shrugged. "We all do our best. It's all we *can* do. And where Max is concerned, this is how I'm doing my best for him."

Alyssa shifted again, then slid deeper into the shadows until all that remained was a faint outline of her face, her eyes glowing. "He nothin' special, jus' one o' us. You no right to take him away." She glared down, her gaze hot. "You leave with Max, Aun' Po, don' ever show yo' face here no mo'." And with that final warning, she disappeared.

I never saw her again.

—◻—

Charlene lay on her mat, as deep in the basement from the cold winter air as she could go. By good fortune for once, pipes radiating generous heat crisscrossed the ceiling. I imagined it'd make the nights, maybe the entire winter, comfortable, assuming one enjoyed good health.

Which Charlene did not.

Whatever she'd caught earlier this fall had taken its toll. She couldn't eat anymore or keep down what little she did nibble. The 'munity-attacking virus, as Leo called it, left her wasted, all skin and bone now, ribs and pelvis showing. Her breathing came in ragged gasps; a slickness coated her nostrils. Though she turned her face as I approached, I felt certain she couldn't see me, not through the glaze over her eyes. But she could still smile. "Posie! Good o' ya ta come," she wheezed, almost purr-like.

I settled by the edge of her mat and tried to be strong. Leo stayed back by the basement entrance, watching for Alyssa. I understood his reluctance to be so close. His mother had suffered a similar wasting away. The smell alone kept strangers back. "Easy, Char. Don't exert yourself. Just rest."

"I have time 'nough for that soon," Char said, though she relaxed back onto her frayed, rumpled grey mat. "And thankfo' fo' it all I be."

"Me, too. I hate this. I do." I'd had time to adjust to seeing Char like this. Still, my sorrow threatened to engulf me. The tears wanted to come. I wanted to let them. But I had one final duty to perform for my dear, dying sister. I had to stay strong one final evening.

"Max?" Char asked, her voice faint. I imagined it preceding her into her long night.

"Tonight. Leo has it all planned. He believes it'll work, that we'll find Max the home he deserves. I trust him."

Char didn't reply, merely closed her eyes and released a long breath, her ribcage collapsing further. I froze. *Not now! Not yet! I need to say goodbye!* At last Char shifted, took a healthy breath, and seemed, in that moment, content. The cold that had gripped me, though, held on. The pipes offered no warmth against such chill.

"I don't want to say this, Char, but we both know.... If I wait...." I clenched my jaw against the rush of emotion.

Char opened an eye, glanced lazily in my direction. "I know. Ya a good sister, Po, comin' by all these years, when ya din' have ta." She took another slow, filling breath. "Never did tol' ya how much I 'preciated it."

I could only bob my head in a parody of a nod. If I tried to speak, I couldn't be sure how I'd sound. But I had to say the words.

"Kids really liked havin' ya 'round, too," Char added. "Well, 'cept for Lyssa, a'course." Her eyes closed, and she adjusted her head on the mat. "Never could account fo' that, I guess."

"It's all right," I said in the silence that followed. "Alyssa and I exchanged goodbyes coming in. She'll be happy to not see me again, I think."

Char managed a weak laugh. "Ya more'n her, I 'magine."

I laughed in turn. "I think so, yes."

At that, neither of us could find words. In the darkness behind me, a machine kicked on, loud and grinding for a moment before quieting to a steady throb. I imagined that, too, might provide comfort during the cold dreary months ahead for someone fortunate to discover this basement nook. When the time came, it wouldn't hurt Charlene to ride the soothing throb away....

"Char, I love you," I blurted then, as part of the dam inside me weakened. Not broke–couldn't let that happen. Maybe tonight, after we saw Max home. Good night for it, too: cold, bitter winds throwing harsh flakes all about, much like the way Fate threw Charlene and I down our different paths. "And I'm sorry for all this. I am. I never meant to end up so happy. It just happened."

My sister lay still for a long moment, her ribs rising and sinking. Then she cracked her eye open again, and this time I knew, through the glaze, she saw me—really saw me. "S'all right, Posie. Never blamed ya fo' it all. Not once," she said. "Glad ta have it happen, too." She managed a smile with the upper half of her mouth. "Had me a good life. Good bunch o' kids. Friends. A warm place ta rest." She sighed, closed her eye.

"S'all right. S'all right."

I shook with emotion, knowing that eye would never open again. I reached out, touched her exhausted body, and felt her feeble gasps. "I'll take care of Max," I whispered. "I promise. I'll make you proud."

Her smile broadened, just a hair, but enough for me to tell she'd heard.

I left my dying sister alone in the dark with her comfortable mat, a crisscrossing of warm pipes, and the gentle throb to keep her company. Leo led me out of the basement, up toward the street where we'd find Max. I felt no urge to look back. Once we'd left with Max, I'd be done with this horrible place forever.

—□—

We found Max at his perch on a nearby banister, mesmerized as usual by the traffic. He made sure to stay unnoticed, out of the way—a gift of awareness from Alyssa. He hadn't been keeping clean. I didn't think it would matter this evening, but another day or two and our plans might have fallen through.

The approaching storm threw more wind and snow at us. It forced our hand. In a way, I was glad. No matter how, this ended tonight.

"Uncle Leo, Aun' Po!" Max saw us approach, dropped from his perch, and rushed over. "Guess how many limos I counted already today! Six! Can ya believe it?"

"Wow, Max, that's a lot for sure." I gave his chin a playful nudge. We stayed clear of the steady pedestrian traffic along the sidewalk. Charlene may not have lived in an affluent part of the city, but it was busy and noisy. "Where do you think they're all going?"

"No ideas, Aun' Po, but I'm sure it's ta somewhere neat!"

A low rumbling from the street drew Max's attention. A large truck, radiating a potent stench even over the steady wind, rolled to an idle at the nearby corner. More than a few pedestrians gave it a wide berth on their way by. Max took a step toward it, intent on the letters decorating its side.

"D–Dar–by... Darby's Santitetion!" he exclaimed after a moment. He turned back with a wide smile. "It say Darby's Santitetion!"

I pretended to look. "I think it does, Max, I think it does." Unable to read myself, I gave him the benefit of the doubt; I was pretty sure it was pronounced 'sanitation,' though. Then a push of wind blew a stream of snowflakes into my face. I turned my head.

"Wow! Windy!" Max laughed. "Lots o' snow tonight, huh, Uncle Leo?"

"You betcha, Max," Leo replied, loud enough to be heard over the bustle. "A lot of snow."

I looked back at Max. "You know your momma's sick?"

His playful mood darkened. "Yeah. Lyssa says I'm not supposed ta go down and bother her. Made me say goodbye."

I moved close, nudged him again. "That's good, Max. Your mom, she's not doing well. She'll probably pass away tonight. Do you understand what that means?"

Max looked down at the sidewalk—now dressed in a dusting of snow—and nodded. "Mom tol' me it all. We spent all last night talkin'. Tol' me to be 'specting you, too." He looked up. "And pass away means gone forever." He stared at me for a moment, then dropped his gaze again. "And maybe that be good fo' her."

"I think so, too," I said. My breath hitched. For one so young, Max seemed aware of an awful lot he shouldn't need to know. I suspected Alyssa's involvement in this but found I couldn't fault her. After a moment, I raised my head and gave him another nudge. I may not have been able to read, but like Leo I could tell time, and a glimpse through the traffic at the clock in the shop window across the street told me the afternoon was passing. "Anyway, we've got to go now, Max."

Max looked up, out at the traffic, then back at Leo and me. "Lyssa say ya want to take me away. Said it was 'cause I was special. She say I could stay if I want."

Now that, I *could* fault Alyssa for. "Yes, yes you can. But that's not what your mother wanted. You *are* special, Max. Your mom hoped for more for you, as do Leo and I. So we're ready to bring you to a better life. Right now. If that's what you want."

The traffic reclaimed Max's attention. "Why can't Lyssa come?" he asked after another truck rumbled by. Another two minutes had passed. The wind kicked up again, blowing a wave of flakes over the streets, the sidewalks, and us. I realized then the passing cars and trucks had their lights on, and the streetlamps were lit. Overhead, the thickened clouds brought a late afternoon gloom. Night would fall soon, whether the clocks spoke of such time or not.

"Alyssa belongs here. She's adapted to survive here. You have not. And you will not." I glanced nervously at the passing foot traffic, worried we were staying in one place too long. We would be noticed, especially Max, and urged to move along, maybe nicely, maybe not so nicely. I saw Leo was growing anxious, as well. "More important, Max, you don't belong here. You belong in a better place."

"But why? Why me? Why not Lyssa?"

I glanced out at the street, where another truck rumbled by amidst the honk of horns, throb of engines, and swish-swush of windshield wipers. "Because ... because of Darby's Santitetion. Wellson's Flowers. Harrel's Barber Shop. All the other words too. No one so young as you can read, Max, and you do it so well. That's a gift; a beautiful gift. This place here is not good for that." I paused. "This place ... suffocates gifts like that."

"Benji can read, too, but he ain't goin' nowhere."

"I don't know who Benji is, but I'm sure he'd want this for you. Max, I don't mean to force it on you, but you *have* to decide. We need to leave soon if we're to make this work."

"Real soon," Leo said, "Like, right now soon, please." Leo had made all the plans and knew what needed to be done.

I said, "So, Max, okay, we need to go now. This is scary, and it's a lot to take in. But you're growing up so fast, Max. You know something of what I'm telling you now—that you're special. You have to decide."

Max grunted. "I don't know, Aun' Po. I don't know what ta do."

Another gust of wind blew the snow gathering at our feet across the sidewalk and pushed another dusting in its place. "Your mother would want you to come with us. I want you to come. Leo wants you to come. It'll be hard leaving, but it's for the absolute best."

Max glanced up at me, at Leo, back at the traffic, then down at his feet. "All right. Mom say that, too."

"You won't regret this, Max. I promise!"

—▭—

Leo set a hard pace. "We're a little late," he admitted in a low voice when we paused for the first time, a few blocks down from Max's neighborhood. "The timing has to be just right, or it won't work."

We waited at a crosswalk. Pedestrians clustered along the curb, hunched against the growing cold. "Will we make it?" I asked, my voice equally low. "We're still a long way off."

I glanced back at Max, who was close to the brick wall of a corner store, still watching the cars, trucks, and even bicycles roll by. The tide seemed non-stop, noisy, and grinding. Though the wind had eased somewhat, the fall of wet, sticky flakes ticked up. The dusting over the sidewalk had doubled. Afternoon deepened into evening with each passing moment.

"We have to hurry, and need some good traffic."

By *good* Leo meant light, which also meant we'd have to cross more than a few streets. Having done it so often, I didn't mind much, and Leo knew best when to brave the asphalt. Max, though, was easily distracted. I could picture him stopping in the middle of the street to look at something heavy and loud barreling toward him. I shivered.

The weight of what we were doing crashed over me. Our destination seemed so far and the obstacles too many. Even the weather conspired against us. "Oh, god, Leo, can we do this?"

Leo smiled. "Yes, Po," he said with confidence. "Yes."

The weight didn't leave me entirely. But Leo's calm gave me hope. *No matter how, this ends tonight.*

Max came to a stop beside me. "This a cool neighborhood. Smells really good!" he said, raising his nose into the breeze.

I gave him a friendly nudge. "It is a nice place, Max, but we're not stopping. We've got a long way to go, and you must work hard to keep up. Can you do that for me, Max? Forget the traffic for a while and just keep along?"

Max smiled and nodded. "Sure, Aun' Po!"

"Max! This is important! You agreed to come. There's no turning back now, so you have to keep up. You *have* to."

His smile disappeared. "Sh–sure, Aun' Po."

Leo said, "Okay, we've got the green."

We joined the group crossing the street and hurried along. Max bravely kept up. Leo stuck close to the buildings and away from the heavier traffic near the street, which helped. We stayed along the main thoroughfare for several blocks, and for a long while, the flow of traffic moved in our favor. The weight on me lightened a tiny bit more.

From time to time, Max lingered, gawking at this or transfixed by that. Sharp words brought him back, and he caught up. But I could tell our pace, block by block, was wearing him down. None of us were used to this pace, and the cold sapped our strength even further.

We made better time sneaking through alleys and cutting across parking lots, finding paths free of the shuffling crowds. In the tighter spaces we faced swirling winds and accumulating drifts, and icy patches tripped our steps. Leo let us catch our breath at just the right times, and every so often the traffic forced a long halt to our progress. But we covered a lot of ground. We made up a lot of lost time.

Our breaths puffed hard when Leo crouched to a stop at an alley entrance, his gaze intent on the expansive hotel entry across the street. "We're all right. Whew!" he said, panting. "We wait now. Shouldn't be too long."

I crouched down a step behind him, Max by my side. "Okay, honey, catch your breath," I told the youngster. "We've just a little bit left to go. We'll continue on in a moment. You did well."

"Okay, Aun' Po," Max replied between gasps. "Wow. Never been this far before. Look at those cars!"

I glanced out of the alley, through the steady snowfall, and at the busy street beyond. The wind had died, but night had arrived early. Lights from the buildings around us, and from the cars and streetlamps, fought with the darkness. The stalemate proved welcome.

Max was right—the cars here seemed longer and gleamed brighter, even in the darkened sky. The people smiled, cheerful despite the gloom. Dressed for the weather, they appeared happy as they hurried about.

"Nice, huh?"

"Never saw cars like this at home! Wow! Look at tha' stretch limo!"

I smiled at the gleaming black sign of luxury that pulled to a stop in the circular hotel entrance across the street. Only then did I realize Leo had moved from the alley to the sidewalk curb several feet away. He, too, was studying the limo.

After a moment, he jerked his head around. "This is it! Get close."

"Max! Stay close now. This is important." I shouted as I moved to the alley entrance. A quick glance showed Max by my shoulder.

"What? Wha's happening?"

"We're crossing the street here, Max," I said. I eyed the pedestrian traffic, searching for the right moment to join Leo at the curb.

Max huddled close, panting. "Here?"

"Yes. Hurry!"

I darted from the alley and joined Leo. Max followed. A car passed in front of us, achingly close. Slush splashed at our feet. We could still see the limo, though, and the legs of the driver as he stepped from his driver's seat and crossed around in front of his idling vehicle.

"When he opens the passenger door, we go," Leo said.

My heart beat a furious tempo in my chest. Insanity to cross here, in the middle of the street, across two lanes of traffic! In the darkness, the car lights made it difficult to judge distances. The slush at the curbs would make it a tricky start. The swirling snow in the street threatened a slippery cold. The distance across looked reasonable—for a warm summer night. Now it seemed a nightmarish gulf, especially with Max in tow. Max, who had probably never crossed a street at any point but an intersection.

"Aun' Po? We can't cross here! Even Alyssa wouldn't cross here!" he said.

"Max!" I turned back. "It's scary. I'm scared, too, but this is important, Max. It has to be here, okay? You'll understand in time. Follow close." Focusing on the two lanes of traffic, the black limo, and the set of legs, I struggled to catch my breath. The weight returned to crush the air from my lungs. *No matter how....*

"Ready!" Leo shouted. "He's opening the passenger door. Max! Po! Now, now!" And he darted into the street.

Trusting him with my life, I followed.

"Aun' Po!" Max's cry seemed far behind. "Wait!"

This close to the road, the scents proved overwhelming. The asphalt vibrated beneath my feet. The rumbling engines deafened. I sensed movement and froze when Leo froze—twice, both times scaring me to death—yet somehow made sure Max stayed close by. Dark shadows passed agonizingly close in front and overhead. Heat radiated from growling, throbbing car engines, like Char's crisscross of pipes. We dodged wheels ... started ... stopped ... started.

All the while the driver's legs moved along the limo's far side, joined a moment later by a set of lady legs dressed more for a glitzy social occasion than the gathering slush. A second set of legs followed—those of a young girl, her red boots vivid in the dim light. The legs Leo and I and Max—though he didn't know it—were shooting for.

Leo led us beneath the limo's front end. The smells proved even more intense. I barely felt the warmth radiating from the dark, ticking metal above.

"Aun' Po! Wait!" Max cried, falling back. Leo and I moved fast now, with a purpose. We emerged from beneath the limo near the front tire, squeezed through the slush and over the curb, and darted across the hotel entrance.

Max's smaller legs wouldn't let him keep up. Despite his frantic efforts, he would be left behind.

"Aun' Po! Wait!"

Leo led me around the limo driver, the older woman, and the young girl. The two adults gave cries of surprise while the little girl shrieked with laughter.

"Where'd those come from!" the driver shouted.

"Oh! Oh my," the woman said, a touch of frenzy in her voice.

"What the hell?" the doorman coming through the hotel's revolving door cried out.

"Aun' Po!" Max called, further behind now as we ran down the slippery sidewalk and out of his life.

The little girl cried, "Mommy. Look at the kitten."

—◻—

Breathing hard, we watched from a nearby alley. Over the traffic's grumbles and roars, the slap of boots on the sidewalk, and through the shuffling pedestrians we heard and saw everything.

Max had stopped, his eyes wide. He looked ready to dart back beneath the limo. Then the girl reached down and scooped him up.

"Mommy, can we keep it?" she asked, holding Max tight in her mittened grasp. He struggled, his little claws dug into the wool of her mittens, but the girl's hold proved gentle and firm.

"What?" the girl's mother asked, bending over to look at the kitten squirming in her daughter's hands. The limo driver and hotel doorman stepped close, as well.

"Where the bloody hell did that come from?" the doorman asked. He glanced at Max, looked in our direction, then back at Max. "My God, he's got some color on that coat, though."

"Sorry about that, miss," the limo driver muttered. "Want me to get rid of it?"

"He's so orange! Can we keep him?" The daughter squealed. "Can we? Can we?"

The mother studied the squirming Max. I was certain he could see us crouched in the alley entrance, especially after the girl held him up for her mother's closer inspection.

"Careful, dear," she said, "he's got his claws out."

"It's okay, Mommy." The girl giggled. "They tickle!"

"Well, let's have a look. Such beautiful orange fur. Goodness!"

"Can we keep him, Mommy? Please. Can we?"

"Oh, I don't know, dear."

Uncle Leo! Aun' Po! Max cried. "Meeew!"

The girl squealed in delight.

The limo driver jerked back. "Goodness, he's a squawker!"

"He's got some lungs in him, all right," the doorman said. "And that fur. Something special, for sure."

"He is kind of cute," the mother admitted, patting Max on the head.

"Meee-ew!"

"Can we keep him?" The girl's smile was wide and bright in the light of the hotel entrance. "Blaze! I shall name him Blaze."

"Let's get out of the cold first, all right?" the mother said. "I want to see what he looks like in the light." She brought her arm around her daughter's shoulders and aimed her toward the revolving door. The doorman and limo driver remained close by.

"Something special, I might think," the doorman repeated.

"Special," the limo driver agreed.

As a group, they disappeared into the hotel.

—◻—

Leo nudged me with his shoulder. "Let's go."

I stared at the revolving door. "We did it, didn't we?"

"We did. Max is home."

Despite my weariness, my aches and pains, and my fur's heavy wetness, I followed Leo with a bounce in my step. I smiled with him. The weight was gone. "We did it, Char," I whispered. "Max is home. Your special boy is home.

ABOUT THE AUTHOR

Charles Brass

Charles Brass is the pen name of a middle-ager who believes in the maxim, "Write what you want to read!" He enjoys science fiction above all other genres and action-adventure tales most within the SF genre—though space opera and epic tales come a close second. He's not into convoluted explanations of technology or how things work; it's science-fiction! Have fun with it.

Charles served six years in the US Navy right out of high school, where he earned his education and training as a Radiologic Technologist (x-ray tech) and served in Bahrain during the first Gulf War (remember that one?). After leaving the service, he worked as a word processor for a few years (where he learned the joy that is WordPerfect!) before returning full-time to Radiology.

In the decades since, he has obtained his credentials in CT and MRI, and currently works in a small city west of the Minneapolis as a CT/MRI technologist for a local, stand-alone emergency center. With a new bachelor's degree in animation under his belt, his business idea will soon claim a majority of his waking hours. But rest assured, he will find the time to keep writing now that the Muse has struck—even if it means his patients in the ED have to wait a moment or two.

Website: www.seabrassproductions.com
Facebook: @seabrassproductions
For Amazon Author Page Search: Charles Brass

TISHY

When Tishy came barrelling through her cat flap, the warm, sweet smell of butter made her mouth water. Heather was loading the washing machine and Laura, ready for school, sat at the kitchen table buttering a piece of toast.

Tishy jumped straight onto Laura's lap and swatted at the toast, trying to snag it away.

"Get off, you nasty thing ... *my* toast." The room filled with the girl's wails as she held her breakfast high out of Tishy's reach.

Tishy leapt onto the table. She alternated lapping drips of butter from the tabletop and stretching up on her haunches to get to the toast, yowling in frustration. It was unlike Laura to be so stingy.

"Could you turn it down, please? If you want breakfast, Tish, don't stay out marauding all night. And Laura, don't get butter on your cardie, it's running down your arm," Heather admonished them both, reaching for a pair of jeans.

Thwarted, Tish feigned uninterest and licked idly at a butter-stained paw, as she watched Heather fish a wodge of tissues from the jean's pocket.

"I wish you would check your pockets before you put things in the wash."

Laura ignored her mum's scolding. "At least Tish hasn't brought anything back this time. I think it must be boring to have a cat that just brings in half-eaten mice and mangled birds."

It's not like you appreciate my gifts. Tish made another move for the toast, but Laura was waiting for it and snagged it away once more.

"I wouldn't have got a black-and-white cat, if I'd known it had some magpie in its genes. Can you feed her, please?" As she spoke, Heather held up a rose-coloured dressing gown.

Something small and cylindrical slid from its folds unnoticed by the women and rolled under the side of the machine.

"I love cold toast. Thanks, you horrible cat," said Laura, getting up and reaching past her mother for a box of kibble from the cupboard.

Tishy meowed her disapproval; kibble was a poor substitute for creamy butter. She forgot the toast and jumped from the table.

Laura went on. "At least with her practically living across the road, you never have to worry about hiring a cat-sitter."

"Silly, who hires a cat-sitter, anyway? Have you seen her latest contribution? I think she must have pinched it from the museum shop," Heather said.

While Tishy swatted under the washing machine to reach whatever fell, Laura read off an inventory of gifts she'd brought to them, and which almost filled the basket sitting on the dresser.

"It's an odd assortment," Laura said. "Golf balls, bunches of keys, soft toys, baby socks.... None of these rightfully belong to Tishy. And after we return the jewellery, there's nothing of real value."

Tish stopped fishing for the object to consider Laura's words. *What does she mean they don't belong to me? Who brought them to you and laid them at your feet if not me?* In her three years as a member of the Robson family, she'd brought home all sorts of wonderful presents. Laura failed to mention the hearing-aid, the piece of yellow tape marked with human writing, and the sponge cake — which had still been warm. *I should have eaten the cake myself; ungrateful humans. And I would have if I hadn't been so full of cake already.* She especially liked to bring them bright, shiny objects. Overnight visitors to the house often left coins or watches by the bed. And she collected any jewellery that the neighbours so generously left lying about for her. Heather and Laura didn't appreciate her, no matter how hard she worked to please them.

Laura held up a metal buckle from the basket — yesterday's

gift. "This looks a bit retro, but it's not in mint condition, is it?"

"Maybe she dug it up?" Heather offered. "Over the road at the fort. Oh, God. They'll be looking for nighthawks pillaging the site with detectors, and it's our moggy! She'll be on *Crimewatch*, in the Rogues' Gallery!"

Tishy sneezed at that. *Do you think I'm so shoddy as to be caught?* She returned to her hunt for the fallen item.

"It's junk, Mum. Don't worry. They won't want it back. I wouldn't. She probably got it out of next door's bin, like she did that inflatable sheep. Have one of your tranx and chill."

Heather pushed gently at Tishy with her toe. "I don't know what you think you're going to find under the washing machine, but if you get trapped there, you'll have to stay put till I get in from work."

Tishy sneezed again. *Thankless, simple humans. Why do I love them so?* She finally snagged the object with the tip of one claw and pulled it out. *Ah ... that little plastic bit tied to Laura's house keys.* Tish had been chewing at it just the other day — however did it come loose?

—▢—

The workers at the museum across the street grew used to finding Tish on their step when they opened. The building was a speculative replica of the original Roman gatehouse, with a tower at either side and a short passageway where the reception desk stood open to the fort. It housed display cases in the two small rooms on either side and a shop in the middle. The fort itself — now a series of holes in the ground — had been built onto at steady intervals during the centuries after its occupiers left. Unlike the more glamorous sister sites up on the Wall, it did not stand on windswept moorland among majestic crags. Instead, it was just outside the town centre, ringed by terraced houses and around the corner from a chip shop and a newsagent.

Tish was always in evidence at the fort on days when there were school parties carrying packed lunches. Potato chips, especially cheese and onion flavour, went down well. The sausage rolls were worth a nibble, and since schoolchildren were getting more sophisticated all the time, she'd enjoyed her first sample of sushi. The site wasn't thrilling for human visitors, being robbed out over the years, but it was cat heaven. There were ankles to rub, snacks to share, and if it was raining, there were cosy places indoors to lay on and be admired, like on top of display cases under the warm lights. She'd heard the cleaners complain about paw-prints on the glass, but otherwise, she was in her element.

In truth, she was in two elements. Unlike most cats, she'd found the Special Cat Flap. Though it was knowledge suckled in with mother's milk, only a rare few could see it, and fewer still ventured through. Of those, most reserved the special flap for use in their own homes ("How the hell did you get in here?"). And some went through intent only upon finding a better basket in which to nap.

Tishy went through intent on felony.

—□—

Quintus Liberalis wanted his belt buckle back. His slave, Titus, had polished his chain mail, but the buckle to his sword belt was missing. He was due on patrol soon, and it would be no bundle of laughs. Welcome to the Northern Frontier. Expect grey skies and sullen little Brits who spoke in a tongue like a gobful of brambles, and whose hair stuck up in spikes of rust. Worse, they'd knife you in the back for the fun, and that was only the women. He'd experienced rotten food, wine from home that hadn't travelled well (and made him positively seasick), rain that ran down the neck even when you were indoors, and a bitter wind off the river that forever sliced through the fort like a hail of arrows. He suffered the enduring feeling of being trapped at the arse-end of nowhere without the prospect of ever dragging his bones into the warmth and light of home again. If you tried to relieve your feelings by taking a hack at the local scum, you'd have to explain yourself to the commander, as at the moment, they were all technically on the same side. That wouldn't last, of course, it never did.

The local tribes were a cat's cradle of feuds and counter-feuds, grudges, vendettas, resentments, sulks, suspicions, and jealous tantrums. They loathed their occupiers, but they loathed one another more, which explained why they were so easily conquered. Incapable of cooperating with one another for more than half an hour at most, they'd demonstrated their neighbourly ill will over the last hundred years or more, on and off. Even the civilised Roman blood that entered the mix of late was unsuccessful at instilling the locals with common sense or team spirit.

Quintus turned, yelling for his slave to find the sodding buckle—*or get kicked from here to Londinium*—when he saw another face he didn't much like. It was heart-shaped, green-eyed, snub-nosed, and peered in a coy fashion 'round the door of his quarters. He looked about for something to chuck at it. He would drown the little thief in a bucket the first chance he got as soon as he found—

"Did you nick my belt buckle, you misbegotten freak?" It sat just outside the doorway, eyeing him, unruffled, looking nothing like a normal cat—with its big eyes, and no scars or patches of missing fur. Its ribs were not showing and there was something about the way it regarded him that gave him the shivers. It looked ... friendly. Why in the name of the Gods was that? Cats, barbarians, and slaves should cringe before him, not beam at him like an optimistic shopkeeper.

Cats were tolerated—just about—when they slunk around the granary with rats dangling from their jaws. But a cat that would rather frisk about, playing with a purloined sock in the middle of the parade ground, was unprecedented, unnatural. Quintus was sure it had been one of his own socks. He'd have to write to his mother for more. Could it not filch from someone else? It sat there now, washing its paw, pink tongue extended. He hurled a clay cup at its head. The cup broke on the ground, spilling red wine, and the cat disappeared. Cats did that.

—▢—

Tishy had no intention of visiting the granary. Sure, there were big, juicy rats, and she could have sorted them out, no bother. She'd found the hard way, though, that if you take one back through the Special Cat Flap as a present for Laura and Heather, they'd get over-excited and run about screaming and waving their arms. The rat would get away from them, and she'd have to take it under the bed to disembowel it herself. Clearly, they never received proper training in their kittenhoods. Instead, she brought them simpler gifts—ones that didn't move. Slow learners, but she'd make hunters of them yet. In the meantime, here was the funny man in the skirt who liked to play chasing games. Skirts were good; you could curl up on them once you'd worn the person out by biffing objects about.

—▢—

Satisfied, Quintus turned back into the room. The cat sat bolt upright on his bed, purring. Either there were two identical cats hanging about, or he would need to see that quack again for his eyes. The animal was now batting something about with its paw—a small glass phial of some type. He reached for the cylinder, but his hand closed on nothing. The cat looked at him again, just out of throttling range. He snatched another cup, poured a hasty swig of wine, noting the odd taste—*Gods, did someone expect him to drink this bilge?*—and lunged at the cat. It evaporated again. Quintus bellowed. His slave peered 'round the door with rather more anxiety than the cat had shown. Quintus crouched to look under the bed.

"If you let that effing cat in here again, Titus, I'll give your skin to the locals to make their tatty drums with." As he got to his feet, the phial rolled from under the bed. He tried to crush it beneath his foot; instead, it buckled oddly, as though the glass was flexible. Quintus grabbed and shook it, but it was empty. He threw it at the slave, catching him on the temple. Titus yelped and ducked away from the doorway.

Quintus, meanwhile, felt a second's unsteadiness; perhaps the result of getting up too fast. Tiny stars flickered at the corners of his vision. He was getting old. Twenty-seven this year. Gods! Ten years of his life in the legion, rising to the rank of eques, one of the cavalry, and here he was, on a soggy island of halfwits, being taunted by cats and mucked about by recalcitrant slaves. Weak sunlight trickled in through the door, which was a novelty. Patrol. He was going on patrol, with his second-best belt buckle. Outside, he looked about for Titus, who must have sloped off again. The man wasn't as good at vanishing as the cat, but by the look of things, he'd been taking lessons.

Quintus called. There was no reply. Something was different, apart from the shocking sunlight, but he couldn't put his finger on it. He walked across the deserted parade ground. Where was everyone? There were no sweating recruits, no swaggering officers, no toiling slaves unloading supplies brought up the hill from the river. And no mooching barbarian scruffs from the huts outside the gate looking for anything not nailed down with iron rivets. Even the birds were silent. He needed a horse if he was to go on patrol. Where was his horse? Where did you put horses when you weren't sitting on them? He fished about for the word, in the depths of his brain: stables. At that moment he couldn't remember where the stables were. The world was, if not revolving, moving about more than usual. He reached a hand to steady himself against the wall of the barracks, but it felt spongy under his fingertips. He shouted again for someone to bring him a horse. No response. Right, be like that, he'd go on patrol without a horse. He had his sword — his trusted spatha.

He shook his head to clear it, almost falling over. Recovered, he strode into the gatehouse as though wading through water. It didn't smell as sweaty as usual, and he was taken aback to see that the soldier on duty was a young woman. She ignored him as he passed, and instead went on arranging what must be votive offerings in the form of small bears, along the top of a polished counter. Another time he'd have reported her for neglect of duty, but he had his own duties to fulfil.

He made his way outside, observing with approval that the cluster of buildings that made up the oppidum — the straggle of huts where the local riffraff dwelt in cosy squalor — was razed to the ground overnight. Just then, something very large, loud, bright, and fast hurtled by right in front of him. He swayed but kept his balance. A huddle of people he didn't recognise clustered together outside the gatehouse. Oddly, they were all of them looking at hand mirrors.

Six or eight milled about. Many seemed to be women, but they were swaddled in clothing too dense for him to be sure. The large, loud brightness that passed nearby had produced no reaction from them at all. He expected them to quail at the sight of *him* though. Quailing was mandatory. *Quail, or be quelled.* However, the group failed to so much as part before him. No one cringed or even glanced his way. Accustomed to dominating from horseback or on foot, even outnumbered, he was stunned to be blanked. Hated and feared yes, but never *snubbed*.

"Shift your carcasses, you lumps of stinking offal, unless you want me take your heads from your shoulders."

He drew his sword. That got a reaction. Two of the barbarians came to stand on either side of Quintus, one held his hand mirror before him and grinned. The others looked at something behind him. He turned. The wretched cat ran from the gatehouse, its tail raised like a centurion's staff and uttering excited cries. They clustered around the creature, babbling in an unknown dialect. As they stroked the cat, it arched its back and chirruped with pleasure.

A podgy man, bald and wearing baggy grey breeches and a flapping white tunic decorated with lions, stood before Quintus. The man held a hand mirror, as well, and was talking to himself. *He must be mad*, thought Quintus; *he should be in irons*. No one else seemed concerned. Another of the fast, bright things passed in a roar. For a fleeting instance, he saw a face peering out as it shot past. Someone had been captured and trapped inside, by the look of it. Well, they'd have to rescue themselves; he couldn't help. Quintus might have assumed it to be Apollo, manifest in his chariot, had he not been certain in his heart that the Sun God would never deign to appear in these parts.

The unfamiliar sensation of not being in command of his circumstances washed over him. Clubbing the lunatic standing in front of him to the ground to enforce his authority was one option, but the man would then have to be dragged away, and there was no one about who seemed inclined to do that. He would have ordered Titus to do it, had the slave not skived off somewhere. The fat man continued talking to thin air and laughing to himself. With a farewell to the cat, the group strolled away from him, into the gatehouse.

—▫—

Though the tourists had failed to offer her food, Tishy was more than happy. The funny man had somehow gotten through the Special Cat Flap, and here he was, ready for a game.

She rolled on her back, showing her belly, and squirmed at the soldier's feet. He raised his sword and swung at her. Tishy dashed out of reach, then stopped, and glanced flirtatiously back over her shoulder. When Quintus came after her, she shot across the road and dove through the gate.

—▫—

The cat had gone too far now, insulting a representative of the empire. He would enjoy killing it and sticking its little skull on a spike outside his door, the way the barbarians did with their enemies. It ran towards a brick building with two storeys that had somehow escaped Quintus' notice in the three years he'd barracked at the fort. There was no time to wonder about that.

The beast was cornered.

"I've got you now! Prepare to die, you flea-bitten succubus!"

The cat vanished yet again, this time through a panel at the base of the door to the structure. Quintus raised his fist to hammer on the door. If it did not open at once, he'd break it down and drag the cat out by the scruff to face Roman justice. A fresh wave of dizziness overtook him. He leaned forward and closed his aching eyes. Upon opening them he found himself on the inside of the building with no clear memory of crossing the step. Somehow the door must have yielded to him. Perhaps it was opened by an unseen person.

He looked about the room. It smelt strange. The cloying scent caught in his throat. Its walls were white-washed, and the glare hurt his eyes more than the sunlight had done. There were things in the room for which he had no name. A rhythmic throbbing and sloshing came from a crate in the corner. The crate had a porthole made of glass of a thickness he'd never encountered. When he put his hand on it, his fingers merged within. The few things about him that seemed familiar, apart from the hellish cat, which was washing its hindquarters while eyeing him in its usual coy manner, were a wooden table and a brown pottery bowl filled with lemons. The floor was a mosaic patterned black and white but of a substance not stone. He reached to pick up a lemon, hoping to mask the smell in the air. His fingers went through it. He tried again, and found, if he was careful, he could cradle the lemon like an egg in his palms. A peculiar wooden throne with a high back stood behind him. He lowered himself carefully onto it. It supported him, just about, without his sinking through, but it was rather like trying to sit on a hammock. He was more tired than he had ever been. The cat had disappeared again.

A girl entered the room. She was perhaps fourteen or so, he thought, and brown-skinned. Her face was spattered with freckles, and she had frizzled hair, indicating African parentage, but the hair colour was reddish rather than black. No surprise.

The Empire was like that. There were plenty of visitors to the fort who could have been her relatives. The confidence of her bearing nettled him. Her clothes were outlandish: a dark-coloured cape with sleeves and a flimsy kilt wrapped around her thighs, leaving her long, bare legs showing. She walked past him, towards the door, ignoring him. Only inches away, he put out his hand to stop her.

The cat came from under the table. The girl crouched to pet it, looked up, and screamed. She appeared angry. She shouted something he couldn't understand, and a woman ran into the room. The cat disappeared again. The woman wore breeches and something flimsy and patterned with peacocks that left her arms as bare as the young girl's legs. She had fair hair loose to her shoulders, and she was tall, with high cheekbones and a long, straight nose. In other circumstances he would have found her almost attractive, for a barbarian.

The girl shouted. "There was a man! Over there! A centurion!"

"What? Where? A what? How did he get in?"

"A centurion! Sitting at the kitchen table. With a sword!"

"From the fort? Somebody came from the fort? What's Tishy done now? Oh, Lord. Your dad'll want custody, if I have to go to court!"

"They wouldn't send a centurion to arrest a cat. He was sitting right there, and then he vanished. And I'm not living with Dad, not after what he's done."

"Vanished, where? An actual man, like a re-enactor? That kind of centurion?"

Quintus had no notion what they were shrieking about. He understood most of the local dialects enough to order people about — and kill them if they didn't jump to it, smartish-like — but he'd never heard this dialect. He caught a single word in the midst of the verbal deluge and snatched at like a drowning man.

The demon cat poked its head back through the flap by the door, whiskers bristling.

—□—

Tishy was delighted. The chasing game would involve the family and the new friend she'd brought them. Happy day! She'd just have to wind them up a little more. She didn't want to miss this.

"Eques! Ego sum eques!" The man's voice bounced off the glaring white walls.

Both women were staring at him now.

Heather pushed Laura behind her. She yelled back at the man. "Pax! Nil ... d-desperandum! Non illegitimi carborundum!" She'd snatched up two long wooden spoons from the kitchen counter and held them in front of her, crosswise.

Tishy watched. As usual, Heather and Laura didn't seem to appreciate the gift she'd brought them.

"He spoke! He spoke in Roman!" Laura said, coming out from behind her mother. "What was he saying, Mum?"

"I think he said he was a horse."

"Oh ... he's gone again! The salad servers must have scared him off. I never knew you spoke Roman, Mum."

"Latin. I don't, really. I wanted to do metalwork instead." Tishy pranced up to her, but she ignored the cat. "Oh, no, now he's back, look."

"So's Tishy, Mum." Laura collared her.

Tishy wriggled in her arms, fought her way free, and ran out of the room into the hall. As usual, they were very slow at getting the message. You had to keep repeating things until they understood. Daft as kittens, all of them.

Laura followed Tishy into the hall.

"Don't leave me alone with him...." Heather called out. "Oh, he's gone again."

In the hallway, Laura picked Tishy up once more.

"And he's back," Heather said from the kitchen.

Tish jumped from Laura's arms again.

"Gone again," Heather reported. "He keeps flickering on and off like a dodgy lightbulb."

Tishy trailed after Laura when she returned to the kitchen. She bent to pick her up once more, and the centurion reappeared.

"It's the cat!"

"Cattus!"

"Tishy, you little horror!"

The three humans spoke at once.

Tishy gave a self-satisfied mew and snuggled against Laura's shoulder. She'd got through to them, finally. Now they could all have fun together.

—□—

He saw the girl with the cat still struggling in her arms, and the way the older woman's eyes had turned to him once more, as though....

"Cattus!"

Quintus and the older woman stared at each other.

After a pause, she said, "He's quite young, isn't he?"

"Mum, no! For one thing, he's probably buried under the floor, and if you did go on a date, you'd have to take Tishy with you, otherwise you wouldn't be able to see him."

"Laura!"

Quintus wondered why they now shouted at each other, instead of him.

"And I'm not learning Latin. I'd never live it down at school either. Meet my stepdad; he's two thousand years old," Laura whined.

"Who said anything about a date? You're rushing ahead a bit there. He does have long lashes though."

"Mum, I know diversity is your watchword...."

They both turned to stare at him again. Quintus rose to his feet, fingertips sinking into the table top. The floor rocked under his boots, and the mosaic spun before his eyes. His stomach lurched. Through his delirium, he'd spied something across the room.

"Puto ego aerogrum." He walked past the two women to a basket of oddments on a shelf, thinking how sweet they both smelt, and how he'd have wrung that cat's neck if only his hands wouldn't go straight through it. There it was, thank the Gods, something of his in this bizarre world. Cupping his hands, he scooped up the shiny metal buckle. There was a rushing sound like the Tiber in full spate. He wasn't sure if it was his ears, or the rocking white crate in the corner.

"Vale, dominarium!"

He pitched forwards into blackness. Down he went, into the water, drowning, gasping, then struggling upwards, he felt himself carried along by the current.

—□—

"Gone again! No mind, Mum. It would never have worked. What with only one of you having a pulse. Even dad has more going for him," Laura said.

Tishy supposed the funny man had gone back through the Special Cat Flap again, but no matter. It must be about time for a snack. She rubbed against Laura's legs.

—□—

Titus stood by his master's bed. He was in a reflective mood. Half an hour ago when he had been enjoying a rest from Quintus' company—his feet up and a mug of the better wine he kept for these private moments—a young boy had come and tugged at his sleeve. Titus was led out of the fort to where Quintus lay stretched, snoring in a patch of nettles behind the huts. There was drool on his mouth. The folk from the oppidum put a moth-eaten blanket over him and helped the slave carry him back to his quarters, smuggling him into the fort by an entrance known only to barbarians, cats, and slaves. Titus tucked him into bed.

The honey-coloured powder Titus had slipped into Quintus'

wine had a rather mixed result. He'd ground it himself from the little round bits in the strange container the cat had brought him. When he'd first tested it on Quintus, the master fell fast asleep. But he'd too soon awoken. This time it appeared he'd used too much. He must find the right amount to leave Quintus docile and pliant rather than off his face or raving. Sure to be in a foul temper when he woke, Quintus would likely have a raging headache, as well. Titus would be out of range by then.

Looking on the bright side, one day he hoped he'd be able to buy his freedom. The little things he'd squirreled away in a hole under the barracks were mounting into a good-sized nestegg, and the contributions from that weird cat, especially the gold jewellery, would be useful. She sat beside him now on the edge of the bed, her fluffy tail twitching across Quintus' face like a runaway moustache. Titus tickled her under the chin.

—□—

Tishy liked this one even better than the funny man, though he didn't play chasing games. He always seemed to appreciate the little things she found for him, without shrieking about and making a fuss, and he knew the best angles for scratching. There was a large pole with a bird on top she'd noticed leaning against a wall in the strong room. It might be a nice present to take home to Laura and her mother, but it was too big for her to carry. This new friend could do it for her, if he could be persuaded, like Quintus, to use the Special Cat Flap. Tishy purred.

Isobel Horsburgh

Isobel Horsburgh, a short story author (and occasional poet) lives in East Boldon, Tyne & Wear, England. When she's not writing, she works at the South Tyneside public libraries and has been a volunteer at the North East Mining Institute since 2012. She also volunteers with the British Heart Foundation. Somehow, she manages to find time to foster cats, as well.

Her short stories and poems have been published by *SpaceSquid, Devilfish Review, Buzz and Roar, The Drabble, The Casket, InkBlink, 2000CC, Urban Fantasist, It's All Trumped Up, Phobos, Gathering Storm, Noir, At The Salad Bar, Secret Stairs*, and *Strange Beasties*.

For a list of available anthologies with stories by Isobel Horsburgh, visit her author pages on Amazon or Goodreads.

INTREPIDUS

He thinks I can't hear him. Or he doesn't care, which is the likelier scenario.

I push open the door to his studio, though he's repeatedly told me not to come in. He's an artist, with the temperament to match. He seems to think my presence alone will ruin his paintings, but I can't help myself.

"Get out!" is his favorite greeting, and I brace myself for it. Tonight, however, he's sitting at his computer table talking on the phone again. He keeps laughing in that nauseating, lovey-dovey kind of way. I haven't seen him remotely like this in over a year, and I hate it. Because we're just roommates, once again I must bear the agony of witnessing his burgeoning relationship with a new female.

There's a strange scent in the room. It lingers on him; cheap raspberry body spray clings to his skin and hangs heavy in the air, sickeningly sweet. The voice on the other end of the phone, the female I can barely hear, is the one who leaves that fragrance on him. I don't have to know her to know that I hate her, and I hate her more for knowing that he loves raspberries.

Their laughter makes me so ill that I leave without saying whatever I had meant to. He ignores me completely.

After an hour, he emerges from his room and walks down the hall toward me. Hope fills my heart that this night will be different from the rest. But he strolls by the couch in silence and continues to the kitchen, where he grabs a can of soda from the refrigerator. I say his name twice; he pretends he doesn't hear me and returns to his room, to the new painting waiting on his drawing table. I have no idea what it takes to make him listen to me anymore, or why I even bother.

Sometimes I think I should just walk out the door and never come back. He's threatened to throw me out enough times. I just

can't leave, not even if I wanted to. No matter how many times
he's declared his acceptance that he will spend his life alone, no
matter how many times love has gone badly enough to make
him stop believing in it altogether, he'll never convince me that's
what he really wants. All I have to do is look into those dark
eyes and see how the loneliness, whether he wants to admit it or
not, is killing him.

I could easily fend for myself. No one like me needs
someone like him.

This is how love makes you weak.

—□—

"All you do is sleep!"

It's the first thing I hear when I wake up on the couch, where
I had fallen asleep last night. I sleep to avoid the shouting, to
avoid thinking about what he does beyond these walls. But I
can't tell him I'm jealous. All I do is gaze up at him, wishing he
would remember how things used to be. *I* can't even remember
my own name anymore.

"And I'm tired of finding your hair all over the place!"

People have always complimented me on my thick, shiny
black hair, but now I wish he'd take a razor to it if he hates it so
much. Make me hairless like him. Whatever he despises about
me, I despise about myself even more. I despise what I've
become.

When we moved in together several years ago, he often
stroked my hair playfully. Sometimes he still does. I believed
our relationship would progress beyond mere roommates, and I
was certain back then it was only a matter of time. But this
female is not the first to come between us, only the latest. Still, I
want to be whatever *she* is, whatever has captured the heart he
pretends he doesn't have. Because every now and then he'll
touch my face as he used to, brushing his fingers gently over my
cheek and under my chin. If he felt nothing for me, he wouldn't

do it—that kind of contact is far too intimate. I almost wish he had never touched me at all.

"All I've ever done is tried to make you happy," I say, "and all you do is yell at me."

He glares at me like he doesn't understand a word I've said, like I'm completely out of my mind to even suggest that he's raised his voice to me, then storms into the kitchen and grabs another soda. Sugar for breakfast, lunch, and dinner. And he wonders why his teeth are bad. Without another word, he returns to his room; he won't leave his drawing table for hours, and it's likely the last time today he'll talk to me.

—□—

My ancestor is *Pseudaelurus intrepidus*, or *Hyperailurictis intrepidus* if you prefer. Either way, the first felids in North America. We were all slender and as large as cougars, with beautiful, leopard-like coats. We roamed the warm, arid plains and grasslands and watched mountains rise, millions of years before the apes arrived here. Many more before the apes "domesticated" what they now refer to as the house cat. I don't know how I know these things, except that it's like a collective unconscious, a storehouse of our ancestral memories. The apes originally coined the concept for themselves, because they're nothing if not arrogant, but all animals have them.

Intrepidus means "unperturbed," and I suppose that applies to me. To all of us, famous for our reserve, our poise. I *am* perturbed, though; I just don't let it show.

Usually.

—□—

When I wake up again, it's dark and rain batters the windows. The bad weather was supposed to hold off until tomorrow. He hates walking in the rain—or used to, anyway. The last time he did it, he ended up with a cold for a week. He's done it enough times for this female, though, and because it's fall it rains often here. I wonder if she's some kind of witch who has cast a spell on him. For someone going on thirty, this case of puppy love seems highly unusual.

Every Saturday night he vanishes until the next afternoon, a pattern over the last three months. While he shouts at me more often than not, the hours without him are like days. I stretch my legs and slide off the couch to see if he's left anything to eat. Sometimes he still makes dinner for me. Whether out of habit or pity, it ignites another spark of hope in my heart. I believe this is just a rebound relationship after the last one's four agonizing years, and he only needs a chance to see what has been right in front of him all this time. Like those love songs say, he's saving the best for last.

His leaving every Saturday night was never an emotional issue for me when I knew he'd return within hours. It's her fault. He must be with her; he comes home smelling like raspberries and sex every Sunday afternoon, and my heart twists so painfully that I wish—hope—I'd die. I can't bear the thought of them together, which of course is all my mind focuses on. We truly are our own worst enemies. Has he even told her about me? How could he hide the fact he's been living with someone for years?

Maybe his disappearances are completely innocent and she's simply an acquaintance, a collaborative partner for one of his art projects. Maybe he's just too afraid to admit his feelings for me. He hasn't brought her home after all this time, so it can't be serious. He has never attempted to paint her, and he's painted all of his significant love interests. There are no pictures of her on his desk. Of course, there are no pictures or paintings of me, either.

I've gotten good at deluding myself. He hides the pictures she emails to him in a file on his computer.

I walk into the forbidden studio so I can feel close to him. An empty soda can sits on his computer table, as always. He doesn't have an overhead light, only desk lamps. The constant squinting has added crinkles around his dark eyes and engraved permanent furrows in his brow. He looks distressed even when he's happy, the latter a rare occurrence until recently. I sit at the drawing table to examine his latest work, not that my opinion means anything to him. It's still in the outlining stage, a series of quick, light pencil sketches on white illustration board—a vaguely humanoid shape that will likely become some kind of monster.

Comics and horror novels fill his bookshelves, along with models he's put together and painted from movies of the same genre. He lives in the world of Barker and Giger; he likens himself to Frankenstein's creature. These things inspire him— bizarre things, dark things, fuel for the mind that never stops creating. His artwork might scare me if I didn't know that buried deep inside is a kindhearted and fragile soul eternally searching in vain for the one thing we all want.

I heard him say she's a writer, and she writes that same darkness. That she and he are so much alike. I hate her even more for that because I could never be a writer or artist, though I shouldn't care at all. When you're too much like someone else, you begin to see all the things you hate about yourself in them. It's a situation doomed to failure.

I go to his room and lie on his bed, smelling him in the sheets he rarely washes. I've fallen asleep here once or twice, only to wake up to him screaming at me. If I do it again, he'll kick me out. I force myself up and catch a glimpse of my reflection in the mirror, large pale eyes staring back at me with the unspeakable sadness of a love unrequited. He doesn't want me the way I want him. How can he be so kind, almost loving, one moment and so cruel the next?

I'll never understand him, and I think he wants it that way.

—◻—

Sekhmet, The Powerful One—warrior and healer goddess—bore

the head of a lioness and breathed the desert into existence. She was also called The One before Whom Evil Trembles, Mistress of Dread, and Lady of Slaughter. She once destroyed almost the entire human race.

Bubastis was a rich and beautiful city dedicated to the worship of B'sst, goddess of fertility and protection. Sacrifices were made to her on the day of her great festival.

Those who murdered a cat, even accidentally, were killed by her angry worshippers.

—□—

At the ungodly hour of three in the morning, the door creaks open, followed by hushed voices and muffled footsteps disappearing into his bedroom. I open my eyes and jump off the couch, creeping down the hallway to listen outside. That same giggling I hear when he's on the phone drifts from beneath the door. Shadows flicker across the dim strip of light there. Then the bed begins to squeak rhythmically, and the sound of labored breathing eclipses the groaning mattress. I tap the door and it opens; he didn't close it tightly enough after all.

The first thing I notice is the smell of raspberries, stronger than ever before. And something even more potent—the primal musk of sex. I don't want to see what I know will confront me inside, but I enter anyway.

He's lying on his back. His body is thin, pale, dusted with dark hair. His eyes are closed, his mouth open in mindless ecstasy as he thrashes with her in the deep red sheets. She has dark hair like mine, and green eyes like mine. I've often wondered about the strange ways in which the apes make love. Why they assign so much significance to such a primitive biological urge, which I suppose is why they insist on looking at each other, or at least facing each other, during the act.

I dip my head and gaze at my chest coated with silken ebony fur.

He can't possibly pretend he never knew how I felt about him. It wasn't enough that I had to suffer for four years with the other one; now he brings *this* girl into our home. I will not accept it. Not anymore.

Everything but the will to destroy her shuts down in an instant. Insane with the visceral urge to protect my territory, I leap at her with the intent to do just that, screeching, "How can you do this to me!" The skin of her arm, the source of the raspberry stench assaulting my nose, gives way under my nails. Blood splashes into my face, into my eyes. She shrieks and flails her arms madly to throw me off, but I can't stop myself. I want to shred her to pieces for taking what's mine, for stealing the only thing I've ever loved. Droplets of blood spatter the walls; it fuels my fury, and I try to lick the scratches in the hope of transmitting a disease.

He closes his fingers around the ruff of fur at my neck, and the wall is speeding toward me. He didn't mean to hurl me so hard, I know he didn't, but white, electrical bursts of pain crackle through my brain. My claws are still extended. I taste blood—hers? My own?—in my mouth. My tail twitches as I slump to the floor, dazed. Out of the corner of my eye, I see small dark spots of blood, absorbed by the carpet as it leaks from the torn flesh of my shoulder.

I think there are tears in his eyes as he cradles his shivering, bleeding lover and stares in shock across the room at me. I stare back. If I had tears, maybe it would have changed the way he feels. If only I could express on the outside what I feel inside, if I could be more *homo sapiens*, maybe he would've given me a chance. His relationships end eventually. I am the only companion he's kept this long. But it's too late for regrets.

He looks like he's about to be sick. "I didn't mean...." He falters. I can't tell if he's speaking to the human female or to me. She squeezes her eyes shut and buries her face against his chest.

"I loved you," I say, but what emerges from my mouth is the stuttering yowl of a wounded cat.

Loved.

We never forget cruelty inflicted on us by those we trusted. But this display of aggression has shaken the circuitry in my brain, rewired it, made me remember who—and what—I am. That once we were gods and these violent, base creatures served and revered *us*. Once we were dressed in golden jewelry and ate from their plates. That, like the gods of old, we are impulsive and impatient, and grow bored of things in which there is no reward for us. That we have long and complex dreams, and in these dreams, we often recall the terrible things done to us. We have nightmares, and sometimes they are violent.

It should have been him all along. He whom I should have hated. He—not her, and not any of the others—who has subjected me to these torments.

Him. Alone.

He thinks he's hurt me worse than he actually has, and I let him. It's the blood, of course; people panic at the sight of it no matter how little. I lie there for a little while longer, thinking. I remind myself that we hunted with Diana, goddess of the moon. That we pulled the chariot of Freyja, goddess of sorcery. That the apes once worshipped us, and some still do.

He lets her go and shifts as if to leave the bed and approach me. I rise—slowly, pretending I can barely stand. My legs wobble. I arch my back and hiss; he smartly draws back but strikes his heel on the bed and tumbles onto it, landing on his lover's wounded arm. I smile when she shrieks, though they see only bared fangs. Aggression. I stalk from the bedroom to the front door and caterwaul a demand to be let out. He's all too eager to do so, though he skirts me as if I'm a rearing cobra with its hood spread. Once he's unlocked and opened the door, he flattens himself against the wall as I pass. Afraid I'll touch him, or worse. He has no idea how much worse it could be, or how he has squandered the gift of love that we are so reluctant to give the apes—and for good reason.

I slink down the stairs, stopping at the bottom to lick my paws and the injury on my shoulder that will heal in a few days. From the sidewalk, I gaze at the wan light behind the second-floor window curtains. Yellow eyes flash from the shadows and bushes. Understanding eyes.

It will fester inside me like a rotting organ. I will dream about it. One day I'll return, bedraggled and pathetic, and he'll remember what he did, how he betrayed me and let me disappear into a cold autumn night. He'll take pity on me that he left me out there to survive on my own. But I won't be alone.

And I will wait. I am *intrepidus*.

Given the right reward, I have all the patience in the world.

Jennifer Loring

Born in Portland, Maine and raised in rural western New York, Jennifer Loring had read Stephen King by age 11 and was writing horror stories within a year. Her first publication was in the Canadian vampire magazine, *Requiem Aeternam,* at age 21. After graduating with a BA in studio art, Jennifer wrote several novels that thankfully never saw the light of day and dabbled in more short stories, including the first draft of "The Bombay Trash Service," which was awarded an honorable mention in *The Year's Best Fantasy and Horror* for 2004.

Jennifer received her MFA from Seton Hill University's program in Writing Popular Fiction, with a concentration in horror fiction. In 2013, she won first place in Crystal Lake Publishing's inaugural Tales from the Lake horror writing competition, which found her published alongside her mentor Tim Waggoner in the anthology of the same name. DarkFuse released her psychological horror/ghost story novella, *Conduits,* in September 2014 (re-released by Lycan Valley Press in 2018); her debut novel, *Those of My Kind,* was published by Omnium Gatherum in May 2015. She has since written a contemporary/sports romance series, *The Firebird Trilogy.*

Her work has appeared in anthologies alongside such prominent names in horror as Graham Masterton, Joe R. Lansdale, Ramsey Campbell, and Clive Barker. In addition, Jennifer presented her academic horror research at StokerCon 2018 in Providence, RI, and at the International Vampire Film and Arts Festival (IVFAF) in Sighisoara, Romania. She is a member of the Horror Writers Association and the International Thriller Writers.

Jennifer lives in Philadelphia, PA with her husband, where they are owned by two basset hounds and a turtle.

Website: http://jennifertloring.com
Facebook: @JenniferTLoring
Twitter: @JenniferTLoring

Pinterest: JenniferTLoring
Instagram: Jennifer_Loring
Amazon and Goodreads: Jennifer Loring

WITCH CAT

No one believed anymore. Old Gert had worked her magics for more than forty years, but she recognized the death knoll of her craft when she heard it. The villagers doubted now, even when they presented their broken children for hexing. Even when they scratched at her back door on the night of a full moon, begging love potions.

Her kind was on their way out, but Old Gert had no intention of going quietly.

"Here kitty, you wretched bag of fleas." She waved a fish tail over the bottom half of her cottage door and gargled deep in her throat. "M'ere, puss. Kitty wants his dinner?"

It was Hilde from Sansburg, her counterpart 'cross the river, that gave her the idea. Bragging, Hilde had been, but her story provided Gert the seed of a plan; the thought that wormed its way deep into her old brain and refused to let go.

"When I'm a cat," Hilde had lied, "I can hear all their rubbish talk, you see? I *know* things 'bout them, and they'll never dare to send *me* packing."

Gert snorted at the memory and waved the stinking fish. Her front bushes rustled, and her dratted, over-sexed familiar slunk onto the cobble path. She'd called rubbish on Hilde, and no doubt earned the woman's ire for it. But though she suspected the brag was false, the idea of it appealed to her.

"Come on, wretch. I haven't got all day to wait for you to clean yer business."

The cat stretched, gave itself another three good licks, and then rose and wandered toward the door and dinner.

Hilde hadn't much skill, certainly not enough to transform. Old Gert could do it, though. She had a grimoire passed down through thirteen generations. She had the cat, the book, and knew her skill to be at least three full degrees above that of Hilde's. She'd always been the superior witch, and tonight she meant to use the old hen's story for her own ends.

She'd take her familiar's form.

She'd go out as a cat and *listen*.

With her head full of the villagers' secrets, they'd never have the mettle to replace her. She'd live out her days as she liked, lazily, subsisting on gifts from terrified people who owed her for one thing or the other—things learned from their nattering.

"C'mere, cat." Gert waved the fish until her familiar leapt for the doorway. She snatched it away at the last second, caught the animal in her arms, and grunted, holding fast against its twisting. "Now cut that out. You can have it later."

The ungrateful beast hissed and scratched at her arms, but Old Gert didn't give up easily. She had scratches on her scratches, and scars from far more diabolical things than an irritable familiar. She lugged the black cat to her work table where a beaker of herbs smoldered and a stout, iron cauldron waited beside her open grimoire. She placed the cat next to the book, holding him still with the wrinkled fingers of one hammy hand.

"Still now," she gargled. The candles set around the room sputtered and flared brighter. The smoking herbs crackled, and Gert's sharp eyes fixed on the words of the spell. "Sit still. This won't hurt a bit.

—▢—

Shadow's belly rumbled, and he growled, but his mind worked furiously. His claws dug neat lines in the witch's table. Not random etching; not the fearful scratches of an ordinary beast. Shadow drew runes into the wood. He dragged each claw with great precision, hiding his efforts behind the snarls and hissing she expected from him.

He'd spent the day behind the cottage, listening to the old fool mumble and plot. She'd finally stumbled onto something of worth, and the cat had no intention of letting the opportunity pass. He'd even less desire to be cast out than the hag, and his kind had seen the end coming far sooner. They'd been planning their escape longer than her ilk could fathom.

As the witch began her spelling, Shadow drew his lines. When her mumbling shifted on a note, and the power built around the table, the cat's whiskers gathered a measure of it for himself. Old Gert cast her spell, her fingers hard lumps against his pelt, while Shadow twisted the threads of her weaving to his own design.

Heat built into a thick blanket. Static energy crackled, lifting the dense hairs along his spine. The witch's voice rose and fell like a hammer, but it was the cat who positioned the nail. It was the cat who guided the power, redirecting and aiming it like an arrow toward his freedom.

The magic flowed over them both, exploding through the witch's fingers and amplified by the cat's runes. His head expanded. He felt her creeping there, a coarse, low nature only intent on saving her own hide. She pushed inward, focused on invading his body, but if she expected a fight, Shadow meant to disappoint.

He leapt upon her thoughts and chased them upward. Like mice, they flittered from him, scurried away, and led him straight into the old woman's mind. There Shadow settled, dug his claws in tight, and shoved against her. The witch fell away, sinking into the cat's body, and her familiar curled himself contentedly into hers.

He stretched to fill insanely long limbs and purred at Old Gert's satisfaction with her new form. In her conceit, the truth that she'd been let in willingly evidently went unheeded. She yowled triumphant and streaked away, a black witch-thing, reveling in the cat's speed and grace, and wholly unaware she'd no way of returning.

Shadow lifted the wrinkly fingers in front of his face. He wiggled them like fat maggots and then bit into one before remembering he shouldn't.

—▢—

Gert knew all along she was clever, but this spell so fully drowned her other accomplishments that it triggered a shiver of cold fear. Perhaps she'd praised herself too soon. She ignored her doubts. She meant to enjoy the transformation, to run amok a bit, and then, more importantly, to gather the town's secrets around her like a shield.

Her borrowed body moved more smoothly than she was accustomed, and a single thought resulted in a flurry of twisting and leaping. She'd cleared the cottage without incident, caught in the frenzy of success. But when she concentrated on moving like a cat, her efforts grew clumsy, and she was forced to slow her pace to focus on shifting each paw in turn.

Rot. She'd never collect what she needed if she spent the spell's duration learning how to walk. A shiver of fear took her once more—a hint of wrongness about her plan. Gert shook it off; it rippled from her whiskers to the tip of her tail. That ripple solved her problem. She didn't need to consciously guide this body. She needed to relax and allow it to follow her commands naturally. The flesh and bones remembered how to be a cat. She sat on the cobbled path and eyed the dusty road at the edge of her yard. Odd. From this low to the ground she could see the ruts and rocks much clearer than the buildings on the far side. What she'd always taken for a smooth thoroughfare now became a landscape with dips and valleys. She pondered this, and something tugged at her from behind.

Turning, the witch caught sight of her sinuous tail. Like a satin rope, the black fur swept from side to side as if punctuating her thoughts. Gert tried to still it, but again, the more she concentrated, the more her tail whisked across the cobbles. Her irritation swelled. She snatched at the thing and was startled at the prick of pain when she caught it between her claws.

Rot. Wasting time. Fiddling with her own tail. Hilde would never let her live that sort of carelessness down. She released the appendage and turned up her nose. She was a witch of thirteen generations, a weaver of power, a woman of immense magic. If she couldn't master a cat's form, she might as well take up sewing and move to a city where no one would ever scratch at her door for help.

"Back to business," she meant to say. Instead, a half-choked mewling tumbled past her rough tongue. *Good enough.* Old Gert had no more time to lose. The village called to her with the voice of scandal. It sang of late night trysts and unconfirmed parentage, of silent murder and unobserved theft.

Inside the cat's head, the witch cackled. Relaxed in her new form, she raced down the street, into a multitude of lives that ignored cats. A village of fools too simple to suspect a transfigured spy prowled among them.

—◻—

Shadow found his new form liberating. Certainly, his limbs moved with less grace and complained at the joints when he twisted too freely. But the voice he howled with echoed to the cottage walls, and the hands were nimble and excelled at picking up objects and placing them down again.

He struggled with the speaking at first. His mind had learned the witch's language years ago, long before she'd grown stingy and switched his sweet cream for her cast off fish tails. Somehow knowing the words and producing them were two separate skills. Shadow drew air through the witch's fat nose, opened her crooked lips, and issued a heresy of speech that sent the birds outside swiftly on their way to a friendlier town.

He meant to twitch his tail irritably but only managed to waggle the woman's wide bottom. Her skirts swished, and the movement of the fabric formed a mesmerizing wave. "Pretty."

The word slipped out with no effort on his part, and Shadow grasped the secret of proper speech. Best not to think too hard; the words will come on their own.

With that small victory, the cat-turned-witch closed the heavy grimoire, gathered the book in his arms, and scampered from the cottage with his skirts swishing. He hesitated only a second at the sight of carts in the road, and the idea of the villagers. Then, confident that he'd blend in, and no one would dare fling garbage or kick at a witch, Shadow waddled into the fray, down the road in the direction of Sansburg.

—□—

Old Gert clung to the window sill and listened. She'd been a cat for most of the day, and only managed to overhear ordinary complaining and petty arguments. In hindsight, she should have known Hilde's plan was riddled with holes, but after all the power she'd wasted pulling it off, her stubborn streak wouldn't let her admit defeat.

Besides, she'd managed a transformation that, alone, would place her in a witchy league well above dabblers like Hilde. In fact, the old bat would never believe she'd done it. That stuck in her craw enough to keep her bounding from one brick ledge to the next, peering into villagers' homes listening for anything that might prove her story when she returned to herself.

The last alley she haunted was deep in the heart of the village, and the window she watched belonged to a man of status high enough to hold secrets worth discovering. All Gert needed was to wait for him to do or say something interesting.

She eyed the dense, woven carpet, the hand-carved furniture and velvet upholstery, and licked a front paw absently. Her target napped in an enormous green chair at the edge of the room. His feet twitched. His snoring vibrated into the alley. As the sun dipped to the far trees, Gert considered visiting Hilde instead.

Her tail dangled, swiping the wall. She smoothed the fur on her right shoulder; it mussed too easily. One short journey through the town and her fur poked up in different directions. Uncomfortable. And Hilde's cottage was across the river, and the idea of that much water jerked at something fearful deep in her cat body.

She'd just have to be patient. Eventually, this boor would wake up and say something interesting. Gert looked back into the room to find a face peering out at her. Startled, she yowled and leapt straight into the air, scrabbling at the bricks to avoid falling. Her fur bristled like the brush she used to clean her hearth.

"Shadow?" A white cat sat just inside the window. Her ears flicked, and she patted the pane with a round paw, blinked green eyes, and meowed with words Old Gert had no trouble understanding. "How goes the plan?"

"What?" Gert clung to the bricks, nails splitting, and tail snapping behind her for balance.

"Has the old bat gotten any closer?"

"The old bat?" Gert's cat nerves twitched. Her whiskers tested the air, stirred by vibrations of secrets and subterfuge. "She's still working on it," she responded cautiously.

"I hope she's as foolish as you believe." The white cat purred and rubbed her body against the thin glass. Her voice came through muted, as though she spoke under water. "If I have to endure the master much longer, I'll drown myself."

"I can imagine," Gert meowed. "But the *plan*...."

"I hope she attempts it soon. This one never lets me out anymore. Nothing but fish and cream." The strange cat rattled off a list of offenses against the man in the chair, as if he hadn't fed and protected the animal, as if he hadn't coddled her far more than Gert ever.... "If you *can* steal their bodies, come and fetch me first."

Old Gert tumbled from the window sill. She landed on her feet in a pile of trash with her heart—her cat's heart—pounding. *Steal their bodies?* The chill returned, and Gert replayed her spelling in her mind: The sense that something was wrong; the shivers of fear; and a flashing image of lines carved into her table. Runes! That dratted cat had—

Her borrowed body stiffened, taut with nerves and panic. There must still be time, a way to unwind his trap. She had thirteen generations of witching behind her. The notion bolstered her. The witch-cat raced from the alley, down the busy street, and straight for the river, Sansburg, and Hilde's shop.

—◻—

Shadow carried the heavy grimoire to Hilde's cottage. The old woman's arms ached before he even reached the ferry and then trembled during the short ride across the river. He hugged the book close to her sagging chest, remembering that he had no reason to fear water any longer.

In fact, he had the oddest desire to take a bath.

Old Gert's brain carried a memory of the route to her rival's shack, but the lanes on that side of the water all looked alike to Shadow. He circled twice before he found the slender pathway that led behind the fishing piers and into the sparse woods at the edge of town. He hurried, eager, hobbling on ungraceful legs and clutching the book as tightly as Gert's failing arms would allow.

Gert and Hilde squabbled more than the all the toms in the village combined. When Hilde opened her door and saw Shadow wearing his master's form, the witch hissed through the gap in her teeth and blocked the doorway with her stooped body.

"Hey now. What you want 'round here?"

"Book." Shadow made the word perfectly, but the old witch only squinted her eyes and growled back at him.

"Go away."

"Book." Gert's arms shook when he thrust the grimoire toward her rival. Shadow forced a smile and imagined he'd brought the witch a fat, half-dead mouse. "Gift book."

"Eh?" Hilde's eyes still squinted, but she tilted her head for a better view of the grimoire. Her fingers un-balled from her sides to become twitching claws. "You lost yer mind?"

"Gift." Shadow imagined what he wanted her to do, what they *needed* her to do. Hilde's familiar, Mist Weaver, had visited

Gert's cottage often. Together they'd sang of the plan while the two witches bickered. They'd see it finished tonight. "Cat spell."

He peered into the shack, around the halo of wiry hair topping the shorter woman's head.

Somewhere in the dark interior, Hilde's cat mewed. "Is that you?"

"You ain't put a hex on it?"

"No. It's me."

"I know who you are!" Hilde stamped a foot against her floorboards and dust puffed around her ankles. She reached for the book but hesitated before grabbing onto it. "An' I know how much you love that book there. You got something up yer sleeve."

"No." Shadow lifted Old Gert's arms to show the witch her empty sleeves.

"Nothing would make you part with it," Hilde argued. "Nothing good."

"Cat spell," Shadow insisted. "Works good."

"Ah, then." The hag straightened and lifted her pointy chin. She whistled through her tooth gap and nodded. "I see what yer at. You tried Ol' Hilde's transformation and couldn't do it!"

"Works good."

"Well you probably did it wrong." Hilde's claws snatched at the book then, and Shadow released it readily. His arms ached, and he'd feared the stupid hag would refuse his offer of magic. "Let's see. Which one is it?" she said.

Shadow followed the old crone into her shack. His eyes scanned the corners of the room, but the human's vision failed to illuminate the darkness. "Where?"

"On the work table," Hilde mumbled.

"Over here," Mist Weaver meowed.

The witch placed the book upon her table, and a smoke-gray feline drifted into the light near her ankles. Hilde wandered to the four corners of the room, lighting stout candles that cast demon flickers onto shabby walls. She returned and opened the book, giving Shadow a distrustful look.

"Which one is it, then?"

Shadow moved to the table and shuffled through the grimoire pages with Old Gert's grub-like fingers. When he found the spell of transformation, he tapped the page. "Cat spell."

"I don't believe you. It won't work."

The gray cat mewed and leapt up to sit beside the book. Both witch and cat stared at him. Shadow tried to remember the battles he'd witnessed between the two witches. The hags sputtered and stamped at each other, but victory shifted evenly back and forth, and he wasn't confident he could best Hilde now.

He focused on the arguments Old Gert had won, searching for an effective tactic. At last. As if on reflex, he shrugged Gert's saggy shoulders and snorted. "Suit yerself."

Hilde snorted back, but her eyes darkened. The defiant jut of her chin hardened and she looked at the book with a challenge in her expression. Mist Weaver purred and dug a claw into the witch's worktable, carving her first rune.

—□—

Old Gert raced between the fishermens' shacks, her cat's heart pounding in her chest, her witch side growling in panic. She'd found it easy enough to sneak aboard the ferry, but as soon as the boat left the shore, Gert was possessed by a new terror that didn't ease until she reached dry land again. Each leap carried her lithe body farther from the wretched water, but even as she entered the lane to Hilde's, her sense of danger built.

Steal their bodies.

She'd raised that cat from a kitten, provided cream she couldn't afford, shelter, and scraps of fish from her own plate. And all along the beast was plotting against her. All the spells they'd cast, all the knowledge she'd spilled forth … the cat was paying attention.

The old fleabag.

Her growling shifted to snarls of fury. She ran on swift black paws; ran until the forest thickened and blocked out the river. Ungrateful. Injurious. Rude! Gert swept down the path, her fur fluffed, and her tail held out for balance.

She raced toward her rival's home and met the woman's cat twenty paces from the front door. "Move aside!"

"Cat." The gray cat yowled. "Gert's cat. What's his name again?"

Old Gert skidded past the gray familiar and slid to a stop. She spun on the other feline and hissed. "His name is dead meat, kitty. And you're next. Plotting against your witches. Shame on you both!"

"Gert?"

"You're damn right, it's Gert, wretch. Soon as I get my book back, ya better move on if you know what's good for ya."

"I'm Hilde!" The cat yowled and rolled onto its back. "You old fool. I did it too! Just look at me." She displayed her feline form proudly to Old Gert.

Gert spat and her claws extended. "You didn't?"

"Think yer the only one who can pull off a transformation, do ya?"

"They've got our bodies, idiot."

"What?"

"And I got a sick feeling they're not gonna rush to give 'em back."

The gray cat sat up primly, tail swishing. "What are you on about now?"

"The cats, Hilde. They've been plotting against us the whole time."

"Why?"

"To get our bodies. An' you just offered yours right up, didn't you? He bring you the book? You didn't think it was a bit odd, me handin' it over?"

"Sure I did. But...."

"C'mon, idiot." Gert raced up to Hilde's shack.

The other cat padded behind her with a meow of protest.

"You done it too."

At the door, Gert leapt for the handle and found it locked. She threw her slim body against the wood, falling away without so much as rattling it. The gray cat appeared beside her, worthless, but at least familiar.

"Go 'round the back," Gert ordered. "Make a fuss. We'll have to wait them out."

"They've got your book," Hilde cat yowled. "What about that?"

"Watch the back door, fool. They have to let us in eventually."

—□—

Shadow covered his ears with Old Gert's big hands and whimpered. The scratching intensified, claws raked against wood. Cat voices screamed to be let in, yowling in feline distress.

"I can't stand it." Mist Weaver hunched beside the hearth in her new human form. The witch's candles had gone out, but a hot fire burned inside the shack and the shadows on the shabby walls waved and taunted them. "We should open the door."

"No!" Shadow scooted closer to her, sweeping the dusty floor with Old Gert's skirts. "We can't. We have to be strong."

"Listen to them!" Hilde's face scrunched into a demon's grimace. Mist Weaver had never been as strong as Shadow, but then, his witch had thirteen generations behind her.

"Block it out," he ordered. "Focus!"

Outside the shack, the two cats yowled and tore at the timbers. Inside Shadow's mind, an angry presence pressed at the edges, trying to force its way back into power.

"I can feel her," Mist Weaver whispered in a hag's voice. "She's still in here."

If they allowed the struggle to continue, he could tell, Mist Weaver would fall. She'd give up her new body, let the witch in, and he'd face more than just Old Gert inside his mind. He'd have a witch outside to contend with as well.

"We have to burn their book." Shadow eyed the fireplace, the flames danced and crackled inside Hilde's hearth.

"What about the rest of the plan?" Mist Weaver asked.

"The cats in this place are plotters."

"And there's plenty of witches about."

"Yes." Gert's body yawned and stretched her tired arms toward the rafters. "They'll have to come up with their own plan."

"Yes," Hilde purred. "Of course they will."

Gert's shoulders shrugged, and her hands tossed the grimoire into the flames. Smoke boiled into the room. It billowed from the chimney with green sparks glittering within. Two cat's voices screamed to the heavens. Two old women's voices coughed and sputtered.

—▢—

If the villagers heard the wails, if they saw the smoke and the sparks that marked the last battle of the witches and their familiars, no one came to stop it.

That night, the two old hags slept on the floor by the fire. At first light, they left for the seaside where they lived together on fat fish and fresh cream and never opened their back door for anyone.

Their neighbors told tales of the Sansburg cats, two odd felines that endured much longer than any cat should. Each night they met by the river, and their encounters inevitably ended in a great show of hissing and flying fur. Their kitty battles became a thing of legend, and many whispered that two old witches inhabited them.

But no one truly believed it.

Frances Pauli

Frances Pauli is a hybrid author of more than twenty novels. She writes speculative fiction, usually with touches of humor or romance, which means, of course, that she has trouble choosing sides. A fan of things outside the box—the odd, weird, or unusual—that trend weaves through her stories, which feature aliens, animals, fairies, and on occasion, an assortment of humans. Once upon a time she was a visual artist but has since come to her senses. When she's not writing, she fills her miniscule amount of free time with crochet, belly dance, and abysmal ukulele playing. Frances lives in Washington state with her family, four dogs, two cats, and a variety of tarantulas.

Website: francespauli.com
Facebook: @AuthorFrancesPauli
Twitter: @mothindarkness
Amazon and Goodreads: Frances Pauli

LISA TIMPF

MOONLIGHT

breeze wafts through open window
small creatures squeak in the grass
and a moonbeam begins a slow march
across the living room floor

you snore, still, in bed,
and I wonder at the fact
that you cannot hear the full moon's call
as it casts its silver gleam upon the lawn

do not scold me when I waken you
asking to be let out —
evening's hours, like all our hours,
are short and bear their numbers

I glance at your face, as you sway,
eyes heavy with sleep, to grumblingly hold
the door ajar —

do not fear, I will be back
if not, do not lament
I live life on my own terms
and the mice await

ABOUT LISA TIMPF

Editor's note: To learn more about this very talented writer see page 138, following her story, "The Open Road." Lisa also contributed a second poem, "A Cat's Confession," page 152.

MAU OF THE PHARAOHS

The Egyptian Mau is perhaps the oldest of all domestic cat breeds, dating back 3000 years. Cats were a sacred animal of the goddess Bastet (who was represented as having the head of a cat) and were a symbol of fertility to Egyptian women.

I am Mau. I have no other name, or I do not remember it. The Nile has flooded twenty times since I was a kitten attending to the amusement of the little princesses. As I am at your service, I am also honored to have served three pharaohs, although one I attended unwillingly, for I believed him to be a usurper and a murderer. As I sit now at your feet Goddess Bastet, in your temple in Bubastis, I pray you will find my story worthy. The journey was long and needs be my last, and this is all in the world I have to offer you.

I was not yet full grown when I killed the cobra. To be true, it was a small cobra. But the Royal Princess (and soon to be Great Royal Wife and Queen) Ankhesenamun, made much of my heroic deed. In the retelling, the cobra grew large — so large and so fierce that I must also be made large and fierce to have defeated it. In this way, I acquired great importance in my mind and in that of Princess Ankhesenamun, and in the minds of all who resided in the palace. No male of my kind dared approach me without invitation. So exalted did I become that, having placed gold rings in my ears and a gold amulet around my neck, declaring me the Royal Mau, Ankhesenamun offered me as a wedding gift to the young Pharaoh.

Thus, from the day of their wedding, I served the Pharaoh, Rathotis, as He was born and known by those closest to Him. To all others, He was Tutankhamun, Son of Ra, King of Upper and Lower Egypt. By any name, no one, not even the Queen, presumed to lounge at his feet as I did, for the young Pharaoh prized me above all others. There was no doubt in my mind of this, and I was proud and emboldened.

To be fair, I was diligent in keeping Pharaoh's rooms free of snakes and vermin (though I have seen no other cobra to this day). As well, I observed closely those who appeared before the Pharaoh, for I have talents beyond assassin of cobras. I can discern falseness. It was known to me when any in His service was deceitful. So it was, I came to distrust Horemheb, the commander in chief of Rathotis' army, of whom I will soon speak.

Rathotis was not well. He suffered from the shaking disease; the curse of many of the Royal Family. When He was young, the shaking was frequent, though it lessened somewhat as He grew older. The throne room being in a distant corner of the palace, a separate room was prepared nearer His quarters for His comfort in receiving His education, meeting with advisers, and welcoming worshipers. As the Royal Mau, I was in attendance on these occasions. Oftentimes, He would hold me in His lap as He ruled—a prodigious honor granted to no other adviser.

Frequently Pharaoh was visited by His tutor, Sennedjem, who instructed Him in the history of those who ruled before and that of the two lands, Upper and Lower Egypt. On these occasions I slept. The past was of little interest to me, and I knew Sennedjem to be harmless.

More often, however, it was Ay, the Grand Vizier, who was with Pharaoh. Of his many titles, Ay was Fan-bearer on the Right Side of the King, Scribe of the King, and Overseer of the King's Horses. I would have willingly died for Ay as for Pharaoh Himself, for we loved our Pharaoh equally and collaborated to protect Him. To seal our alliance, Ay would frequently bring me tidbits from the kitchens, and in return I would allow him to stroke my belly; an honor permitted no others but Pharaoh and His Queen.

In those early years of Tutankhamun's reign, much good occurred. The God Amun was reaffirmed as King of Gods, and the effigies and writings of all pretenders were expunged. It also came that the first harvest upon Amun's return to prominence was plentiful, and so the devoted followers of Amun were rewarded. Much prosperity followed.

While the peoples of Egypt relaxed in the bounty of Amun, the threat of war with Nubia persisted, and the Kingdom of Amurru was lost to the Hittites. Horemheb, the commander of the army, traveled Egypt and its colonies often during these years, seeing to matters of war and foreign diplomacy in the name of Pharaoh.

It was on the occasions of Horemheb's return visits to Thebes to record his accomplishments that Rathotis grew besotted of Horemheb and his tales (greatly embellished, I am sure). Rathotis was the living God, but so was He a young boy, admiring of Horemheb's strength and good health and covetous of his adventures. As with all males of His age, Pharaoh's interests were in horses, chariot racing, and hunting ibex, giraffe, and wild boar—all activities at which Horemheb excelled. Upon each return of Horemheb, Pharaoh would order a hunting party formed. These excursions would last several days. I received no invitation to accompany Pharaoh on His hunts, and so He was left undefended in the face of Horemheb's influence.

Always Horemheb would bring gifts from the border colonies to enchant and flatter Pharaoh. At one such time, he returned accompanied by a Nubian prince bearing gifts of gold, incense, ivory, and praise for Pharaoh. During the prince's visit, a long-desired treaty of peace between Egypt and Nubia was agreed upon, with the mutual promise of military protection for trade routes. Pharaoh was greatly pleased with Horemheb on this occasion. So much so that Horemheb was designated the Hereditary Prince if Pharaoh should die childless—a situation that was unthinkable at the time. Still, I cautioned Rathotis against this action, but He did not listen. As was often the case, Pharaoh silenced me when I endeavored to use my voice in earnest. While tutored in many languages, the subtle language of the maus was difficult for Pharaoh, though I spoke as simply as I could.

If I failed Pharaoh, it was in one thing, oh great Bastet. But this one thing was of such consequence that it provided the means for the impostor to pursue his evil designs. For all other faults but this, I beg your forgiveness.

As Rathotis grew, so grew his desire for Ankhesenamun. In your service, great Bastet, I slept many nights beneath their couch, and twice from thy blessing Ankhesenamun became with child. Alas, as punishment for my pride and notions of grandeur, in both cases, the child was stillborn. History will forever attribute all that occurred thereafter to my failure in procuring your blessing, and thus, a living heir for Pharaoh. Such is the sacred duty of all mau.

Only you can know the truth of this, but on one occasion when Pharaoh was practicing with His chariots, I left His quarters to seek the company of a male. This was a time when Ankhesenamun was heavy with Pharaoh's child. As I was passing through a common room, I observed Horemheb offering Ankhesenamun a drink from a golden goblet inlaid with colored stones. If it was water or wine, or something else, I cannot say. The following day, the child was lost.

As before, I continued to watch over and protect Ankhesenamun as diligently as my duties allowed. Still, one year and three months later, a second child was born dead (on this I have no suspicions). Thus, Tutankhamun was without sons to succeed Him. And so I failed in my ultimate duty to the Pharaoh and to you, my most cherished Goddess.

Being in Thebes upon the death of Pharaoh's second child, Horemheb organized a hunting expedition as a diversion for the grief-stricken Pharaoh. After only three days, the party returned bearing Rathotis on a length of linen carried between two of the palace guard. Rathotis' leg had been broken. It was an ugly sight, with the splintered bone jutting from His flesh. The Pharaoh had lost much blood and was fevered. The priests did what they could, which was little but to make Him comfortable. During these days, I lay on Ankhesenamun's lap and watched over our Pharaoh as she applied linen soaked in kapur to His forehead.

In the Pharaoh's presence, as He lay on His couch unable to respond, Ay and Horemheb exchanged heavy words and threats. Both asserted their authority to act on Pharaoh's behalf during His confinement — Ay as Vizier and Horemheb as Hereditary Prince. I made no attempt to express my opinion in this, for Ay's argument was unassailable, and I was sharpening my claws for attack should matters turn violent. It was rightfully noted by both Ay and Ankhesenamun that Horemheb's assertion of power could only be honored upon Pharaoh's death, and Pharaoh was still much alive. With Amun's blessing, He would soon recover. However, Horemheb did not waiver.

But for a skirmish that occurred in the Asiatic colonies, which soon turned to rebellion, the disagreement may have escalated into something much worse. Horemheb had no choice but to lead the Pharaoh's army to quell the uprising. Thus, Ay was left to act freely on behalf of Pharaoh during His recovery.

It pains me to recall as if it occurred this day, but Rathotis did not recover. Within ten days of Horemheb's departure, even as Ankhesenamun, Ay, and the priests administered to Him faithfully, the great Pharaoh Tutankhamun, Son of Ra, King of Upper and Lower Egypt, began His journey in the afterlife.

Prayers were said, hymns were sung, and processions honoring Pharaoh were assembled in Thebes and throughout Egypt. Funeral rituals and spells were observed as befitting the Son of Ra, and Tutankhamun's earthly body was preserved to sustain His soul in the next realm. For much of this I was not present but learned of as the ceremonies were recounted in detail by the priests in residence at the palace.

On one occasion, I accompanied Ankhesenamun in her litter to view her husband's tomb (for I provided solace during her time of mourning). This was done late at night and in great secrecy, as only a few could know the location of the tomb. I was honored to be among them.

This was not the intended burial chamber of Tutankhamun,

but a smaller one that Ay had been granted permission to build for himself during his service to Tutankhamun's father. At His death, Tutankhamun's great tomb was not yet completed. (The lesser tomb of Ay's being easier concealed to my mind.) When we entered, we saw a scribe working by lantern light to complete inscriptions on the tomb wall, and something engraved there upset Ankhesenamun greatly. Upon our return to the palace, she sent for Ay though the hour was late.

Unbeknownst to me, Ankhesenamun and Ay were conspiring to destroy all official record of Horemheb's designation as the Hereditary Prince. I believe this to have been a foolish undertaking, for those in the palace and many elsewhere knew well of Horemheb's appointment. At learning of their plan, I was at first offended that they had not confided the details to me from the start. However, as I thought about it then, my disapproval of their actions would have been correctly predicted by both. Regardless, it was the title of Hereditary Prince next to the likeness of Horemheb himself that Ankhesenamun had witnessed being engraved on a wall of Pharaoh's tomb. Their plan, poorly conceived, was abandoned.

Upon learning of Pharaoh's death, it was expected Horemheb would immediately return to Thebes to claim the throne. However, it was not to be. Word came to us that the Asiatic uprising had gained strength and more troops were dispatched to aid Horemheb in the fight. It is not to my credit when I say to you that I prayed often for Horemheb to die with honor upon the battlefield, as was his due.

So it transpired, as Rathotis basked in the Realm of Osiris and Horemheb was far from Thebes, Ay succeeded Tutankhamun without contest as the Pharaoh Kheperkhiperure.

—☐—

I had been always loyal to Ay during Tutankhamun's reign. He did not give me reason to be otherwise, nor ask me to perform a task that would reflect badly upon or cause harm to my beloved

Rathotis. Regarding Ay's reign as Pharaoh, I can neither praise nor condemn. He was a just ruler and dutifully honored the King of Gods, Amun, acting in His stead in all things. His legend, however, does not chronicle great accomplishments or heroic deeds. To his credit, he did not discourage the citizens from continuing to deify and pray to Tutankhamun as another might have. As to Ay's sanctity as the Son of Ra, I do not know nor will I speak. Egypt neither prospered nor declined under his rule.

Upon becoming Pharaoh and having no sons, Ay, well advanced in years, proclaimed his son-in-law, Nakhtmin, as Hereditary Prince. At Ay's ascension, his wife, Tey, was thus Queen. Tutankhamun's beloved, Ankhesenamun, no longer Queen, was but a widow with no sons to protect her. She feared for her life. I believe her fear was unjustified, though understandable. The crowning of a new Pharaoh often brought upheaval and danger to members of the Royal Family. This was so even in times when the claim to the throne went unchallenged.

Ankhesenamun, in her despair and acting on her own behalf, wrote to a Hittite Prince with an offer of marriage. While I did not see this letter myself, it was said that she *begged* the prince to take her in marriage. That she would consider a Hittite, or any man of foreign blood, to be a suitable consort speaks to the extent of her perceived danger. Of course, this prince agreed at once (no doubt he was astounded at the offer) and made haste to Thebes. Upon his arrival, Ay had him put to death. As Ankhesenamun herself was not harmed, and with her fears allayed, she retired to her rooms. Except for my visits to console her, she was seen little in the passageways of the palace for many weeks thereafter.

It was during this time, however, that the Queen, Tey, became ill and died. Some whispered she had been poisoned at Ay's order. Others maintained the order came from Ankhesenamun. Rumors abounded, but I chose to believe Tey died of natural causes in absence of evidence otherwise. So it was that Ay took Ankhesenamun as his Royal Wife and Queen.

His status as Pharaoh being thus strengthened, the intrigue of Ay's court subsided. Short of a year after their marriage, Ankhesenamun choked on an olive pit and died. As I was a witness to her death — my efforts to save her being in vain — the cause of death was accepted without speculation.

Ay's reign as Pharaoh was short, a scant four years and one month when, on an early morning, he was found dead on his couch. As Tutankhamun lay in the tomb of Ay, so Ay, upon appropriate ceremony, was to be interred in the tomb once intended for Tutankhamun.

Though I was not among them, many considered it a coincidence upon Ay's death to learn that Horemheb, returning victorious from the Asiatic colonies (the rebellion having been settled three months earlier) was camped only days from Thebes. The envoy sent ahead to announce Horemheb's arrival was by chance present when Nakhtmin, son-in-law and successor to Ay, was found floating in the Nile. His servants, assumed to have fled in fear, were not in attendance when he was discovered.

So it was that Horemheb arrived at the palace in Thebes, riding triumphant at the head of Egypt's army, and declared himself Pharaoh.

—□—

When Horemheb had departed for the Asiatic colonies, only days before the death of Tutankhamun, he had thought to take with him a papyrus upon which bore the seal of Tutankhamun, naming Horemheb Crown Prince and rightful heir should Tutankhamun die without sons (further proof that Ay and Ankhesenamun's scheme could never have succeeded). As this was the case, and inasmuch as Ay's reign as Pharaoh was brief and unremarkable, and the Egyptian people continued to worship Tutankhamun without break, Horemheb's claim to the throne went unchallenged.

To further secure his claim, Horemheb married Ay's daughter, Mutnodjimet, thereby fulfilling Ay's desire to have his son-in-law inherit. Thus, the papyrus was neatly wrapped with a string of leather, and a commoner, without even the smallest drop of Royal blood, now rules as Pharaoh, Son of Ra, King of Upper and Lower Egypt.

Assured of his throne, among Horemheb's first acts as Pharaoh was to wipe the face of Egypt clean of all mention of Tutankhamun and Ay. For Tutankhamun had been, and still was, greatly loved, and Ay had served Tutankhamun, His father, and His grandfather, and had been himself the father of many Queens, most notably the great Nefertiti. Thus, if not worshiped, he was revered.

Although Horemheb meant to be thorough in expunging all reference to Tutankhamun and Ay, including bringing down Ay's intended tomb and reusing the stones to build edifices to honor himself, he has yet to find the tomb of Tutankhamun. I believe I am the only living soul left to know of its location, and Horemheb would never stoop to ask me.

Horemheb has ever tolerated me underfoot, as by your command, great Bastet, slaying any mau in Egypt remains punishable by death (though perhaps not for a Pharaoh). However, he removed the gold from my ears and neck and degraded my position as Royal Mau, Adviser and Protector to Pharaohs, to that of Royal Rat Killer.

It is now three years into Horemheb's reign and, barring assassins and cobras, he will stay Pharaoh for many years to come. He is still young and healthy. Being a commoner, he does not suffer the shaking that distinguishes the Royal Family. Though I know him to be a pretender and believe him to have murdered Ay, Ay's successor, Nakhtmin, and perhaps even an unborn son of Tutankhamun, I do not believe that Egypt will suffer under his rule. For, as I often lay in the sun these last three years and watched the rats parade by, I sometimes reflected upon the fact that Horemheb chose to forego his earlier claim as Pharaoh and instead remained willingly in Asia to protect Egypt's interests. It soothes me to think of this.

So, great Bastet, my story ends. Those whom I loved and served are in another world, and it is my wish to join them. Having expended all that is left of my strength traveling to your temple to prostrate myself before you, I pray you will accept my offering as worthy, and set me on my journey to the next kingdom.

—▱—

The priestess entered the inner temple and slowly approached the small figure lying at the feet of Bastet. Unfurling a length of the Goddess's finest linen, the priestess bent and tenderly wrapped the cat in its folds. Bowing to Bastet, she raised the body of Mau for the final blessing before carrying her to the mummification chamber to prepare for her journey.

Robin Praytor

Robin Praytor spent her corporate years drafting legal documents and creating training materials. To distract from the deadlines and to-do lists that kept her awake at night, she invented complex and quirky stories that demanded written versions. Thus, her debut novel, *Transmuted*, book one of the Dark Landing series, and a 2017 Kindle*Scout* winner, finally saw daylight. The second book of the series, *Mass Primary*, was published in May 2018. She is currently writing the first book in a new dramedy series, *Evelyn Granger, Vampire Detective*. Each book will be a stand-alone mystery set at different points in history, or in the near- and far-future.

Managing Editor of Post-To-Print Publishers, Robin splits her time between her publishing duties and writing novels and short stories. A Michigan native, she now lives in Phoenix, Arizona, with her patient and long-suffering husband. She is a card-carrying nerd and Comicon aficionado, with a penchant for science fiction and the paranormal.

Blogsite: Disclaimer: I Could Be Wrong
Facebook: @RobinPraytorAuthor
Twitter: @RobinPraytor
For Amazon and Goodreads search: Robin Praytor

BIG EARS

Wallace made a final dash for the tall grass at the bottom of the hill. His pursuers, the folk of the village Culloden, descended upon him in a scrum. Their hands grasped at his back and haunches, fingers sliding off sleek fur. After several unsuccessful attempts, the large sausage-like appendages of Mr. MacGowan, the smith, wrapped around the tip of his tail. Wallace tried his best to ignore the pain. The man had a tenuous grip but a grip nonetheless. Should he threaten a bite or a swat to free himself? The other humans would likely have him.

He thought about his friends and fellow toms. He thought about Snowbell, the molly he loved and with whom he shared his kills. He was their living memory now. They could only live on if he lived on. Capture, and the certain death to follow, wasn't an option.

He ignored the pain and pushed forward, suppressing a yowl as he dug his back legs into the dirt. A pop sounded at the base of his tail followed by a bolt of pain that shot up his spine and cascaded over his body. It was unbearable, but Mr. MacGowan no longer held him. No time to stop, no time to think. Had he lost his tail? He was unsure, but if he slowed to check now, it would most certainly mean death. His pursuers tripped over one another as they tried to recapture him.

As swiftly and silently as his feline grace allowed, he ran to the tall grass that clung to the miles of hilly terrain just outside the village. The grass was a good place in which to get lost. With his body squeezed as thin as possible, he navigated through the stalks. From their higher vantage point, he feared the humans could see the blades split as he passed. When his pursuers grew closer, they stomped big, clumsy feet in spots in the grass where they thought he might be. He dodged the trampling, putting as much distance as he could between himself and the deranged humans.

With long, furtive strides, he labored up the sharp slope. He could slow down on the other side, a safe distance from the madness that contaminated the village Culloden.

His mind wandered back to his comrades, to Snowbell. He lamented the fate of his clowder—his family—wishing he'd never turned that corner in the village square where the heat from the flames scorched his whiskers. Someone caught up in the madness of it all, had grabbed him by the scruff and thrown him unceremoniously onto the nearest bonfire. The errant toss was more a favor than either he or the villager that tossed him realized.

The people of Culloden skewered most of the cats with a wooden spit before placing them onto the bonfires. Not having a wooden stake shoved up his ass allowed Wallace to gather himself and leap away before the blaze did real damage. With chaos crashing around him, he was able to make it to the edge of the village square before they noticed he'd escaped and picked up the chase.

A surge of pain rushed through his body, emanating from his tail. He paused long enough to inspect the appendage. It hung unmoving between his back legs, his efforts to lift it, to no avail.

The fires crackled in the village behind him, and the smell of singed fur and cooking flesh assaulted his senses. As they often did with their kills, the humans cooked them but oddly did not claim the meat. Instead they let them roast beyond palatability. Wallace didn't know much about what the humans called "cooking," but he knew that if they applied the flame for too long, the meat soured. It insulted him that they would let his people's perfectly good meat go to waste.

What caused this strange behavior? Was it the pox that had infested the village weeks prior? It spread through the town quickly, killing so many. Wallace paid it little attention since the cats were unaffected, but perhaps he should have. Maybe he would have seen the genocide coming. He concluded it was the only logical reason for the humans' recent insanity.

He thought of the milk girl that lived in the small farmstead near the barn where he sometimes slept. Had it affected her? No. The night prior, he'd lay in the rushes of the modest dwelling. A sweet, fat rat entered in the middle of the night. The rats had grown bold of late; this one did not fear as it should. The milk girl found Wallace early that morning, lying with the remains of its corpse. As usual, when he caught a rat in the barn, she rewarded him with a fresh bowl of milk and stroked his fur as he lapped at the liquid. He did not see her amongst the throngs in the village square. That reassured him, and he hoped that she was okay.

What about the rats? Were they connected to the pox? He heard that if the humans caught it in the morning, the worst symptoms manifested that same afternoon, and they died by nightfall. The piles of bodies steadily grew higher along the hills outside the village proper, forming mounds of pink, rotting flesh, marked by knots of arms and legs. The fetid odor kept all but the most uncouth of cats away. The rats however, feasted upon the carnage. Rats breed when food is in abundance, and they grew fat and plentiful on the decaying corpses. Doubtful it'd been the rats; they had naught within them to achieve something as insidious as this.

For now, he'd escaped, and that would have to be enough. What should he do next? Go to a city in the highlands, Inverness perhaps? There was a forest nearby. He could hide there, hunting field mice and small birds. He'd miss the farmstead, and the creatures in the forest weren't as easy to kill as the rats, but he'd get by.

When he exited the tall grass, his musings crashed around him. Atop the hill sat the largest animal Wallace had ever laid eyes on. It held the limp body of one of the plague victims like a toy between its paws and looked down at the fires in the village with a passing curiosity. Wallace trembled as he regarded the creature's sleek ebony coat, the fur dancing off its body like the smoke of some great fire. A single splotch of white in the center of its chest marred the creature's darkness. But its most significant feature was the large, tufted ears that lifted into the sky like great watchtowers.

It seemed not to notice Wallace, or if it did, chose not to acknowledge him. The black-striped tomcat took that for his opportunity to creep silently back into the grass. He sought to hide there until the monster got bored and wandered away.

The giant ears twitched in aggravation. "Take one more step," its brogue sounded regal inside Wallace's head, like a highland lord, "and I will string your entrails from the hillside to the center of that shithole down yonder."

Wallace's ears flattened against his head and his back arched. He stopped all the same, emitting a soft growl, but the threat was empty. The creature ignored his protests. It reached out one paw, lazily stretching it so a single claw, caked with dried blood, protracted. The claw was a massive, curved blade that reminded the tom of the swords humans carried during war. It ran its tongue along the back of the claw, its eyes never leaving the village below.

"Got away did ye?" it asked, "The last wee little refugee of Culloden?"

"A-Aye, I got away," Wallace wasn't sure if the thing could hear his thoughts, but it was worth a try.

"I would avoid all the villages and towns if I were you, wee refugee," the creature said, before tearing the dead body open across the midsection and dipping its claw into the guts. It stirred them around as if the corpse were a pot and the innards a stew.

Wallace found that he rather disliked the creature. "I'll keep that in mind. Thank ye for the tip."

"This madness is everywhere," the creature's voice cracked, its eyes widening as it looked down on the village. "It's watching us right now, angered that you are beyond its reach."

Wallace looked back the way he came. Over the grass, he could see only the fires and the humans who still searched for him at the bottom of the hill. They did not seem interested in climbing, or even to look up at the great cat that sat at its crest.

Wallace was unsure what was happening, but he still believed it too weighty for the rats to carry out. They were agents of chaos, disorganized, they could not achieve something so elaborate.

"Are ye sure about that?" The creature asked. "They are crafty li'l buggers when left to their own devices."

"Aye," Wallace conceded, "but their attention spans hinder them from pulling something of this magnitude. The humans like them less than they like us. So I don't think they'd allow themselves to be so easily manipulated, especially by pointy-nosed vermin. If you said dogs were to do this, I might be inclined to believe ye. But dogs are far too loyal, and quite frankly not resourceful enough to think of something like this. Yet ye speak of this madness as if it is sentient—as if it can see us?"

"Some think it is. That answer, however, is irrelevant. What it is, is a fire. As you know, fire is all-consuming. This country, or even this continent, will nae be enough. It won't stop at the humans either; it'll mutate, change so that it can go after the livestock, then maybe the dogs, or the trees, or whatever else it can."

"So why doesn't it kill the rats?"

"They made a deal for immunity." The creature flattened its ears as it looked at him. The sound was like great, leathery wings folding in on themselves. "Tell me, wee refugee, what did the humans in your village do? What did those bastards do to my wee little ones?"

It awaited an answer, its intense, jade eyes filled with a deep knowledge and an equally deep malice as they gazed upon him. The creature was intimidating to look upon, and more so when it looked back. Wallace wanted to run, but there was nowhere to run to. The village was not an option, and he did not think he could get past the creature.

"They turned on us," he said, "gathered us up in the village square. They started by breaking our necks. They did that to my youngest. Those were the lucky cats. Eventually they opted to impale us on spits before throwing us onto great bonfires. They burned us like they do their witches, they did. We died yowling. Ye can see the bonfires from here." Wallace stopped for a moment, tears forming in his eyes.

"Aye, ye can," the creature said as it pulled the entrails from the corpse and then shoved them into its mouth. It sucked up the meat, making a slurping sound. "Arg, tis no haggis."

"That is how they came for us. They spared no molly, no tom, and nae even a catling. They killed us all, everyone, except me."

It smiled at that bit of news, a playful, musing look on its face. "It is a delicious bit of irony!" the creature said, casting aside its meaty plaything. It laid its head down between its paws, like a domestic anticipating a bowl of milk. Its eyes grew wide as it looked down at Culloden, giving the impression of some deified-kitten about to pounce on the village as if it were an unsuspecting mouse.

"I guess ye deserve an explanation," the creature said. "Do ye know what the Taghairm is?" Wallace had heard of it once but knew little. "So that's a no?" The creature continued, "It is a ritual. The humans perform it in the hopes that a demon will appear and grant them a wish."

"I thought that was supposed to bring a faery?" Wallace asked.

"Faery, demon, Cait Sidhe — they cannot tell the difference anymore. They've strayed so far from their gods, and lost themselves in that strange, foreign religion. Though, they tend to revisit us when their new god does not respond to their prayers. Sometimes we appear, sometimes we don't, and still sometimes, if they don't get everything exactly right, we are free to do as we will." The creature seemed eerily pleased at the last prospect.

"What would a faery have to gain from the death of cats?"

"Nothing. They figured out long ago that if enough cats suffer, I show. I don't want my kin to suffer, so I do what I must, let them bind me, submit to their will and all that. Of course, in exchange, the ritual must be performed exactly. One misstep, one failed 'tribute,' and I gain free will. So when the humans perform the Taghairm they must be a mite careful." It looked at the village again, a slow rumbling growl far surpassing Wallace's earlier attempt, rolled from it. "The pox struck down the population of neighboring lands. It culled them as the farmer culls his wheat. These humans planned to attack their neighbors, to take advantage of the situation.

"They amassed a great army in preparation to take that southern kingdom after the plague finished its work ... but it wasn't finished. Death crossed the border, feasting upon the great army. No mail of rings nor sword of steel could protect the soldiers from the rot developing inside of them. Under threat of mutiny, the generals turned tail and ran, like cowards. Ye can't run from this, however. Ye just bring it with ye, and they did. Brought it home to their mollies, and their catlings they did. It ravaged every village, town, and highland from Edenborough all the way to the Isle of Skye. Now they grow desperate. They want to keep the plague from killing their human clowders."

"Will ye?" Wallace asked. "Will ye keep it from killing them?"

"Even if I wanted to, and I've no strong *want* to, they have already sealed their fate by performing the Taghairm."

"How so?"

"The death infests the countryside, sitting in the town squares on a throne of corpses. It's in the water, the earth, and the air around them. It chooses them randomly, pointing its finger, calling their names, using their fear as an appetizer before consuming them whole. In their desperation, they kill my kin to summon me. They commit senseless slaughter to bind me into saving them. As they kill my cats, they doom themselves.

"Could they have stopped the plague, kept it from their cities?"

"They could have contained it. The plague transmits via the fleas. Nae, you were right wee little refugee, 'tis not the rats who are causing this, but the fleas that feed off them. The rats made a pact with this death god, but the fleas serve him."

"The fleas?"

"Aye, the rats cart the death in their blood. The fleas drink from them, infect themselves. Then, as carriers, the fleas drink from a human and pass the death on. Unchecked by the clowders and feeding off the corpses, the rats over populate. They in turn feed the fleas, who make the human cities into havens for the death god. In time, the human dead will pile as high as their buildings. They can't stop it, and they've killed the only thing that can contain it … my cats."

Wallace looked once more at the great animal and then back down the hill at the village. The bonfires burned bright in the village square. He thought he saw the spirits of his loved ones riding the plumes of dark smoke into the blue, afternoon sky.

"Run along, wee one," Big Ears said. "Go to the forest, feed on the birds, and mourn your losses. Leave knowing they will beg me for the solution, for the balm to, at the very least, temper this death god that steals away their children. Your survival means I am not bound to the Taghairm. They cannot bend me to their will."

"Will ye kill them? Do to them what ye did to yon plaything?"

"Will I? Should I?" Its eyes narrowed into slits. It pushed its butt up into the air, haunches at the ready, as if it were about to pounce on a beetle. The creature filled Wallace's field of view. Maw opened, the fangs of its grin were easily as long the tom's body from tail to head. He suddenly felt very small, insignificant. "Tell me, wee one," its voice came on waves of excited breath. "What should I do with them? How should I repay their kindness? Split them with my claws? Chew them with my teeth? Gobble up their children in front of them, one by one? Ye suffered by their hands! Let's repay the debt."

"Do none of those things," Wallace shouted, closing his eyes, expecting the Cait Sidhe to punish him for his insolence. It did not. When he opened his eyes again, he saw it staring at him, a curious look on its face. "Tell them not to hate the cats," he continued hesitantly. "Tell them the truth, not to look upon us as ill omens, and tell them to stop killing us. Maybe, when our numbers return, we can help them stave off this death god before it's too late."

"Spare them?" it asked, trying to hide the offense in its voice.

"Nae, not exactly. The death god will have his way with them for generations to come. To kill them now only hastens the inevitable and is a mercy. But while the pox is distracted by its playthings, our numbers can swell. When we've grown enough, we can turn our attention to the rats. Kill the carriers and the fleas will become immaterial. The rats and the fleas are the only creatures with immunity, and the lifespan of the fleas isn't long enough to make the disease much of a threat."

"Aye," said the Cait Sidhe, "and as long as no one else makes a deal like the rats, we should be able to stop the death god. But why?"

"As ye said, eventually it will turn its attention to something other than the humans. Maybe to the dogs, maybe the livestock, maybe us — probably us. Before that happens, let's kill it in the human cities. We can't do that unless the humans understand that we're not their enemy, know that we're not the reason this is happening."

The Cait Sidhe sat up to its full length, looking down at the tom. Wallace once again felt like an insect about to be swatted from existence. "I will spare yer humans, Wallace of the Culloden clowder. You are to find a molly and have many catlings. You are to tell your progeny to have many catlings, as well, for it is they who will attack the rats. Should this work, do not look for the Cu-Sidhe in your last days the hound will not come for ye. Instead I shall meet you where the path diverges. I will claim you as one of *my* clowder."

With that, Big Ears no longer stood before Wallace. It did not move past him, nor vanish with any flair, it simply ceased to exist on the hill. He looked back at the village of Culloden one last time, and thought of his life there, thought of his catlings, of Snowbell, and finally of the girl who brought him milk as he lay in the rushes. There was nothing he could do for his loved ones, but he hoped that he gave the milk girl a little more time. He tried his tail again and found that he could lift it if ever so slightly; it was a start. The forest beckoned. There he could lick his wounds, mourn his losses, and maybe find a molly.

Wilfred R. Robinson

Wilfred R. Robinson is a writer of weird fiction (which, in his opinion, falls under the all-inclusive category of "genre fiction"). In 1992, he took first for his age bracket in the Philcon Young Writers contest and was at one time the head writer for the now defunct comic, *The Friday Knights*. His work appears in the anthologies *Trysts of Fate,* Issue 5 ("Everspring"), and *DarkFuse* #4 ("The Intruder").

Wil lives in Philadelphia, PA with his wife, Laura, and their young son.

Blogsite: http://www.wilfredrrobinson.com/
Facebook: @lazycuthulu

NICE WORK IF YOU CAN GET IT

A Maine Coon—a country-sized cat, built for the extermination of country-sized rats—is an anomaly in the city. Before I was inadvertently liberated from the Manhattan luxury condo set, I was a custom-ordered cat. Now, freewheeling on the sidewalks of New York, I am sometimes mistaken for a bobcat, an escapee from the park zoo.

I ask you, have you ever seen a tortoiseshell bobcat? An epic Jackson Pollack riot of cordovan brown splashed on and swirled through long black fur? I take great pride in my stylish coat and often lament the loss of my regular salon appointment, a song which sets the other street toms yowling in scorn. They do so from a distance, the better to preserve their personal safety. Even on feral rations, I outweigh them by a good ten pounds. Nor do I, a debonair cat about town, care to risk being marred by a lucky swipe in a street brawl. I happily put in the hours it takes to maintain my sartorial elegance. Not that I'm competing with those other toms. No, indeed, it is much more satisfying to woo the human ladies.

The ladies who lunch that is. One strolls up to the tables so strategically placed on sidewalks or inside opened French doors, and presents an immaculately groomed coat, drawing attention to it with a plumy wave of the tail. One pays homage to their equally stylish turnout with a rumbling *basso profundo* song. Then one gazes upon the delicacies, culinary and otherwise, with wide and soulful golden eyes.

Such a performance is always rewarded with tidbits from their plates, so it's important to choose the proper venues. The best are ones which serve fish for lunch, though I am not opposed to the occasional morsel of chicken or beef, or even more exotic treats such as can be found in the city. The trick, however, is to eat and run.

In the unlikely event that one is snubbed, one merely retreats to cover. A tortie coat, I've found, provides excellent camouflage. The timing must be perfect. Commandeering a meal should occur between the departure of the guests and the arrival of the bus person. It's nice work, if you can get into the right places. Lunch sittings are best, as people rarely order dessert, and the table is bussed directly after the entrée while the fish is still warm from the grill, succulent, and not too muddled with the veg. Mind you, I'm not opposed to an occasional slurp of melted gelato, a nibble of cheesecake, or a discarded corner of tiramisu.

Oh, but show me the fish, baby.

I'll admit it freely, salmon is my downfall. Grilled, smoked, raw rolled in rice, cream cheesed in a bagel—it's all delectable. The lure of salmon has provided me with more adventures than I care to mention, from shameless cat lady pandering to crashing a ballet gala party.

Granted, that last soiree not only landed me a forever human but found me a job with the 86th Precinct. I present Officer Atticus Finch, feline familiar, and protective companion to the one and only Alejandro Valdez, ballet star.

Spiffy, if I say so myself.

But it almost didn't happen. Now, you'd think, as expensive as I was to acquire, that bleached-blonde attorney, who couldn't tell a field mouse from a subway rat, might have pinned up a few "Lost Cat" flyers, or at least posted something on social media. Then again, there was plenty of incentive to do what the humans call "sweeping under the rug." Which has nothing to do with cleaning the floor, but much to do with pretending certain things didn't happen and with keeping their fat bank accounts intact. For instance....

The neighbor's pit bull is not your pony.

If I had thumbs, I would gladly have spent an afternoon's detention writing that phrase on a blackboard one thousand times. As it is, I am one of the largest domestic cats in the world. Almost as big as the neighbor's mutt. Which no doubt embarrassed the neighbor, who also happened to be an attorney. And there was copious use of the *L* word.

Litigation.

Humans, it seems, are even more competitive about territory than tomcats. A piece of prime Manhattan real estate, once occupied, is not to be surrendered over a trivial matter.

Though the matter wasn't trivial to me. It had everything to do with the food chain and one's hierarchy within it. I was acquired because Bleach-Blonde thought she'd seen a rat. After two years of mind-numbing confinement in her luxury condo, I'd battled nothing larger than the occasional cockroach. Not much in the way of sport for a cat like me. On the other hand, the neighbor's pit bull promised a great deal of sport. Not to mention I felt the mutt owed me.

I could hear the beast through the walls, whining for attention, snoring, and most annoying to me, clicking its toenails in mockery each time it passed by my door. That damn dog got to go for romps in the park when all I could do was sit in the window and watch. There came a miraculous evening when Bleach-Blonde was coming in just as the beast was going out.

The neighbors stopped in the hallway to chat, and Bleach-Blonde stood there on her ridiculous high heels, holding the door open. I had plenty of time to determine the rules of engagement with the slobbering beast.

Rule number one: There are no rules.

I crouched, tail waving. An obvious warning, but the humans paid no attention.

The flag is up, and ... we're off!

One pounce and Bleach-Blonde and the Litigator were left flat-footed. The mutt was off its leash, and the bandana hanging around its neck helped me board. I dug in with all claws, riding to victory, or so I thought. Howling and yowling, we blundered into the open elevator. Its door closed behind us.

I almost lost him as the beast whipped in circles in the enclosed space. But the elevator opened into the lobby, and we raced past a befuddled doorman to the Outside World. The mutt was frantic, ready to throw itself into traffic. I shifted my weight, dragging its head away from the street, but it wouldn't reverse. The next I knew, we were galloping down a flight of stairs.

When the mutt came to a stop in front of a crowd of people, I managed a graceful flying dismount, and, spotting a pair of doors sliding open, ducked through before the dog could follow.

Elevator, right? Upstairs to home?

So very wrong.

This fresh hell was a downtown subway train. Thus began my odyssey as a free-range feline. One would think assaulting a pit bull and stealing a ride from the transit authority would set the pet police after me, but no. It was the salmon.

There came a balmy day between spring and summer when, while skimming a lunch seating, I spied party supply trucks circling my favorite performing arts complex. Just the sight of them had me salivating, quivering from ears to tail in anticipation.

Gala night.

Pavilions would go up, red carpets would go down, and tables would be laden with all manner of delicacies. Including, but certainly not limited to, smoked salmon. Suddenly, the mid-week matinee ladies lunching in front of me weren't up to scratch. I did snarf a few leftovers, of course. One must keep up one's strength on a stakeout. I was soon across the plaza, tucked into a prime surveillance spot.

Bring on the caterers, baby.

I passed the time studying posters for the event. A ballet charity gala, so the eye candy on display was plenty prime, the most prominent being Alejandro Valdez, appearing in something called *A Tribute to Nijinsky*. When I saw him arrive at the stage door, I was astonished to learn that he was a mere slip of a human. All muscle, to be sure, but not the immense form displayed on the posters. When I took a second look, as a cat should, I saw his aura.

It was not only as bright as the star he was, it was *massive*. There was, however, a tinge of darkness around the edges, trying to work its way in. Intriguing, certainly different from most of the other talent in the building, but not my concern. My quarry approached from another quarter. As the catering crew unloaded their goods, my superior schnozzle detected the unmistakable scent of salmon. Content to bide my time, I settled in for a nap.

An inundation of human voices roused me. I'd slept through the evening performance, and VIP guests were swarming the tent. A flash of sequins on the periphery marked Alejandro Valdez, fresh from the stage, doing his fundraising duty by mingling with the patrons. I gave myself a good stretch, flexed my claws, and sniffed the air.

Ahhhh!

A delectable platter of salmon, so thoughtfully unattended, lay in the midst of the social schmoozing. And how nice of them to rent such lavish greenery in which to hide. The ambiance was also to my liking, perfect for turning my tortie coat into camouflage. No snatch-and-snarf job here. This fish deserved my full attention.

I prowled the periphery, judging the angles, waiting for the right moment. When it came, I was a mere shadow slipping across the outdoor carpeting, flitting over the table. As I savored the fillet, I was a gentle breeze barely ruffling the fichus.

"A treat tastes best when you've worked hard for it—eh, *gato grande*?"

I looked up to find Alejandro Valdez also hiding in the fichus. I gave him a wink between bites.

"I confess," he whispered, "I snagged a few bites of red velvet cake myself. I don't like these events. There are too many unhealthy people here. The Shadow of Death looms large tonight."

Licking the last of the salmon from my whiskers, I eyeballed the dancer. Alejandro Valdez could see the things most cats could but most humans couldn't.

Like the Shadow of Death, hovering over a group of self-indulgent slobs stuffing themselves full of rich food and strong drink. I gave his leg a jowl rub in empathy and turned my attention back to the table. The waiter was nowhere in sight, and I was feeling like a second helping. We parted ways, the dancer and I, he to a table of diamond-draped society ladies, and I to the buffet.

As I applied a delicate claw, contemplating my next selection, a shout broke my concentration.

"Hey! Get outta there!"

Cheez it! The penguins!

There are tuxedos, and there are *tuxedos*. In Bleach-Blonde's guide to life, the cut of a man's tux indicated his station. On the scale from Milan to Manny's Cater Waiters, the penguin suits coming at me were bad news for a cat with his paws in the people food. So, I did exactly what I was told.

I got outta there.

Or I might have, but I took off with the filched fillet in my jaws. I am nothing if not determined. Unfortunately, the penguins were even more determined, and I was quickly surrounded. They weren't gonna put that fish back on the table, so I backed them off with a few growls while I finished it. I was considering snagging a third helping on my way through their legs when something dropped over my head and tightened around my neck. *For the love of Bast. A catch pole? Seriously? I'm a friend of Alejandro Valdez. We shared a fichus.* Oh, the indignity. Apparently, there is no right of appeal in the court of Animal Control. Dogs may whine and whimper when apprehended, but I am a feline and go stoically to my fate. Hauled off to the cooler, I'm sent directly to the treatment room. I feel the prick of the needle and prepare myself to enter the great cat condo in the sky.

Gradually, I awaken to a bright, white light. Though I'm not moving toward it, nor is it moving toward me. After a brief inventory, it appears all my parts are present and accounted for.

Er ... maybe not. The injection wasn't lethal to me, but to my future offspring. My pedigree status is no longer worth the paper it's printed on. Now that I've been nip/tucked, I'm just another shelter cat.

A three-striker, as they say here in stir. Too big, too boisterous, and doesn't play well with others. There's not much in the way of intelligent life coming through on two legs looking to spring me from the pokey, either. Though I know I've got a limited shelf life, I just can't put on the cute kitty act for these slack-jawed humans and their screaming, slobbering, spoiled spawn. After being hauled out for inspection, having my tail *and* my ear tufts pulled, and listening to the brat wail when her lollipop got stuck in my fur, I hoped being taken to the treatment room meant trading in one of my nine lives for a do-over.

Nope.

It meant getting a bath and a blow-dry to get the candy outta my fur, which rather gave me a new lease on life. The shelter staff agreed.

"Let's make Bowser the centerpiece of the adoption event. He may not get adopted, but he'll sure make people stop and look."

They weren't kidding. Bright and early the following morning I, along with a selection of my fellow inmates, was caged, packed into a van, and stacked for display on a midtown sidewalk. I drew a crowd, all right. A crowd of people who adopted every cat but me. The traveling cages weren't exactly spacious for ordinary cats. I couldn't turn around without shaking the entire stack. Which, as cage after cage was emptied, gave me an idea. I got ready to rumble.

My mitts were too big to reach through and fiddle the door latch. A good bounce on the pavement, however, ought to pop the thing right open. I meant to do it, too. I knew this was my last chance, but timing was crucial.

The sun dropped behind the skyscrapers. I was the last cat standing in the last hour. The lone attendant looked at his watch. I kept an eye out for the return of the van, when who should I see coming toward us? Mop of raven hair, sculpted Spanish cheekbones, blazing aura.

"Alejandro Valdez!" Most of the humans around me heard

nothing but a desperate yowling. Alejandro, however, snapped his head around and looked me right in the eye. When he smiled, I knew he remembered me from the gala. I felt a great sense of relief when he came over to my cage, put a finger through, and scratched my ears.

"Hey, *gato grande*. That cage is too small for you." He pulled a credit card out of his wallet and turned to the yawning attendant.

"How much for this cat?"

"Two hundred dollars. Cash."

"You're kidding."

"Nope. Better hurry up if you need to find an ATM. Our permit's only good for another half hour, and the van's gonna be here any minute."

I rattled the cage to get the dancer's attention, but he was off down the street without giving me so much as a second look. I kept him in sight as long as I could and thought I saw him enter a bank. At least I hoped it was him and hoped it was a bank. I was hoping like mad to see him come out and return with my bail, when my view was cut off by the van.

"Don't worry too much, Bowser," the attendant yawned again. "We'll leave you on the sidewalk till the last minute. Maybe he'll come back."

My only answer was a dismal yowl. What I wanted to do was growl, but that would've given the game away. I was still hell bent on my original escape plan, and now I intended to track down Valdez. His good intentions toward me shouldn't cost him so dearly.

Besides, I was ready to cause as much trouble for that obnoxious attendant as I could.

Nobody calls me "Bowser," and gets away with it.

"Tough luck, Bowser. Time to go."

Damn skippy, jerkface.

I snagged his thumb with my claw as he picked up my cage. He let go, cursing, and I threw my weight so one corner of the door hit the sidewalk first. The latch popped, and I barreled out into the gathering dusk. Taking advantage of the heavy pedestrian traffic, I crouched in the shadow of a nearby doorway, watching the fun.

"We gotta catch that cat!"

The van driver shook his head. "That cat's halfway to the Bronx by now. Just say some kid let it loose. Not like that's never happened before."

"Yeah, they'll believe that. Let's get out of here before the parking cops show up."

Curled into the smallest bundle of fur possible, I watched the van pull away. As it cleared the intersection, Alejandro appeared on the other side of the street, shopping bag in hand, watching it go. His shoulders slumped, and he turned back the way he'd come.

Mustering my remaining nerve, I broke from cover, yowling and running for my life.

"Alejandro! Wait! I'm still here. Don't leave me. Alejandro Valdez!"

No one in Manhattan pays attention to crosswalk signals. I was no exception. I stuck close to a woman pushing a stroller, heedless of an oncoming bus, and tried to remember what Valdez was wearing. The perspective from pavement level was daunting. Concentrating on making the opposite curb, certain Alejandro must be at least a block ahead of me, I slammed into a pair of muscular legs.

"Hey, big fellow! You make a clever escape, no? But of course, you had to. I thought I was being careful of the time. Where we are going, you must have the proper accessories."

I followed Alejandro into a sheltered doorway. He hunkered down, and I put my front paws on his shoulders to rub my face against his, purring enthusiastically. I rubbed him all over, to be certain I wouldn't lose track of him again.

"It wasn't your fault," I assured him. "The van came early, and those lazy bums didn't want to wait." I swatted the shopping bag.

"What's in here? Is it for me?" This last was muffled, I was halfway inside, curious.

Alejandro pulled it away, taking out a dog harness of neon orange and a black leash. I didn't mean to seem ungrateful, but my ears flattened at the unfashionable sight.

Alejandro laughed.

"I know, *gato grande*, it is not very stylish, but I was in a hurry, and this was all they had in your size. Tomorrow we will go to the pet boutique in Chelsea. They handle the custom work for the cats of the 86th Precinct, and because you are so clever, we have two hundred dollars to spend."

"Okay. I'll wear this for tonight. Where are we going?"

"To the cathedral. So behave yourself."

As he adjusted the harness and snapped on the leash, I raised my right paw. "I promise. What is the 86th Precinct? And why do cats work there? May I work there? Are we going in a taxi? May I sit by the window?"

"The 86th is a paranormal unit. Every sort of familiar, and all manner of practitioners work there. My boyfriend works there."

"Things that go bump in the night?" I thrashed my tail, ready for battle.

"Yes, and when bad things go bump, the 86th bumps back. They police their own kind, as well as things the mundane police can't handle — or won't. You'll see."

"I see you, Alejandro Valdez. You shine. Most humans are dull. You shine."

I was babbling, but I couldn't help it. My plan for an eleventh-hour reprieve had worked better than my wildest dreams. I might have made a complete fool of myself if Alejandro's phone hadn't chimed.

"Hey Mike, we're on our way. You are not going to believe who I found. Remember the cat, the one who stole the fish at the gala? I adopted him. Don't worry, you're gonna like him."

We got out of the taxi on the corner, and I made use of the local shrubbery for a spot of personal business. Trotting jauntily at Alejandro's heel, I basked in the attention as heads turned, drawn by the sheer radiance of his being.

A tall, chestnut-haired man in the dress uniform of a high-ranking police officer was pacing the porch of the cathedral, glancing at his watch. I could hear organ music as we climbed the steps to meet him. He looked down at me with strange, hazel eyes.

"You didn't tell me he was the size of a pit bull."

I leaned forward, brazenly sniffing the trouser cuff of this person who dared question my rescuer. With my ears flat, I looked up at Alejandro.

"You didn't tell me your boyfriend was a ghoul."

My reward was a flicker in the undead eyes. I was now being taken seriously. Mike folded his six-foot-two frame to my level.

"Detective Mike Hodges. I'd ask you how you managed to hornswoggle AJ, but the service is about to start."

"Atticus Finch. Pleased to meet you. I eat pit bull for breakfast."

"And smoked salmon for dinner, I hear. We need to go inside. I was hoping for a kitten in your pocket, AJ. I don't know what the bishop's going to say about this."

"He will say that is the finest tortoiseshell he's seen in many a day and definitely the largest."

When I approached the bishop, I gave the gnarled hand extended toward me a gentle rub and touched my nose to the ring it wore. The old man smiled.

"Just stay in the back, gentlemen, if you don't mind. And you, my fine fellow, stay under the pew. Try not to be mistaken for a kneeler. I'll expect you back on St. Francis Day."

The children about to receive their first communion were lined up in the narthex, ready to fall in behind the main procession. Taking his place, the bishop smiled again as one little girl ducked out of her line, her face transformed by a brilliant smile.

"Uncle Mike! Uncle AJ! Wow, where'd you get the cat? He's huge!"

Mike shushed his niece.

"Not now, Peggy. You can meet the cat after the service. Mind your manners and get back in line, or your mother will have all our hides."

Peggy got back in line, and we waited for the procession to make its way up the aisle before slipping into a back pew. AJ— Alejandro, that is—sat on the aisle so I could peer out. Peggy's place at the rail was within my view.

What a delightful child. I hope she isn't a tail puller.

Neither of Mike's nieces were tail pullers, though Mike's sister, Caitlin, wasn't happy about the necessity of *al fresco* seating at the restaurant afterward. She pouted until a girlfriend showed up with a Chihuahua in her bag. Then the sidewalk table was Caitlin's idea, because *wasn't it a beautiful evening?*

Whether the mutt sensed an alien presence beneath AJ's chair or more likely because it was simply bad-tempered and spoiled, the ankle biter kept up a persistent yapping. Conversation became impossible as the woman insisted on holding the dog in her lap. I was content to be patient, knowing the mutt wouldn't be able to contain itself. It soon jumped down, and I chose that moment to stroll out of my hiding place. I sat at AJ's right leg, staring at the yammering dust rag.

A nearby diner, in a staged voice, asked a waiter to get the manager. I swiveled my head, looking up at AJ in mute appeal. He, in turn, looked across the table at Mike. After all, the dust rag belonged to Mike's sister's friend, even though the ladies in question were oblivious to the disturbance. Mike must have given AJ the okay, because, with a wicked grin, AJ gave me a nod and a wink.

I commenced a rumbling growl, slowly rising in pitch and volume until it cut through the dog's yip yap, ending in a prolonged hiss. The little fur duster answered with its own comic growling, punctuated with snaps of its tiny teeth. The women persisted yammering.

The dog's bravura terminated in a loud yelp as it went tumbling between the tables. I ducked back under AJ's chair, out of sight. Several nearby diners applauded, even as Caitlin and her friend rushed to the Chihuahua's rescue.

The manager appeared, and Mike dug out his credit card.

"I'll get the check," he told AJ. "You get Atticus out of here."

The next morning, I went with AJ to the 86th Precinct where I met Officer Pookie, the large, gray tabby familiar, who was Mike's partner. With a feline snigger and an emerald wink, Pookie indicated that Mike was on the phone. Much to my chagrin, I found the subject of conversation was me.

"Actually, Caitlin, the manager put it on the house. Yes, he did. Seems he dislikes toy dogs as much as everyone around us last night. In fact, he's invited us to bring Atticus to dinner any time we like. No, he will not be allowed to make a habit of bitch slapping Chihuahuas, but the cat did only what the rest of us wanted to. If Atticus hadn't tossed that dog, the manager was going to insist that your friend leave. As far as I'm concerned, the cat let you both off the hook. 'Bye, Caitlin. Love to the girls."

For a moment I thought I was bound for the shelter once more. Then Mike hoisted me up to his shoulder, giving me a vigorous rub.

"My sister is a piece of work. You can use those pocket pooches for bowling balls any time you like."

"I shall only indulge myself when given provocation, sir. I promise. And if you don't mind, just a little to the left?"

Ahhh.

So long to the ladies who lunch. Nowadays I get to sit at the table, across from Pookie, each of us in our 86th Precinct harnesses. Anyone who has a problem with it gets a gold detective's shield flashed at them. AJ shines bright, on stage and off, which makes the things that go bump want to put out his light.

Not on my watch. For a burly familiar like me, this really is nice work.

Karen Ovér

When not negotiating with the cat for desk space, Karen Ovér can sometimes be found clinging to a ballet barre, attempting to realign the vertebrae sent in all directions by hours of maniacal word processing.

Karen currently lives and writes in New York City (after fifteen years in Austin, Texas). Her work has appeared in *Collective Fallout, Sweater Weather, Sci Phi Journal,* and is available on Amazon and her blog site, *Ballets and Bogeys.*

THE OPEN ROAD

The breeze teasing my whiskers carried a cornucopia of scents. Some, like the taint of jet fuel and singed plastacrete, struck me as less than pleasant. But I detected animal smells too, and the aroma of growing things. Best of all, I breathed real air under an open sky, not the re-circulated stuff that had tainted my lungs aboard the passenger liner *Sargasso,* whose company I had so recently departed.

Cruise liners hadn't been my favorite vessels over the years, but I'd sought out the *Sargasso* for old time's sake. After all, the *Sargasso* resembled, in many ways, the *Elizabeth*—the ship on which I'd been born.

Like my mother before me, I'd taken up the profession of ship's cat. And yet, after my stint on the *Sargasso,* I wondered how Mom managed to serve all those years in such an atmosphere. Sure, a passenger vessel comes with its perks: comfortable bunks, a secure food source, doting passengers and crew. And yet, like most things in life, the ship's cat role on such a ship has its drawbacks—like having your tail or whiskers pulled by children who are old enough to know better, while their parents watch indulgently. Passengers screaming in disgust when they find a headless rodent at their door—you'd think they'd be grateful. And—

Forget it, I told myself, lifting my head. *That's behind you, now.* The siren song of the open road echoed once again in my tattered ears. Best to heed it.

I gazed northward, taking in the verdant green of the far-off mountains. *Would it be so bad to remain planet-side for a while?* I wondered. A thinly settled world by human standards, Degna teemed with rodents and small animal life. Perhaps—

The clatter of an automated luggage train reminded me that the ground transport lane of a busy spaceport is no place to pause and meditate. I turned my attention to the vessels surrounding me and assumed a business-like air as I assessed them one by one. Merchant ship—been there, done that. N'Kisi warship—I shuddered. Formidable warriors, the N'Kisi tended to shoot first, ask questions later. Understandably, this had a way of taking its toll on crew safety, not that they seemed to worry overmuch. Much as I hated to admit it, I'd be better off securing another berth on a passenger vessel rather than signing up to serve with the N'Kisi.

That left the last ship, positioned off to the side—Galactic Space Ship *Meech Lake*. Named after a place on Earth if my AI-enhanced memory served me correctly.

I paused, weighing my options. I could bunk in at the spaceport hotel, see what else showed up. The accumulated pay on my collar's credit chip would accommodate a lengthy stay.

On the other hand, I had yet to serve on a GSS vessel. *Why not?* I thought.

Only one way to find out whether the *Meech Lake* required the services of a ship's cat. I sauntered toward her, tail held high.

—□—

The man supervising the cargo loading had straw-yellow hair and golden irises. His seven-foot height seemed tall by human standards. *A colonist, most likely,* I mused.

I noted, with a grin, his six-fingered hands—just like my front paws, for I've inherited the polydactyl trait that was once deemed good luck by Earthbound sailors.

"Hey there," he said, his voice cheerful. "Lookin' for work, are you?"

"Yrraaaooo," I reply, extending my neck toward him so he could scan my collar chip.

He toggled through his hand-held comp-pad. "Quicksilver. Male, neutered." He glanced down at me. "Sorry, buddy."

I twitched my tail.

"Good record, distinguished service," he muttered. "Up to date on the specifications of all known pest species." A woman with short blonde hair approached.

"Hey there, Vlad," she said.

"Hey there, yourself, Minna. What do you think of acquiring a ship's cat?"

She shrugged. "Good stats?"

"Yeah," Vlad replied. "Jumps around a lot—his longest term in any one place is a year."

"Lots of experience," she said, peering over his shoulder to study the readout. "I vote yeah. He can bunk with me."

"I'll clear it with Commander Salvar," Vlad said, grinning. "But it looks like you're on, bud, pending the boss's approval." He dropped to one knee and held out his hand. We shook to formalize the deal.

—◻—

"This way, pal," Minna said, glancing back over her shoulder as she led me down the narrow hallway.

So far, so good, I thought. The ship gleamed, her floor and walls immaculate. I approved.

Minna paused and gestured through an open door. "This's it."

I glanced through the opening, seeing the small work desk, the bunk bed with its brightly patterned quilt, and there, beside it—

The swagger oozed out of me, for curled up on a blanket to the right of the bed lay the dark lining to the silver cloud I thought I'd landed on. A *dog.*

"Nrrroooow," I said, feeling the hair on my back rise of its own accord.

The dog rose to her feet, yawning and stretching.

"What do they need a dog for?" I hissed, taking a step toward the black-and-white mutt. "Someone to bark when the doorbell rings?" I sat and put my right paw under my chin as though thinking. "Naw, that's not it. Let me guess. They need a place for the fleas to congregate, so they don't attack the humans."

"Nice to meet you, too," The Dog replied. Her gracious politeness made my throat constrict as though a walnut-sized hairball had lodged itself in my gullet.

"This here's Pepper," Minna said, her tone conciliatory. "She's an AI-enhanced border collie, a member of the combat team." Minna glanced at the dog, who cocked her head and looked at Minna adoringly before turning her scrutiny back in my direction. "Pepper, this's Quicksilver, our new ship's cat."

"Pleasure," Pepper said.

"All mine," I replied stiffly, making sure the look in my eyes would suggest to the mutt I didn't mean a word of it. If she had the brains to clue in—which I doubted.

Minna, meanwhile, fiddled with the mag-rack on the wall. She turned back to face me, and I saw she'd adjusted the ledges to create a ladder. On the topmost surface, she arranged a fuzzy blanket. "You'll bunk here, Silver, if that suits you."

I nodded. To show Pepper I wasn't afraid of any dog, no matter how big—or in her case, how medium-sized—I marched right past her long nose and flowed up the wall using the footholds Minna had provided. I curled up on the soft fabric on the top ledge, kneading it approvingly with my front paws.

"I'll just belt ya in for liftoff," Minna said. She rummaged in an under-the-bed storage drawer and pulled out a swatch of compact webbing. Then affixed magnet clips to the shelf, belted me in, and performed a similar service for the mutt before seeking her own bunk. "Here we go," she said, and I heard the familiar rumble of takeoff, felt the huge hand of gravity pressing down onto my body with all its force.

I'd made my choice, now. No chance to bail until the next port of call.

It's all good. I purred, very softly, to reassure myself. *It's all good.* And I repeated it, like a mantra, until I fell asleep.

—□—

Any ship has its routines, and the *Meech Lake* proved no exception. I welcomed the structure.

I did the normal patrol for the inevitable pests, but found fewer than one might expect, for Commander Nibo Salvar demanded meticulous care of her vessel, and the crew took pride in keeping all surfaces gleamingly clean. Still, I have yet to see a ship fully free of vermin, and the *Meech Lake* had just enough of them for me to earn my keep.

With time on my paws, I also attended Minna's training sessions with Pepper. Sometimes the two of them drilled with other team members, and sometimes they went through their routines alone. I always found their activities intriguing.

One day, Minna invited me to join in a game of hide-and-pursue, and I took up the game with great relish, learning to follow hand signals. And as for the conditioning sessions—I had thought myself, when I came on board, at the peak of fitness, but I soon learned that I was sorely mistaken on that point. Minna taught me how to use the hover-treadmill—easy on the joints, since one's paws landed on air rather than a hard surface. With the help of Engineering, she rigged an exercise device with a steady climb where I was able, with a swipe of a paw-pad across the controls, to adjust both height and speed.

All seemed well until the day Pepper jostled me in the shoulder in passing, during one of our drills. Instinct kicked in, and I hissed and swiped at her, barely missing her sensitive snout.

I apologized later, of course, but Pepper, with the obsessiveness typical of her breed, wouldn't let up. Under that relentless pressure—trust me, you don't know the definition of "relentless" until you meet a border collie—I curled up on the bunk and stammered out the story I'd kept to myself for so long.

—□—

The Incident happened when my brother Frisky and I were six

months old. Mom had a small litter that season, only the two of us. With so much affection to give and a habit of having to spread it much farther, Mom might well have indulged us, turning us into favoured, pampered creatures. But she knew that wouldn't stand us in good stead in the long run, so she insisted on getting an earlier-than-usual start on tutoring us in the finer points of ship's cat duties—specifically, identifying and catching pests, while also upholding good shipboard morale.

As the *Elizabeth* went to hyper-jump after a short stop on Harrison's Planet, Frisky and I found ourselves in high spirits. We'd enjoyed our first planet-side romp, albeit a short one, and despite our young years now fancied ourselves quite the space travellers.

The hydroponics chief, having noticed that some unknown party was nibbling down the fresh herbs Cook Jonas took pride in spicing the food with, had summoned my mother to check into it. And of course, where Mom went, Frisky and I went too.

After locating and dispatching the naar mice responsible for the damage to Cook Jonas' prized greenery, we were making our way in a small procession through the passenger quarters, Mom in the lead and Frisky second. Easily distracted in those days, I tended to dawdle, my attention drawn by a flash of movement here or a cryptic scent there.

That tendency to hang behind saved my life.

Just as Mom passed the door to Room 44-A, a square-jawed, powerful dog easily four times my height at the shoulder leapt out. By rights, such a beast ought to have been restrained and muzzled.

Ought to have been.

I stood, stunned, as the dog pounced on my mother, shaking her several times before throwing her against the wall. The beast advanced toward Frisky while I gave voice to my terror. I jumped on the dog's head and clawed at its muzzle as it clamped its teeth around Frisky's small body.

With a jerk of his massive head, the dog dislodged me.

Frisky fell to the floor with a thud, and I backed away a few paces, my sides heaving with emotion as I attempted to suck air into my lungs.

The dog met my eyes. His lips curled in a sneer that revealed his curved, canine teeth.

I held up my right front paw and hissed, unwilling to give ground. I observed the dog's muscles bunching. *He's about to lunge at me,* I thought, crouching involuntarily.

Like the sword of doom halted in mid-stroke, the dog paused to savor the moment. Though every fibre of my quivering body screamed *run!* I sensed that giving in to the impulse for flight would prove my undoing, for the beast would doubtless catch me within four strides. Instead, I took the offensive, leaping at his smug face and raking my claws everywhere I could reach. I ripped the skin open just under his right eye and drew in a tortured breath as I considered my next move. The scent of blood seared my nostrils, plunging me into battle-fury. Spurred by a surge of rage as I contemplated the fate of my brother and dam, I leapt up on the brute's broad, muscular back. It was a struggle to maintain my balance, but I managed to grip his right ear between my teeth. I dug my claws into his muscular shoulders and clung to him like a burr as he flung his head left and right, trying to shake me off.

The dog's efforts to dislodge me had their effect. I began to slide off his back, knowing if I hit the floor, he would be upon me within seconds. Despair and a rising certainty that I wouldn't escape this confrontation alive flooded through me.

The sound of footsteps pounding down the corridor brought an unexpected resurgence of hope. I glanced up. *Security.*

I hurled myself away from the dog just as a blast from the guard's stun gun hit him full force.

It's over. Relieved of the need for action, I huddled in the corridor, winded and despondent, until the gentle hands of Doctor L'Gondu collected me.

—□—

When I finished recounting my sad tale, I crouched low, panting. In the re-telling, I'd relived the roller-coaster of emotion once again.

"What kind of dog?" Pepper asked, when my breathing returned to normal.

"How should I know?" I snapped. "Big head, square face, jaw like a vise, body a bundle of solid muscle...." My voice trailed off.

"Yeah," Pepper mused. "It fits."

"What fits?"

"Those dogs—they're bred for fighting." She paused. "Not their fault—their owners use cats for bait sometimes." Her brown eyes were pools of concern. "Listen, we aren't all like that. I would *never* hurt you." She added a warning, "Unless you hurt Minna."

"Why would I hurt Minna?" I felt the hair on my back rising again, and I followed up my comment with a hiss of displeasure.

"By letting her get attached and then leaving," Pepper said, simply.

"Don't worry." My tail twitched. "I won't be here long enough for that. I never stay in one place for long."

"Have you ever wondered," Pepper said, her voice soft, "why that might be?"

"Oh, so you're a psych-analyst now, as well as a soldier?" I sneered. "Don't stick your long nose into places it doesn't belong."

"You couldn't have prevented it."

"Who said I thought I could?" I stared at my right front paw, willing her to shut up.

"It wasn't your fault."

I growled, low in my throat. Whatever I might have said next was cut off abruptly by Minna's arrival.

Her forward-leaning posture and tense muscles indicated excitement.

"Briefing session, in the mess hall," Minna said tersely. Pepper leapt to her feet and raced into the passageway, her hindquarters skidding to the left as she negotiated the corner. "You can come, too," Minna told me, sidling over to my ledge so I could clamber onto her shoulder.

I rode in style to the meeting, my only disappointment being that Pepper disappeared ahead of us, so I was unable to lord it over her.

We arrived to find the mess hall packed—not surprising, since it was designed to accommodate dining in shifts. Even Doc Wilson doffed his lab coat to attend the meeting.

Commander Nibo Salvar had no need to call for quiet. The moment she stood at the dais, the room fell as silent as a Hybernian sea-cavern during a mid-moon ceremony.

Commander Salvar's green face creased in a grin that showed her pointed white teeth, and her spiky green hair stood straight up, betraying her intense emotion. Rumor had it there was nothing the commander liked more than a good fight.

Though I was not officially a part of the combat crew, I sensed the electric tension in the air and leaned forward.

"We received an urgent message directing us to proceed to Fortuna, to aid the government there. It's a frontier planet," she said, and the image of a desert setting, beige sand stretching to the horizon, appeared onscreen. "There's rioting in Central City, and the local forces have requested our assistance."

My enthusiasm waned as though I'd been plunged into a bucket of icy water. This didn't sound like the kind of action I'd envisioned while performing the drills with Pepper and Minna.

I allowed my attention to drift, kneading Minna's shoulder absentmindedly. I started purring.

"Pay attention," Pepper growled, glancing up at me.

"—with the exception of Minna and Noah. I have a different assignment for you two. A local named Vido Aubin disappeared two days ago, and the Colony's law enforcement staff is stretched beyond breaking with this issue in Central City. I'd like the two of you to search around his habi-dome, see if you can deduce what happened to him."

I swivelled my ears forward.

"As everyone knows, frontier planets can hold nasty surprises, and not much is known about the outback, here — a desert-like land with scattered holdings." Commander Salvar gestured, and the image of a dark brown habi-dome appeared onscreen with a beat-up hovercar in front of it. Another image replaced it, this one showing straggly, purple-green vegetation bounded by a force-fence. It looked like a forsaken land, and the images instilled a sense of foreboding that dampened my ever-present curiosity regarding new things and places.

"Earth atmosphere, so no need for helmets for either assignment, but wear flak vests. We don't know what we might be facing. Include your body-cams and collar mics, of course. We'll be watching from the spaceport, ready to deploy reserves via speed-flitter to either location as needed." Nibo glanced around the small room, eyes glinting. "Good hunting."

"Okay if I bring the new guy?" Minna asked, matching pace with the commander as the meeting broke up.

Commander Salvar considered for a moment. "An extra set of eyes never hurts. Get the Armoury to fab up a flak jacket for him."

My lashing tail betrayed the volatility of my emotions as Minna hustled back to her cabin to suit up.

This isn't what you signed up for, I told myself. *Risking your hide for these people.* Still, I couldn't repress a surge of excitement, for love of the hunt is encoded in my genes.

I glanced down at Pepper, who padded beside Minna, her jaws open in an anticipatory grin.

Besides, I can't let some dog show me up. I'd never live it down.

Another thought struck me as I glanced ahead.

Fortuna has a spaceport. Wouldn't hurt to check who's finned down there.

As Minna strode down the corridor, I heard a sound like a humming engine. With a start, I realized the source — me, purring again.

Make up your mind, I thought. Still, I knew if we passed a mirror, my eyes would glow hunter's green.

—▢—

Minna and Noah approached the habi-dome, weapons drawn.

"This's the real thing," Pepper said, her tone animated. "It's not a drill. Just stay out of the way if we get into it."

I stopped walking and stared at the dog, incredulous.

She means it. She really thinks —

"What do you know about how I react under fire?" I snapped.

Minna cleared her throat, and Pepper and I, our spat shelved for the time, turned our attention to her. She gestured to Pepper to check the area for scents, and the dog jumped to it, her downward-tucked ears and low-held tail signalling her shame at allowing our argument to distract her from duty.

Me, I licked my paw to feign casualness but felt a tinge of remorse. Wasn't discipline one of the very things Mom had dinned into Frisky and I from the start? *Focus,* I chided myself.

I sniffed the air dutifully and exchanged a glance with Pepper, who'd completed her brief survey. Clearly, no one had been there for days. Pepper signalled Minna, who relaxed slightly.

The dog lowered her head near the door, sorting scents with her keen nose. Then she painstakingly traced a trail to the lean-to garage, where a rusting ground car sat idle. She paused there, then followed the scent to the back of the building.

"Check for a persacomp, a note, anything that might indicate Vido left of his own volition," Minna said, waving Noah toward the habi-dome. He nodded and trotted to the entryway.

Pepper raised her head and looked at me, her forehead creased.

"Strange scent, here," she said, gesturing with her muzzle. "Ever run across these things?" I padded over and drew in a deep breath, catching a gamey odor in some slight depressions in the sandy soil.

Squirrel-like, but not a squirrel. The smell reminded me of meerkat, with a dash of weasel—a combination I'd never run across. I glanced up at Minna, seeking direction.

She stood motionless, her expression blank.

"Minna!" I heard the comm crackle. Commander Salvar's voice. "Officer Henderssen, come in. Report!"

No answer.

I turned toward Pepper, who might as well have turned to stone for all the awareness she displayed. *What?*

And then, as I slowly swivelled to face in the direction of Minna's gaze, I saw them. Half a dozen animals the size of jackrabbits stood on their hind legs, paws folded over their cream-colored bellies. They had an element of meerkat about them in their subtle striping, their upright postures. And yet, they possessed a weasel's sinuosity and carried the bushy tails of squirrels.

And teeth. Nature had endowed them with a generous supply of pointed teeth.

I looked at Pepper again and cocked my head. The border collie stood as though transfixed, her usually bright brown eyes dull and staring.

I hissed, low under my breath, and called on my store of knowledge about pest species. Years ago, Earth scientists had debunked the notion that cobras hypnotize their prey. However, as mankind stepped out into the space lanes, they'd encountered species on other planets capable of doing just that.

I shivered.

You couldn't save your own mother. Self-doubt, a familiar companion despite my outward swagger, chose that moment to return with a vengeance. *You won't be able to save them. In fact, it might be best if you ran. Those teeth—*

I detected motion. Careful not to make eye contact, I turned my head just far enough to monitor the animals' behaviour. *They're moving forward.*

Run! There's too many of them!

My muscled bunched as if of their own accord.

Think! I fought the impulse to flee, the strain causing my muscles to ache. *Think! If the animals are using hypnosis —* I launched myself in Pepper's direction, raking my claws across her long snout and drawing blood in neat furrows. Pepper shook her head, scattering droplets of red fluid.

"Whaaaaa —"

"Don't make eye contact," I said crisply.

Minna lowered her head, glanced sidewise at the weasel-beasts, and snarled.

"We need everyone in play." I shot a meaningful look in Minna's direction. Clawing Pepper was one thing; laying a paw on Pepper's master would be quite another.

Pepper began nudging the woman, gently at first, then with increasing agitation.

"No good," she panted. "We need to break their concentration."

With pleasure.

Angry at myself and fearful of witnessing harm to my comrades, I was only too happy to have an excuse to act. I leapt upon the nearest of the weasel-things, catching it by surprise and grasping it by the nape of the neck. I bit down hard. A brief struggle, a flailing of limbs, and it slumped to the ground. *One down.*

I dared a sideways glance in time to see Pepper fling one of the creatures to her left. She pounced on the next one, shook it fiercely.

A crackle of laser fire, to my right. Another of the beasts twitched and stilled. Our actions must have shaken Minna out of her trance. I heard approaching footfalls and a terse warning from Minna to Noah, who quickly joined the fray. I leapt onto the back of my next victim and hung tight, seeking my death-grip as the creature lurched beneath me like a wild horse striving to buck its rider. An intense rage swept through me, and in my mind, I was confronting, not a weasel-thing, but the square-faced dog that had attacked my mother and brother so many years ago. I raked the beast with my claws and bit down hard on its neck again and again, even after its struggles ceased.

I raised my head in time to see Noah finish off the last of the creatures with a well-aimed shot from his laser-gun. Panting, I crouched in place until the battle-fury ebbed from my muscles.

"You're hurt," Minna said, bending to examine my shoulder, from which a trickle of blood oozed. I purred under her touch and licked her hand to reassure her that I'd be fine.

"Minna, something strange." Noah's voice bore a sombre tone out of keeping with his normal carefree demeanour. "Vido disabled the force field."

"Who does that?"

He shrugged. "Sector NE-5. That way." He pointed.

"Let's go."

—◻—

Pepper located the settler first, but even with their inferior sense of smell I'm confident Minna and Noah could have done so, as well, given time.

Vido had, indeed, disabled the field at one of the gateways. His body lay just beyond the perimeter of the field, face-up in Fortuna's brilliant sunshine.

Despite the fact that the incident had occurred days ago, it wasn't difficult to piece together what had happened. He'd succumbed to an attack by an animal with sharp teeth—a hungry animal, judging from the gaps in his flesh.

"Those—whatever they are—are appealing, in their own way," Minna said. "Do you think they lured him out through the gate?"

"The force fence would've kept them out. They must have intrigued him enough to want to have a closer look. But with the gate disabled, they could enter the compound. That's how they got to us."

"Commander, did you get all that?" Minna asked, speaking into her collar-mic.

"We were with you on video and comm," Commander Salvar responded. "We'll warn the settlers about the animals and the need to keep their force-fences operational."

—□—

"You did well back there," Pepper said as we lounged in Minna's room. "I'm … sorry about what I said to you, planet-side."

I turned to study the dog's face. Her brown eyes radiated sincerity—and something else, something I couldn't quite decipher.

"I overheard the commander say she thinks the Central City conflict will be resolved within a couple of days." Pepper paused.

"So?"

"The open road, remember?" Pepper met my eyes, then looked away. "There's ships here, in port."

I lifted my head, waiting for the pull—and not feeling it. "Maybe the open road is overrated," I replied, then yawned and studied my right forepaw.

The fact was, though the realization had been years in coming, I finally understood that my frequent changes of scenery had been motivated, not by some romantic attachment to freedom, but rather as a defense against the terrible sense of inadequacy I'd felt after the dog incident all those years ago.

Pursued by the fear that I'd be forever unable to protect those I loved, I'd assumed a nomadic life to avoid attachments. And so, I'd run from place to place, as though seeking in that way to escape the terrors of the past, never realizing that they would always pad remorselessly in pursuit until something happened to change my self-perception.

Confronting the weasel-things didn't alter what had happened back on the corridors of the *Elizabeth*, but it changed the way I looked at those events. I'd been a kitten then, and had done the best I could against a powerful adversary.

But today, by confronting the weasel-things and saving my companions, I'd been able to garner ammunition against the seductive voice of self-doubt.

"The longer you stay, the more you'll hurt her when you go." Pepper gestured toward the bunk where Minna lay, her persacomp tablet in hand.

"Maybe," I said softly, "I won't go." I studied Pepper's face. "Would that disturb you so much?"

"I suppose not," Pepper said, her expression thoughtful. "As long as you cut out the dog jokes."

I frowned.

"Naw, just kidding. I actually like them." Pepper's lips parted in a broad grin.

"Knock it off, will you, you two?" Minna said, her tone conveying drowsy contentment. "I'm trying to concentrate here."

"I could sleep," I said, and yawned as I kneaded the soft fabric beneath me.

"When *couldn't* you?" Pepper tilted her head as she peered up at me. "Is it true that cats can sleep twenty hours a day?" She looked away and began to trample down her bed, circling once, twice, three times, and then easing herself into the soft mattress with a groan of contentment. "Never mind. Don't answer that." I heard the sound of snoring rise from her bed less than a minute later, and Minna joined not long after.

Their snores were the last thing I heard before I, too, drifted off.

I experienced no nightmares, for once, and was fully recharged when I awoke from my nap, summoned by the chime of the dinner bell. As I followed Minna and Pepper to the mess hall, I tested the ship's air, as though trying to sniff out the road ahead. The future, as it so often does, remained inscrutable. All I knew for sure was that a different kind of road lay ahead from this day forward. And though I did not possess a seers' capability, it seemed likely that adventure might lurk around the next bend, and the one after that.

And I found that suited me just fine.

Lisa Timpf

Author and poet, Lisa Timpf is a retired HR and communications professional living in Simcoe, Ontario, Canada. Her past experiences sharing her home with dogs, canaries, guinea pigs, and a cat have provided her with abundant raw material for writing both fiction and non-fiction.

Lisa's work has appeared in a variety of magazines, anthologies, and zines. Her publication credits include three *Chicken Soup for the Soul* anthologies ("Christmas in Canada," "My Very Good, Very Bad Dog," and "The Spirit of Canada"), as well as stories/poems in, among others, *New Myths, Outposts of Beyond, Scifaikuest, The Martian Wave*, and a *Dogs of War* anthology. She self-published a collection of creative non-fiction stories and poetry titled, *A Trial That Twines: Reflections on Life and Nature.*

When she's not writing, Lisa enjoys organic gardening, bicycling, and bird-watching. A fair portion of her writing is influenced by her interest in nature, animals, and preserving the Earth.

Blog *The Writing Journey*: http://lisatimpf.blogspot.com/
On Goodreads, search: Lisa Timpf

Editor's note: In addition to her story, "The Open Road," Lisa Timpf also contributed two poems, "Moonlight," page 78, and "A Cat's Confession," page 152.

MULGRAVE'S RESOLVE

I'm tired.

The keepers have been loud today. Louder than me when I am hungry or unwell or lonely. The big one throws things at me until the soft one comes to cuddle me quiet. Only a few of their sounds have meaning for me—the things they say that I care about. But when they make the ear-hurt sounds like now, I do not hear my special words, so I wander away.

Above the sounds they say, are the sounds of the things thrown to the floor. There are sharp things and smooth things and smelly things, all there for me to explore. I scamper about at the edges of the room, but when I move close to play in the piles, I am brushed aside.

Now there are new sounds. The thumping of the carry cases they bring out for long sleeps away from me. When I see the special bag—the one with the peekaboo holes—it means I am going on a noisy, smelly journey that will end with poking and prodding. I run away to the back of the tiny-place with the tall stacks of things that no one looks at. When I am there, they grow too tired to crawl and shove things aside to grab at me, so it is a safe place to hide.

Today they do not come to look for me. If not for the scary bag, I would mew for sympathy or howl in annoyance. The noise and mess and old-eat smells are troublesome, but I am too afraid to voice my displeasure, so I stay in the dark corners, eyes wide and ears alert.

The yelling and moving around of things continues. It is good I took many naps yesterday. I stay awake in case they come for me and I need to run to a new place.

—□—

I'm waiting.

It has been a long time. I hear more things hitting walls and floors until I wonder how any can be left. There are more mouth noises, deep and breathy and unformed, and then bumping and thumping.

Suddenly, it is quiet.

It is like the world has been reset. I had forgotten the bliss of nothingness in my ears, and I revel in the silence. Never has it been so easy, it seems, to hear the scritching of the many-legged creatures on which I like to snack. But I ignore the one scurrying across the floor in front of me now because the quiet is still too new. I will not be fooled so easily. I wait. I hear the door that leads to the not-here place. Then nothing. Still, I wait.

I have not forgotten the time the big one tried to put me into the special bag. He did not heed my warning and struck me when I lashed out at him in self-defense. I retreated to the way-back part of the tiny-place where I knew he could not reach me. When things grew quiet and I thought he had gone away, I was surprised to find him waiting for me. He pounced, and I suffered a torturous time at the place with the animal smells and strangers that poke things into spots where they should not go.

I will not be lured out again so easily. And I will be a long time forgiving that transgression. Noise or no noise, I will wait. I have confidence in the safety of my fortress.

But it has been so long, and I am so tired.

—□—

I'm bored.

I emerged today from my hiding place to find the piles scattered into an uninteresting mess. It is still quiet, and I am happy not to see the big one anywhere, but the soft one is not here to pat my rump or chase me up and down the stairs or toss my fuzzy ball to me.

The door to the sleep-place is closed, and no one has answered my cries to open it so I can explore. I pace the hallway and stretch my claws on the big chair, but no one comes to scold me.

I bat at the ball in the roundabout toy, watching it whirl and tease me on its carefree journey. My paws can only reach through small spots to send it spinning again, and I think of the day I will spill it from its shell and knock it across the floor at will.

I climb to my perch and watch the many birds through the window. Like the ball, they think they are safe from my reach, but I chitter my threats. They pretend to be unconcerned, confident that the window will keep me from them, but I have seen it open. I have felt fresh air riffle through my fur and smelled the mysteries that await in the not-here place.

One day the birds and I will meet, and I will win. I chitter and watch, tracking their flight across and down and up and back again. The day is bright. It is warm on my perch. As much as I would like to study the movements of my enemies, soon they blur into a fuzzy blob of feathers and pointy noses, and I nap.

When I awaken, I watch the birds again. It is still quiet. It is still warm. I jump down to stretch and see if anyone has come back and remembered me. I have hope the soft one will return soon to clean up the mess, so I do not have to pick my way across the floor.

My box smells. The clumps cling to my paws and I shake them until they fall on the floor in the spaces between the things. The "between" spaces seem to be shrinking, but I feel no joy at the prospect of climbing across things formerly forbidden.

I cannot find my ball among the debris. There is no place to run and swat and slide. I do not like this now-place. I want it to be as before. I cry, risking the wrath of the big one, but he does not come. No one comes. I cry and huff and nothing changes, so I climb back to my perch and watch the birds until I sleep again.

When I awaken, it is dark. It is still quiet. It is still warm. The warm creates a smell in the room, of things used and left behind. It is not a pleasant smell, and it makes me realize something new and unsettling.

—□—

I'm hungry.

I check my food dish several times in my wanderings. The same thing awaits, empty with yesterday's crust and today's sprinkle of dust. The big one never gives me anything. Like with all things for me, the soft one takes care of it. But the big one is not here to drop crumbs from slobbery lips that before I might have ignored but today I would gladly sniff and sample. And the soft one still has not trilled my name, given me licks from a cream-covered spoon, torn pieces of chicken for an extra treat, or even refilled my bowl with dry and crunchy kibble.

Sometimes when they leave, and my bowl and belly are empty, the lady with the funny voice and shaky hands comes from the not-here place to give me food and water. She tries to pet and hold me, and I run from her. We do the same thing each day till my keepers return, and it is like she does not exist for me, until the next time. Today, I might let her rub my head. But she has not come.

There is water in one dish, but I lift the edge with a claw and let it drop back into its holder anyway. It is how I let them know I need more. It makes the loud clanging noise that angers the big one and brings the soft one running. I lift and drop, lift and drop, lift and drop, and still no one comes. A little water splashes onto the mat below. I sit and watch it dry, refusing to believe more will not come soon.

I yell again to vent my frustration. The food things on the floor are no good for eating—warm and soft with the smell of rot. There are tiny food bits in my remaining water. They do not belong there, and there is no one here to remove them.

I move into the food-place and sit and stare at the spot where my kibble lives. The soft one moved it there after I chewed open the pouches when they were left out. I pull and push at the door with my paw as I have done so many times before, with the same result: nothing.

Now I am waiting and bored and hungry and thirsty, and my paws are sore. No one is here to care. I have been alone before. I have been lonely before when the soft one is away too long. But now I am alone and lonely, and things are not like they have ever been.

It is too dim for the birds to flit about like they do in the daytime. It is too messy to run and play. It is too smelly for me to think straight. There is too much bad all around me, and I can only hope for someone to come soon. Even if it is the big one, I will rub against his legs to let him know it is better than being alone.

I sit and wait. It is quiet and dark, and no one comes. I wait until I hear the birds again, and the light begins to spill into the space beyond the window. Still no one comes. I whine. When no one comes, I whine louder. It is time for my morning feed.

But this time the big one does not shout "Mulgrave!" to shock me into submission. And the soft one does not coo "Gravy" to smooth my heart-hurts. Instead, I pout and moan until I fall asleep, dreaming of a bowl brimming with tasty treats.

—◻—

I'm angry.

I have pulled the last remaining things from the shelves. I have chewed on shiny strings and super-smooth pages. I have devoured crispy plants and left the remnants of their leaves in drying piles on the floor. I have scratched on carpet corners and couch cushions. I have jumped on the surfaces where I am not allowed and left a film of fur as evidence of my passage.

No one has come for me. I have no food. My water is three licks from gone. My box is a minefield of lumps and clumps, rivalled only by the mess of things all around this here-place. The smell is as upsetting as the noises the keepers made in the recent long-ago. The birds mock me in my prison, and I save my hateful energy for a day that may never come.

Now there is a loud noise outside as if all the not-here is blowing at me. Like when I sit on the soft one's chest and feel the puff of breath on my rear to tell me to stop swishing my tail in her face and turn around. Except this is more than just a puff and does not sound playful. It is like the noise the big one makes after he drinks too much smelly water.

Things start to thump and bump, and I run upstairs to see if the keepers have come back to resume their loud sparring while I was asleep. The hallway is empty. It is less messy but much warmer up here. And now I am closer to the roar from the not-here place, and less happy.

I scoot back toward the stairs but stop when I see the door to the sleep-place. I have tried many times before to open it, but it does not budge. I long to run in and jump up to the spot where the soft one lies. To be comforted with the smell of her, the hope of her, the promise of things the way they were.

I stalk over to the door. I bump my head hard against it. It rattles but does not allow me entry. I slide a paw under until I can feel the other side, and I pull. It is still closed, but I feel it shift. I pull harder. The not-here noise becomes louder, echoing my own frustration. I slide my other paw underneath and pull until—faintly under the roar of the wind and my own stubborn grunting—I hear a scrape and a click.

The door pops open, and with it comes a compressed version of all that is around me. It is a cloud of heat and rotten stink that makes me back away without a conscious thought. There is something in the smell that is familiar but forgotten. It holds a potential that already feels lost. I sit in the hallway and bare my teeth and shake my head. I will not go in.

But I must.

The room is small, with the up-high and down-low spaces very close to each other. The big one always bends his way into this place, staying compact and uncomfortable, while the soft one always fills it perfectly.

It is she who is once again filling up the space.

I jump onto the sleeping-place and find her there, spread

across its surface. She is the forgotten familiar smell of lost potential. She is broken and still and silent and too soft. I push my head under her hand, but her fingers do not tickle the spot between my eyes, and she does not murmur "Gravy baby," in time with my purr.

The smell and the sight and the feel of her yielding, puttied flesh forces me back into the hallway. I look at the door and howl. I look down the stairs and howl. I walk the hall to my hiding spot and curl up in the farthest corner, away from the light and the smells, surrounded only by shadows and the howling wind of the not-here place. I think it must know how I feel.

I am finally not alone, but more alone now than I have ever been before. If there is mercy to be had, I will not wake again only to die a slow and pointless death.

—▫—

I'm content.

I have a new home with new keepers. There is a new soft one to cuddle me, and a new big one with a voice that sounds scary but is not, and large hands that give great rump thumps but are also patient enough to brush me from head to tail until I sleep.

I have not been here long, but it is a place of light and order and stillness mixed with joyous noise. There are winged ones outside and captured swimmers inside. Food and fresh water appear before I ask.

I do not like to think much about the other place; about my other soft one as she melted into something even softer in the old sleeping-place. I do not like to think about tiny creatures squiggling on the floor between piles of rank and rancid decay. I do not like to think about the days I cowered and hungered and thirsted and soiled my fur as I grew too hopeless to leave my sanctuary.

There is only one thing I like to remember about the final

days in my before-life.

It is when the big one returned, sometime between the just-past time and the forever. He trudged through the mess and bellowed for the soft one. He cursed the smells and stomped the wrigglers into wet spots on the putrid palette of the floor. I watched him from the gallery above, then slunk down the hallway as he neared the stairs.

Clomp. Clomp. Clomp. Each step he took brought him closer to me.

Clomp. Clomp. Clomp. I was smaller now, I could fit more easily into the way-back part of the tiny-place, yet I didn't run.

Clomp. Clomp. Clomp. A pause. A sniff.

Clomp-Clomp-Clomp. Faster now, the big one rushed into the sleep-place.

Nothing. Then noises like I make when I need to bring forth some fur or grass. Then the howling. Not nearly as mournful as my own—less about grief and loss, and more about being denied something you think is owed you.

He staggered to the doorway, wiping his mouth, and looked up. We stared at each other from doorways at opposite ends of the hall. His eyes opened wide, and he roared nonsensical words at me as he ran in my direction. I was weak and slow but tired of hiding. I ran between his legs and stopped outside the sleep-place.

I turned and showed him what a grieving howl should be, full of memories of chasing dangling string tied to sticks and getting belly rubs, and sneaking extra treats under the table, and licking the soft one's nose when she lay in bed whimpering after he hurt her with his hands. I keened the whole of my heart and soul and I looked at him because we both knew he was the one who had taken it all away from me.

He roared again and rushed at me, and once again I ran between his legs, swiping with my claws as I went. This time his howl was one of genuine pain. As he fell back against the wall, clutching the bloody marks I gave him, I decided how we would come to our end.

I crouched in front of him, just out of reach. I wiggled my rear, bouncing lightly on my feet, waiting. "Meow," I invited him, taunted him, teased him. Predictably, he lunged, and I jumped.

I landed on his chest and raked my claws down his face. He staggered backward as he wiped at his eyes. I scrambled to bite his neck, disorienting him until he staggered too close, missed the step, and we went tumbling together down the stairs.

Once again there was the painful quiet after much noise. I was alone again, and I felt regret. Not about the big one; never about that. But I wondered how things might have been different if this had happened before he'd ended the soft one.

Then it occurred to me that the big one was devious and might try to trick me, like the time before when I was hiding in the tiny-place. I licked the marks on his face, but he did not move. He was still, like the pall that had long-since settled over the here-place. I licked again. The taste of salt and other things, the moisture; they revived me. I took a bite. And I thought perhaps this was not to be my end but could instead be my new beginning.

When the strangers burst through the door, they found me atop the big one where I had remained, napping and nibbling to save my strength. They cooed at me and came at me and I didn't resist. I was not a wild and savage thing though I must have presented that sight. I was a survivor.

They took me away and cleaned me and fed me. They poked and prodded and I endured it all because I knew it would not be worse than where I had been. I showed them I was well-behaved and loving and they put me on display until the new soft one and big one claimed me as their own.

My new days have been only the best of what I had in my old life. I am coddled and revered and the center of everything. The low rumble of my purr is a regular thing, and I wear my smirk of contentment proudly. I do not think things will go badly here.

But if they should, I know what I must do.

ABOUT THE AUTHOR

Michelle Mellon

Michelle Mellon discovered her love of writing at age nine and was a published poet starting in high school. In her twenties, she shifted her focus to short fiction. In addition to the ever-bizarre world around us, Ms. Mellon draws inspiration from her experiences growing up as an Army dependent and her varied occupations as dental assistant, project manager, copywriter, and communications manager.

In August 2015, she and her husband relocated from San Francisco to Germany, where Ms. Mellon has been a stay-at-home cat mom while finishing a story collection, writing for speculative fiction anthologies and magazines, and publishing a blog about her expat adventures. She recently joined a software startup as a content writer and is close to completing her second fiction collection.

Michelle Mellon has been published in nearly a dozen horror and science fiction anthologies. Her collection of short stories, *Down by the Sea and Other Tales of Dark Destiny* (HellBound Books), is available from Amazon.

Website: http://www.mpmellon.com/
Twitter: @mpmellon
For Amazon and Goodreads search: Michelle Mellon

LISA TEMPF

A CAT'S CONFESSION

Forgive me, master, for I have sinned —
I know you hate it when I capture birds
but that black-capped chickadee at the feeder,
I honestly thought his reflexes would be quicker.
You know what they say.
Survival of the fittest.

Forgive me, master, for I have sinned —
I smacked the dog in the nose again.
It was her fault. She keeps trying to herd me.
Besides, her breath stinks
and she doesn't even know how to use a litter box.
I have no idea why you keep her around.

Forgive me, master, for I have sinned —
I sharpened my claws on the couch. Many times.
Perhaps you can take it back and get a new one.
I prefer a fabric with a thicker nap, myself.

For these my sins, I offer
my most insincere remorse.
Then again, the other day
you let the kibble level fall so low
I actually saw the bottom of my dish
so I consider us even
Now, if you would be so good
as to let me out —

ABOUT LISA TEMPF

Editor's Note: To learn more about this very talented writer, see page 138, following her story, "The Open Road." Lisa also contributed a second poem, "Moonlight," page 78.

THE CAT'S APPRENTICE

When James cleaned and rearranged the extra bedroom, Malcolm thought nothing of it. Guests came and went, for his human was a powerful and well-connected wizard, a prominent member of the United Sorcerers League, the Mages Union, the Arch-Wizards Fraternity, and other magical organizations. Of course there were guests—especially on the occasions his wife, Lillian, stomped from the house, screaming and swearing, as she'd done again, only two weeks ago.

So, while annoyed—James's guests were not always as respectful as they should be—Malcolm merely yawned and curled up on the living room armchair, letting his wizard get on with it.

The next day, James took the car, leaving Malcolm alone. Still Malcolm thought nothing of it—James was always going out. He continued his blissful nap, stretched out in the sun on the living room window ledge. It was only when James returned that Malcolm realized there was a problem.

Awakened from his sound sleep, Malcolm jerked up, fur raised, at the crash of the door smacking against the wall. James had returned sooner than expected. He staggered in, weighed down by an enormous suitcase. And there was someone behind him as heavily laden but much younger, thinner, and anxious. Someone Malcolm had never seen or smelled before.

Malcolm stood and hissed. The thin person jumped and cast an uneasy look his way.

"Oh—that's Malcolm." James put down his suitcase and shook the cramp from his hand, panting. "My familiar." He strode over and scooped Malcolm up. "Come over here, boy."

Malcolm glared at his human; why did James issue orders and then make sure Malcolm had no chance to disobey? It really was unfair. He slumped in James's grasp and glowered as the wizard held him out to the stranger.

Malcolm stared into a long, awkward, pimply face with two large, anxious brown eyes under a mop of black hair. *What an ugly, skinny human*, he thought, disdainfully.

"This is Enrique Mendoza," James said. "He's my new apprentice. He'll be living with us."

"Hi, Malcolm," said Enrique, reaching over to scratch Malcolm's ears.

While he didn't understand it all, he comprehended the *living with us* part and stared in horror. This *new apprentice* wasn't a guest. He was moving in permanently! Malcolm wailed in protest and lashed out at Enrique, who leapt away with a yelp. He squirmed and wriggled, trying to free himself from James's grasp to launch at the interloper's face but only succeeded in liberating his front half, flopping forward over James's stomach. James still held tight to Malcolm's back end, while Enrique gasped. With another yowl, Malcolm batted at the boy again, claws unsheathed.

"*Bad* Malcolm!"

Malcolm issued a painful mew under the psychic force of James's anger.

The wizard held his familiar out in front of him, glowering into his spitting face. "*Bad* cat! You *don't* hurt Enrique, understand? No!"

He subsided, still growling. *So that's how it is?* James expected him to make way for this usurper? Unbelievable!

James chucked Malcolm under the sofa and helped Enrique bring the rest of his luggage into the house, both grunting and heaving, while the familiar watched from the shadows; a small, malevolent presence. All the time, James chatted with Enrique in the most disgusting display of betrayal Malcolm had ever seen.

"You can have your pick of the bedrooms," he said. "My wife's not here right now. But I've prepared the room in the front, and you might prefer that."

"It sounds fine," Enrique said in a high-pitched, tentative voice. He cast another uneasy glance in Malcolm's direction, only to be rewarded with a growl from the dark under the couch. Enrique looked away quickly. "When will your … uh … wife be getting back?"

"Don't know," said James, words clipped. "It depends."

"On what?" Enrique asked, clueless.

"On how quickly she forgives me." James smiled grimly.

"Oh." Enrique looked more uncomfortable than ever. He gave his bag another heave. "So, uh, why aren't we carrying this stuff by magic, um, Magister?"

"Please, call me James," James said warmly. "And we're not carrying your luggage by magic because magic is tricky stuff, understand? It's not like in the movies. If you want to transport your suitcases magically, you'd need to study the spell first. Then prepare, which usually involves inscribing a diagram, chanting the spell—minding the intonation—all the while concentrating hard on each individual suitcase, and consciously controlling the outflow of waste power."

"Oh," said Enrique, with a laugh. "So, basically, it's easier to just carry the suitcases?"

James laughed with him. "Much easier."

They disappeared upstairs.

Malcolm heard loud thumping and the occasional snippet of human voices from above. He slunk from under the sofa. They'd forgotten all about him, it seemed. He prowled down the steep stairs into the basement, where he lurked behind the rusty old bikes, brooding in the dank darkness that exactly matched his mood.

It's more than enough, he thought, *that Lillian is constantly screaming at James and storming out, disrupting my house and routine. The guests are an added nuisance, but this…!* Malcolm's home was being invaded and his privacy and routine violated by yet another human. It was obvious that James cared more about Enrique than his adorable, long-suffering, ever-loyal, feline familiar. He curled up on the damp basement floor, awash in self-pity. He'd sacrificed so much for his wizard, and this was the thanks he got. He mewed pitifully in the dark.

Malcolm refused to come up, even for dinner, despite the scrumptious smells wafting down the staircase. Only after James and Enrique had stopped eating, talking, clacking dishes, watching television, talking more, running water, and roaming around, did Malcolm slink up to the kitchen.

At least James hadn't forgotten to put out his food, though it was crusting over. Malcolm sniffed at this added betrayal but settled down to eat. Behind him, the refrigerator droned dolefully. When he'd finished, Malcolm returned downstairs, where he lay curled, a small furry lump of misery, in the darkest corner.

He was going to hate Enrique.

—□—

The next few days confirmed Malcolm's worst fears.

Enrique was everywhere, and James—*Malcolm's* wizard— was everywhere with him. They ranged all over the house, James grabbing common household items—clocks, silverware, basins of water—to illustrate complicated magical principles that Enrique drank in with a wide-eyed attentiveness that Malcolm found disgusting. When he wasn't roaming the house, Enrique was in the workroom, from where the ozone-scent of magic drifted out and made Malcolm's fur crackle for days. And, when he wasn't doing *that*, Enrique was out, usually in James's company.

Malcolm slunk around; he might as well have been one of the sofa cushions for all the notice the humans took of him. From a corner of the living room or the stair landing, Malcolm glared at the adolescent wizard with resentment: it was *his* fault. His fault, that James no longer petted Malcolm or cuddled him in front of the computer or the television. His fault that James no longer spoke to his familiar but to his apprentice instead. His fault, that James forgot he belonged to Malcolm.

It didn't end there. Enrique had no sense of boundaries. He constantly wandered about Malcolm's house with his phone glued to his ear, talking, talking. He'd set up his laptop in his bedroom, and Malcolm was agitated by its endless, electronic racket. Even worse, Enrique, grinning to himself, often invaded Malcolm's basement refuge for one of the bicycles, returning it with much clattering of the backdoor and bicycle gears, all reeking with human sweat.

Malcolm raged; he would have sabotaged Enrique's room if he could, but James had long since cast enchantments against that sort of thing. Not that James took any notice of poor Malcolm nowadays; no, it was Enrique this and Enrique that, and magic this and power levels that, while Malcolm skulked and sulked around the house.

His depression lasted for days before James's attention finally swung back to him — but in a most unwelcomed way.

"Come on, Malcolm," James said, scooping him from the floor and his now-standard slinking prowl, "time to get to work."

Malcolm, draped over his wizard's hands like wet laundry on a clothesline, glared and growled.

James knew exactly what Malcolm's problem was. "Don't look at me like that," he said. "I know you're unhappy, but Enrique is here to stay, whether or not you like it. Time to stop brooding."

This only fueled Malcolm's resentment, and he hunched, fur bristling, as James hauled him into the workroom. Enrique, an apprehensive presence, followed them.

James shut the door before releasing Malcolm, who dashed for a corner far from the humans. Since the workroom was hexagonal, there were plenty corners to choose from. He hid beneath the worktable, eyes gleaming in the dim light.

James turned to Enrique as though there was nothing wrong. "Can you tell me what exactly a *familiar* is?"

Enrique eyed Malcolm with concern, but offered gamely, "It's a kind of, ah, assistant, right?"

"Close. The familiar does assist you — there are several spells and enchantments that are difficult or impossible without one —

but a familiar is more than just a helper. A familiar is a *channel* or *connection* to magic and the natural world. Magic is a natural force, never forget that. Sometimes it comes easier if you maintain a link to the animal kingdom." He nodded at Malcolm. "Like Malcolm, here."

Enrique gaped at him. Malcolm laid his ears back.

James continued lecturing Enrique while getting out the chalk, incense, and herbs. "Since the familiar is a channel, the connection can extend in both directions, from you and toward you. There are advantages and disadvantages to this — can you think of one?"

Enrique fidgeted. "Ah ... something unfriendly could travel toward you through the familiar?"

"Not *travel* — he's a cat, not an interstate highway." Enrique grinned, and James continued, "But an entity might be able to spy on us through him. This is why you should always put protections in place. See, here...."

James and Enrique crouched, drawing with chalk on the floor, scattering incense, and muttering enchantments and instructions over handfuls of herbs. Eventually, James motioned Malcolm over.

"Come here, boy...."

Since it was James and it was magic, Malcolm came over, albeit slowly, hunkered down with his ears still laid back. James swept him up and placed him in the middle of the completed pentagram.

"You just observe this time," James ordered Enrique, who looked relieved.

Malcolm also perked up, sitting straighter. *Just me and James, at last.*

"This is a basic I-spy spell. Watch and listen."

Enrique stepped back while James took several deep breaths and his expression changed to one of blank concentration. The atmosphere in the room grew tense and heavy. Enrique watched, rapt, while a blue glow spread over the wizard's body.

Malcolm purred and stood, his fur crackling as the spell

fizzed to life. A blue light tracked along the chalk lines on the floor.

James chanted.

The magic flowed in Malcolm—James's will directing it like a beam through the familiar's brain. He allowed it, willingly assisting his wizard's intent. The spell amplified, focused, found its target—

—and rebounded.

Malcolm shrieked in alarm, and Enrique leapt back at the sudden flare of excess power. James's eyes widened, but he moved smoothly on to the counter-spell, canceling his previous enchantment.

Too late.

Malcolm felt another's will move up the path of magic toward him. He tried fighting it, but suddenly recognized the new presence. *Oh. Well, that's all right then.* He opened his mouth and let the other magician speak through him.

"Well, James," Lillian said. "I might have expected something like this."

"What's happening?" demanded Enrique. He stayed back, tense, eyes flicking between Malcolm and James.

James, breathing hard, said nothing. He stared at Malcolm, pale faced and gawping like a fish.

"Spying on me?" Lillian continued. It was a strange sensation, a human speaking through him; Malcolm shook his head and sneezed. "What? Jealous, James? Typical." Under Lillian's control, Malcolm's eyes flicked to Enrique. "And who are you?"

To his credit, Enrique didn't appear intimidated. He folded his arms and loomed aggressively. "I'm James's apprentice. Who are *you*?"

"Lillian," James spoke through gritted teeth. "My wife." He'd rallied by now and drew himself up. He muttered the repulsion spell, and the blue light shone from his hands.

Lillian laughed scornfully—which made Malcolm's mouth hurt. "Oh, no you don't! You can't repulse me without hurting poor Malcolm here. That's what always got on my nerves about you, James! You're total thoughtlessness!"

Enrique flushed. "James isn't thoughtless. He's a great wizard."

Lillian issued another cynical laugh. "He's the most selfish wizard who ever lived, kid. And the most insecure. Why do you think I left him? Always snooping around, spying on me—and now in front of you, too. He probably thinks I'm cozying up to a luscious incubus—"

James laughed at this, hard and nasty. "Yeah, right. I was using you as a target, Lillian, because I knew exactly where you were. Saves all that tedious locator magic. And I knew you'd be doing nothing that couldn't be seen by a teenager." He sneered. "Nothing at all."

Malcolm felt the beam of Lillian's spell narrow and sharpen with anger. "Nothing? If you think that, you may be in for a surprise, James."

James's eyes widened. "What?"

Lillian laughed again, making Malcolm cough. "Oh, *nothing*. I merely advise you not to spy on me again. You won't like the results."

With that she broke the connection, like a light turned off.

Panting, Malcolm fell forward onto his stomach, legs stretched out before him; being used as a speakerphone was hard work. He wanted to wash himself, but his mouth was too dry. He wheezed. To his astonishment, it was Enrique who picked his way across the spell to lift him up.

Enrique cradled Malcom carefully and turned to James. "What was that about?"

James, stared straight ahead, his mouth slightly open, and took a moment to answer. "Nothing," he said at last, shaking his head. "Nothing. Lillian's a bit melodramatic, that's all." He laughed, a little ruefully.

"It sounded like she hates you." Enrique shifted, securing Malcolm's back legs.

"Nah—things just get rocky between us now and then."

James shrugged, turning away to get the cleaning supplies. "It's always been like this. She'll forgive me, eventually—if I do nothing else to annoy her. Take Malcolm downstairs, will you? He needs food after this ordeal."

Food! Malcolm purred loudly, but Enrique ignored him, his arms tightening as he drew himself up indignantly.

"She doesn't have the right to threaten you like that," he said. "Not a wizard like you."

"Enrique," said James, gently but firmly, "it's nothing. Go feed Malcolm; I'll clean this up. A broken spell goes septic if it's left too long."

"Feed Malcolm?" Enrique said disbelievingly. "Now? After what just happened? We should at least report that woman's threats—" Enrique broke off as James turned a steely eye upon him.

"'That woman' is my *wife*," James said icily. "And our marriage is none of your concern. Go feed Malcolm and make him comfortable. A wizard gives his familiar the same care he gives himself, remember. And when you're done with that, read Magister Hartwell's article 'Thaumaturgic Backlash from Broken Spells.' *Occult Theory*, volume seventeen, issue two. You'll find his discussion of interrupted spell transmissions most educational."

—▢—

Enrique was still seething when he carried Malcolm into the kitchen.

"I can't *believe* him," he raged as he dumped Malcolm onto the floor and rummaged through the cupboard. Malcolm purred loudly and rubbed against his leg. He might not like Enrique, but he was willing to make an exception where food was concerned.

"I mean, this woman outright *threatens* him, and he says, 'It's okay; it's nothing. Go feed the cat!'" Enrique snorted as he knelt to retrieve Malcolm's bowl and placed it on the counter.

Malcolm purred louder.

Enrique peeled back the lid, still fuming. "It's ridiculous for a wizard like James to put up with something like that." He decanted the food into the bowl and set aside the empty tin. "I mean, he really is the greatest wizard I've ever met. And his wife treats him like scum through his own familiar! Here you go, boy." He squatted and placed the loaded food bowl back on the mat and Malcolm darted in.

Chicken flavored. My favorite. He watched Enrique from the corner of his eye as he ate.

Enrique sat back on his heels next to Malcolm, arms locked around his bent knees. "I can't believe he's *married* to someone like her. He says she's always running out on him. She sounds awful! And now something like — *this*. She could really hurt him if he's not careful." He shook his head. "No. Not James. But she could do some serious damage." He sat silent a moment, watching Malcolm eat.

When he spoke again, it was slow and quiet. "Someone should do something. I bet I could at least find out what she's up to and warn him. Stop her before she even starts." He fell silent again.

Malcolm bit down hard on a particularly stiff lump of food.

Softly Enrique repeated, "I could do something."

—▯—

In the days that followed, Enrique was quieter and more elusive, spending long hours locked in his room or frowning over great leather-bound books at the dining table. Malcolm didn't mind. If Enrique was reading, it meant he wasn't crashing around, and even better if he locked himself away.

"You haven't heard from your wife again, have you?" Enrique asked casually one evening at dinner, a few weeks after the incident.

"Lillian? No." James hardly looked up from his chicken and rice. "She's doing all right though, as far as I know."

"I was worried about you."

Malcolm coiled himself around the legs of James's chair, hoping some chicken would fall.

James laughed comfortably. "Me? Don't worry about me. Lillian might cast the odd curse—or two—when she's mad, but it's never anything serious."

"A curse?!"

Malcolm hopped lightly onto James's lap, where he eyed the wizard's plate greedily.

James shoved him away, and Malcolm growled in frustration.

"Oh, you know, the random sending. A minor demon. Things like that. *No*, Malcolm." He pushed the cat to the floor.

Malcolm slunk, sulking, under the table.

"A demon." Enrique's voice sharpened. "She sends *demons* after you?"

Malcolm emerged from under the table, glaring. *Humans are so greedy.*

"She's handy with spiritual beings. She could probably teach you a thing or two, when she comes back."

Malcolm stalked off to the living room, where the humans' voices were muffled but still audible.

"She's coming back?" Enrique did not sound pleased.

"She always does."

Malcolm jumped onto the armchair, ready for a good long sulk.

"Like I said, she'll give you a better course in demonology than I ever could. If she's not too pissed off."

"I don't believe that," Enrique said passionately. "You're the best wizard I've ever met."

James chuckled. "I'm not Merlin, Enrique. There's plenty I don't know. Let's get started on the dishes, huh?"

Malcolm's ears pricked up. If they were starting on the dishes, it meant he would be fed. He leapt from the chair and bounded to the kitchen. James was indeed peeling back the lid of a cat food tin. Malcolm rubbed ecstatically against his legs. For once Enrique was silent, but he had an odd gleam in his eye.

—▫—

Malcolm awoke suddenly to the long, soft stroking of a human hand on his back.

"Hey there, boy," whispered Enrique. "We've got work to do."

The cat growled but allowed Enrique to sweep him up into his arms and carry him tip-toeing up the stairs. The house was dark now. Pale light slanted in from only a few windows, where the moon peered through the warped old glass, as Enrique carried him into the workroom.

Malcolm's tail lashed. Enrique closed the door behind them, still holding him. Something was wrong: it was dark, and James was nowhere to be seen. Enrique was too quiet; too furtive. Malcolm struggled, hissing softly, but Enrique kept a firm grip, carrying him to the middle of a sorcerous diagram already drawn on the floor.

The familiar recognized it and struggled harder. Only James had the right to use him for this. But Enrique was relentless, stifling his grunts of pain when Malcolm got in a few good scratches before being dropped into the center of the diagram.

Malcolm immediately leapt free—or tried to. He struggled to escape from his sitting position and call for James to save him but failed at both. His back legs wouldn't move. And he couldn't cry out. The foreign magic was in his throat too, creeping like a tide of frost. He could only whimper and whine.

Enrique stood at the edge of the diagram. He appeared nervous, jigging to and fro, eyes over bright in the dim light. "Sorry, boy," he whispered, "but I need your help."

Malcolm spat at him, a tiny, weak gesture compared to his normal level of hostility but one filled with hate nonetheless.

Enrique gestured, and the spell sprang to life, its light much brighter in the darkness than in the daylight. He raised his hands and chanted.

This was not his wizard, and Malcolm was able to struggle harder than usual, holding back the apprentice's intent. But Enrique's spell was surprisingly strong and determined. Little by little, Malcolm lost ground, until the beam of Enrique's intent lanced through him as strong as if it were James's.

There was no magical rebound this time. Slowly, an image rose before Malcolm's eyes: A small room, painted white, with white furniture and a white bed. In the bed was a long white mound with a spill of dark, tangled hair across the pillow. Lillian.

Lillian. Surely, she would save him! He wriggled, desperate to lift the hideous, foreign weight of Enrique's presence from his mind and strained to call out. But Enrique's will was like an iron clamp, moving his senses around Lillian's room; sweeping for spells, for any sendings and enchantments she might be constructing. Malcolm moaned miserably as the boy's mind walled off his own, squeezing it like a vise—

Squeezing too hard.

It was only an instant's slip, but it was enough. Malcolm directed a psychic scream, an incoherent shriek, at the sleeping Lillian.

Enrique scrambled to pull him back under control—a second too late.

"What the—" Lillian sat up, blinking in surprise.

Malcolm's magical vision fractured and blurred under Enrique's shock. His control already shaky, Enrique slipped once more, and a blurry image of Malcolm materialized in the air over Lillian's bed, flailing desperately at her.

"Malcolm?" she said in surprise. Then her eyes narrowed. "*James*...."

Enrique hastily reeled in, pulling Malcolm back like a fish on a line, jerking them both into normal consciousness. But he was still too slow.

Lillian's enraged shout cut through, "James, you bastard!"

Malcolm came back to the workroom to find his fur standing on end from the force of Lillian's scream, and realized immediately his legs were freed and he could move again. He purred in relief and leapt out of the pentagram. It delighted him to see that Enrique wasn't nearly so sanguine. Enrique's dark eyes bugged out, and his chocolate skin was turned a terrible milky color. His breath came in squeaky, ragged wheezes, and his knees buckled.

Malcolm purred louder and sat down to watch. *Excellent.* His pleasure didn't last long.

It began with a silent pulse, infusing the room. Enrique's head jerked up, and Malcolm's fur rose once more. He stood, hissing, as the shadows in the room writhed and bulged.

Amorphous patches of darkness lurched and slithered forward. Great, formless arms reached out. A distant, dismal wail, as if from the bowels of Hell, sounded, and Lillian's sendings advanced on Malcolm and Enrique.

For once, boy and cat were in perfect accord. They both dove for the door.

Enrique wrestled it open as the first shadow lunged at him. With a great moan, it collapsed in a repulsive heap on the exact spot where Enrique had stood. It heaved in frustration at not finding him there. Other sendings inched toward their prey. The wails grew louder as Malcolm and Enrique pelted along the hallway.

They threw themselves at James's closed door. But Lillian knew this door well, and her demons had beaten them to it. A great, howling face, resembling Lillian herself, bulged from the wood, shrieking and jerking, as though trying to wrench itself out of the door. In unison, Enrique and Malcolm screamed and reeled away.

"James! James! Magister," Enrique yelled.

Malcolm screeched.

James would never hear their voices above the unholy racket of Lillian's sendings, and, even if he heard their pleas, he could not come through that door. The demon writhed across its surface. And there was no time to wait for him; the shadows were even now surging down the hallway toward them.

They ran for the staircase. Malcolm leapt down the steps headfirst with Enrique clattering beside him, breath ragged. But the staircase was another place Lillian knew well, and the carpet crawled beneath their feet, the banister coiled and heaved like a snake, a gaping mouth opened on each spindle.

Enrique sobbed, and Malcolm glanced back. Like the sendings, Enrique staggered and lurched, his face an awful, ashen white. Malcolm's nose twitched at the sharp, sour stink of panic radiating from him. He might have relished the boy's fear if he wasn't terrified himself.

The living room had come alive. The carpet rolled like waves at sea. The chairs lumbering back and forth toward Malcolm and Enrique, trying to block their way. The fireplace opened and closed with great, loud sucking noises, and a bookcase slid between them and the front door.

They were trapped. Enrique cowered in a corner while Malcolm crouched at his feet and yowled. The urge to escape sent electric shocks through his limbs, but there was nowhere to go. The shadow-demons had reached the bottom of the staircase and were advancing on them.

Malcom's yowls turned to mews of fear. He didn't know what Lillian's demons would do, but he knew it would be dreadful, just as she'd promised. And it was Enrique's fault. He let out a last despairing yowl and waited for the end.

Then—

"Stop!"

Enrique stepped around Malcolm. He loomed in front of him, arms outspread. Malcolm could still smell the fear oozing from him, but his voice was loud and firm. "Just stop it. This is all my fault. Hurt me if you have to. But don't hurt James or Malcolm, okay? It's not their fault, it's mine." He paused, gulped. "I—I wanted to see what you were up to. I wanted to impress James—to show off. I was *stupid*. Please don't hurt Malcolm or James."

Malcolm stared at the tall black shadow of Enrique. Was this useless human—this interloping, kidnapping, irritating *boy*—

actually protecting him?

The demons were equally surprised. They faltered and fell back before the force of Enrique's honesty and selflessness. Enrique stood taller. At his display of mounting hope and bravery, the demons retreated still further. More confident, Enrique stepped forward. Then *magic* burned around him, white as lightning and as electrically vital.

At his approach, the demons screamed and drew together, moaning in frustration and fear. Their nightmarish mobility faded. The house and furnishings stilled as the shadows clustered together in a single, pitch-black node. The node shrunk, growing tighter, denser, until it abruptly disappeared from existence.

Enrique gave a strangled gasp. His mage-light went out, and his knees gave way. He slumped slowly to the carpet.

Malcolm circled him, staying just out of reach. He watched Enrique as the last gleam of mage-light disappeared from his eyes and his body relaxed in relief.

"We're alive," Enrique said, with a weak shaky laugh. "Oh, god. We're alive. I'm s-sorry, Malcolm. So sorry." Then his expression changed from relief to dawning horror. "Oh, god, this is the end of my apprenticeship, isn't it?"

Malcolm perked up at this. *Is it really?* He purred happily.

"Enrique?"

James. Malcolm bounded over, mewling with delight, as James, disheveled and confused, came down the stairs. He bent to pick up Malcolm, and the familiar snuggled into his wizard's arms, safe at last.

The same could not be said of Enrique. With difficulty, he stood, nervous, trembling.

As James stroked him, Malcolm glanced up to see a gleam of blue mage-light flash in James's eyes. He said nothing at first but stepped to the wall and flipped the switch. Malcolm and Enrique winced at the sudden, bright light that exposed the disheveled living room.

James turned slowly back to his apprentice. "You've been

using Malcolm, haven't you?" he said quietly. "In a spell. Without my permission?"

Enrique gulped, but nodded. "Yes."

James stood immobile, his voice quiet and ominous. "May I ask what for?"

"I, uh ... I...." Enrique shuffled, face red, and stared at the floor.

"To spy on me, James."

Enrique stepped back in horror, and James whirled around. Malcolm stiffened.

The shadows were back, gliding through the living room wall in a soft, dark billow. Malcolm hissed, but the demons merely placed their passenger gently on the carpet and withdrew into their dark node.

Lillian, clad in jeans and an oversized t-shirt, hair just barely brushed, smiled at them. "I'm afraid your new apprentice thinks you're something of a hero, James," she said warmly. "He used poor Malcolm to spy on me; to make sure I wasn't causing you harm. Isn't that right, kid?"

Enrique looked like he wanted to sink into the floor forever, but he nodded, jerkily. "I was ... worried."

"So, you attempted a spell far beyond your abilities, using *my* familiar?" For the first time, anger colored James's voice. "My god, Enrique, have I taught you nothing? You could have killed Malcolm! Not to mention yourself."

Enrique bowed his head. "I know." It was a strangled whisper, barely audible.

Malcolm snuggled deeper into James's arms and purred, eyes slit in contentment. Here it came, the long-awaited moment when his wizard got rid of Enrique forever. Any minute now, James would open his mouth, unleash the devastating news, and Malcolm would watch Enrique creep away in misery —

"You know, James," said Lillian, thoughtfully, "I think I'd better move back in. It looks like you will need two wizards to control this one."

Enrique looked up, hope warring with disbelief. "You

mean—you're not terminating my apprenticeship?"

"Not this time," James said, with something of a glower. "Though whether that remains true depends on your future conduct. I hope you understand me."

"Oh, yes, sir." Enrique was nodding fervently, eyes shining. "Absolutely, sir!"

Malcolm stared. He couldn't believe this. After all the trouble Enrique had caused—after kidnapping Malcolm—after bringing Lillian's demons down on them—he was *staying*? He sat up in James's grip and issued a yowl of protest.

James hugged him, stroking. "It's okay, boy, he won't do it again."

Malcolm yowled louder. *It is not okay!*

Lillian watched with amusement. "I think, Enrique—that is your name, right? I'm Lillian—that, as part of your punishment, you should be the one to feed Malcolm for the next couple of weeks. And buy him treats."

Malcolm stopped wailing. *Treats?*

"And bathe him, and take him to the vet, and...."

Malcolm resumed his howls.

"Later, Lillian." James crossed the room to put an arm around his wife. "For now, let's go upstairs to revise Enrique's curriculum. Malcolm? Where you going, boy?"

Malcolm twisted out of James's grasp, rigid with outraged disbelief. He stalked to the sofa and crouched underneath, glaring out. *Traitors, all of you.* He'd been used and betrayed, and *he* was the one being punished by this intruder's continued presence? He growled miserably.

Lillian looked at James, a smile tugging at her lips. "Think he'll ever forgive us?"

James laughed. "Maybe. With the right application of time and chicken...."

Lillian gushed in laughter and threw her arms around James, kissing him on the cheek. He swept her into an embrace, barely remembering to issue a final order to Enrique. "Make sure you tidy the living room and clean up that spell diagram before you go to bed, Enrique. I'll be checking in the morning."

And, before Enrique's bemused gaze, the magical couple swept upstairs, laughing together in perfect contentment. Soon, muffled giggles sounded from behind the closed bedroom door.

After a minute, Malcolm crept from under the sofa, keeping well away from Enrique, who still stood, gaping at the staircase.

"What *was* that?" the boy murmured. "I thought they hated each other...."

Malcolm sighed. It appeared Enrique really was staying. He padded over and sat close to his feet.

The movement startled Enrique; he jumped and looked down at Malcolm. For a moment they gazed at one another, and then Malcolm, with another sigh, stepped those last few inches closer. *Oh, very well....*

Enrique laughed and crouched to scratch Malcolm's ears. The cat angled his head for maximum pleasure, eyelids half shut; Enrique was a good scratcher.

"Magic's a lot more complicated than I thought," Enrique said slowly. "So's James. And I guess, so's Lillian. Even you." He paused. "Do you think you can help me, boy?"

So young; so stupid. But smart enough at least, to appeal to Malcolm's greater wisdom.

Malcolm butted his head against Enrique's leg and the boy laughed. "Thanks."

Enrique stood and took a few steps toward the staircase, then stopped to look back at Malcolm with an inquiring expression. "Don't suppose you'd help me clean up the magical residue...?"

Malcolm purred, turned, and jumped up on the sofa where he curled and closed his eyes. He would help Enrique—he certainly needed it—but not with cleaning up.

Rose Strickman

Rose Strickman is a fantasy, science fiction, and horror writer living in Seattle, Washington. Her work has appeared in the magazines *Aurora Wolf, Luna Station Quarterly* and *Feed Your Monster,* as well as various anthologies, including *That Hoodoo, Voodoo That You Do, Robotica, After Lines* and *Sword and Sorceress 32.*

A researcher and information professional by day, Rose has held previous positions as diverse as quality control technician at the Library of Congress to clerical temp at the Port of Seattle. She is a compulsive reader and devoted cat lover.

LinkedIn: https://www.linkedin.com/in/rosestrickman/
For Amazon and Goodreads, search: Rose Strickman

STRAY CAT STRUT

Spring finally broke over my little part of the Bronx. The frozen drifts of gray-black slush that had built over the gutters slid down the storm drains, leaving nothing but bad memories. People walked the streets with their coats open and their heads bare. The street musicians crept out from their underground caves, and a song or two floated on the warming breeze. I was lounging in front of my crate on the deli's back stoop, enjoying a belly full of beef scraps, when a jingle jangle came padding down my alley.

She was a pretty little thing, no doubt about that. A smoky gray Siamese, with big blue eyes and high, black boots. She had a certain sway to her. Fresh-groomed, and still wrapped in her winter undercoat, she didn't look like she belonged on the street. Course, one look at the black leather collar around her neck, with its swinging diamond tag, told me that. I kneaded the splintery lip of the box I was lying against and stood up when it was clear she wasn't going to tuck tail and go back the way she'd come.

"You lost, kitten?" I asked, looking down at her.

She jumped straight up when she heard me and splashed backward through a puddle of standing water. When she was confident I wouldn't pounce on her, she took a moment to shake the water off her forepaw.

"No," she said, putting a bit of a purr in her voice. "I'm looking for Leo."

"Uh-huh," I said, licking a few stray drips of grease from my chops. "And why do you want Leo?"

"It's my sister," she said, taking a few, hesitant steps forward. "She's missing, and I need him to help me find her."

"I'm sad for you," I said, dipping my head into the heavy, plastic bowl for a drink. "But I don't see how that's my problem."

She offered a nervous smile with too many teeth in it. "Tig told me you'd say that."

That got my attention. I shook the water out of my whiskers and gave her another look.

"Tig told you where to find me?" I asked.

"He did," the Siamese said. "And he told me to remind you that you still owe him for Newcastle. He said you would know what that meant."

"What's your name?" I asked after a long, awkward moment.

"Duchess."

Of course it is. "All right, Duchess, tell me what happened to your sister."

She padded closer and hopped up onto the stoop next to me. She settled onto her haunches, with her tail tucked neatly around her. I did my best not to loom over her since she smelled all kinds of nervous. It wasn't easy, given that the little lady was maybe half my size without accounting for my coat.

"Her name is Princess, and she's two years younger than me. We were adopted by a lovely couple named Patrick and Diana. We live with them in their home in Manhattan. Princess was just a kit when they took us in. She's known no other life, but she thinks she'll have it better out here on the streets."

"And who put that idea in her head?" I asked.

"His name is Hunter—at least that's the name he answers to." Her ears laid back just saying his name. "A tiger-striped short hair with a notch in his left ear, he has green eyes, and a splash of white on his throat."

"I'm guessing he's not a neighbor's boy?" I said.

Duchess sniffed. "*Hardly.* No one in the building lets their cats outside, and there's a strict leash-and-collar ordinance. If we weren't on the ground floor, I doubt he'd had a chance to do more than catcall Princess. As it is, he made her promises if she'd sneak out the window and join him."

"He make any promises in particular?" I asked.

Duchess shook her head and set her tag swinging. "The usual nothings. That she would see the real city. That he'd show her a time she'd never forget."

"Did she talk to you about it?" I asked.

"We fought about it. She told me she'd be fine, and that she would be back before anyone noticed she was gone. I tried to tell her she had no idea what sort of risk she was taking. She hissed at me, and I hit her." Duchess's ears drooped. She looked away. "I tried to apologize, but there was no taking it back. She spent the evening curled up in Diana's lap, and I thought she'd get over it. But when I woke up the next day, the apartment was empty."

"How'd she get out?" I asked.

"She pushed out the screen on a window. Patrick left it open to get fresh air. Its screen never sat securely in the frame."

I nodded. "And when was all this?"

"Three days ago. Patrick and Diana have been frantic. They've put up posters and made dozens of calls. I didn't know what to do, and Tigger overheard me through the window of the upstairs apartment. I told him what happened, and he said if I was willing to come down here to ask, then he was willing to spend his last favor to help. He said he wasn't going to need it where he was."

That part was true, at least. Last I'd seen Tig, he was getting ready to hand in his balls for a cushy spot with a plump lady in cat-eye glasses who handed out treats like they were about to expire. I bent down and took another drink. Duchess watched me. I could feel the weight of her gaze and the hope she'd pinned on her trek down here. I sighed and shook my head.

"I'm not making any promises. But if Tig is calling in his favor, the least I can do is ask some guys I know if anyone's seen your sister."

Duchess perked up at that. Her motor started again, and she purred excitedly. "Thank you, Leo!"

"Don't thank me yet," I said, hopping off the stoop. "Let's see if I can help first. The blanket in the crate is clean and dry, and Mario will put out a bowl around dinner time. Just wait here, and I'll be back when I have something."

I padded down the alley, avoiding the bulging bags of trash the deli set out every other hour during the morning rush. I wove between a jogger and a suit, crossed against the light, and followed the smell of coffee. Flopped in front of a plate glass window, his big, square head resting on his paws, was a pit bull named, Doc. He glanced up when he saw me, the thin leather of his leash creaking from where it looped over a mostly empty bike rack.

"Ain't Tuesday yet, is it, alley cat?" Doc asked, his tongue lolling from the side of his mouth as he grinned at me.

"Need a quick favor, Doc," I said.

"Oh?" He lay his head to the side. "That's a rare thing. What does the king of the concrete jungle need little ole' me for?"

"You see the uptown sway that wandered into my spot?" I asked.

Doc nodded. He didn't miss much. "She too ferocious for you to handle by your onesome?"

"I need you to keep an eye on her," I said. "I gotta go take care of something, and I can't have her with me when I do it."

Doc nodded again and scratched at his ear. It was ragged, and when he tilted his head back, I could see the scars along the side of his neck. They'd been made by teeth and claws before his pit got raided and he was put up for adoption. They'd faded since then, but even if he didn't feel them anymore, they weren't the sort of things you forgot about. Doc yawned.

"And you expect me to do this from the goodness of my heart?" he asked.

"Course not," I told him, settling on my haunches. "You give me your eyes, and maybe a bark or two if someone looks like they're prowling, and I'll snatch a bag of ham bones for you the next time the butcher's shift is over."

"What do you want me to do if I bark at 'em, and they don't scat?" Doc asked.

I nodded toward his leash. "That thing as strong as it

looks?"

Doc chuffed. "Probably. Still not as strong as me."

"Then if they don't scamper, show them your bark isn't the worst part of you."

Doc sniffed and thought about it. He was getting older, and his boy didn't give him anything that cracked or splintered to chew on when they were at home. The pit bull nodded and lifted his front paw. I tapped it with mine.

"How long you gonna be?" Doc asked.

"Don't know," I said, stretching my forelegs, and then my back ones. "Gotta go have a talk with Reggie."

Doc nodded and turned so my alley was in sight. "Good luck with that."

I started walking. Two blocks north and one east, brought me to one of the little memorial parks that dotted the city. There was a statue on a plinth, a couple of paths just wide enough for the exercise nuts, and some token places where the city planners had put down old rubber for kids to play. Most importantly, though, one of the ubiquitous hot dog carts had taken up residence near the four-way intersection in the middle of the park and was doing a brisk trade. When I was sure the cart wasn't going anywhere, I settled under one of the benches to wait.

It took the better part of an hour before what I needed came strolling by. He wore a plum suit with frayed sleeves and was trying to comb his hair over a noticeable bald spot. His order was three dogs, all the trimmings, no onions. The steam rose, and he inhaled deep as the condiments were layered on. The suit had two dogs put in a brown bag and was starting on the third, as he headed to my bench. He plopped down with a groan that made the aluminum slats creak, put the bag between his feet, took out his phone, and tapped at the screen. With his attention diverted, I snatched the rolled top of the bag in my teeth and made a break for it. By the time I heard his shout, I was already halfway to the gates. I darted across the street, tucked into a blind alley with a busted fence, and came out near the subway stairs. After taking a moment to get a better grip on the bag, I trotted down the cracked, concrete steps.

The station wasn't the worst I'd seen. It stank of tired bodies and old urine, sure, but it looked like someone had swiped a mop over the faded tiles at some point in the last week. No one was sleeping on the benches, and most of the garbage was in the cans rather than on the floor. A train was unloading when I reached the platform, so I ducked and weaved between the forest of legs until I reached the far wall. When I'd made sure no one in a uniform was coming my way, I pushed my head against the safety gate that keeps passengers from wandering off down the tracks. It squeaked open, and I darted through before it sprang closed again.

The tunnel was the true underground. There were no carefully hooded fluorescents down there. No garish ads plastered on the walls to get you to spend everything you earned that day on something you didn't need and wouldn't use. It was all concrete and steel, with the musty smell of a well-used den. Water was dripping somewhere, and other than the rare lantern along the tracks, it was the kind of deep dark you never saw up on the streets.

"Here kitty, kitty, kitty," a voice chittered out of the darkness ahead of me. A fat shadow loomed, and red eyes flashed. It hissed as it slithered, its tail rasping along the concrete.

"What'cha got in that bag, fluffy?" another voice asked from behind me. "Smells pretty good."

I set the bag down. "Smell is free. I'm here to see Reggie."

"Greylord ain't seeing petitioners today, longhair," the rat in front of me said, taking a few steps closer. "But what say you leave that bag with us? We'll make sure he gets it."

Nails clicked on the concrete behind me. I pressed against the wall, whipping my tail up to the side just as the shadow at my back lunged. He skidded on the ledge where I'd been standing, and before he could get his balance, I butted him in the side with my shoulder and he fell over the edge, squeaking as he hit the tracks. The other rat came at me, teeth bared, and I slapped him hard on the side of the head. The love tap flipped him on his side and knocked his head against the wall. I put my foot on his belly and let him feel my claws. He lay there, breath whistling from his nose.

"My name is Leo," I said. "Reggie is gonna wanna see me."

"Hey, sure thing," the rat said, waving his forelegs. "Whatever you say!"

I let him up and walked back over to my sack. He huffed to his feet, shaking his head and rubbing at the place where I'd bounced it. Without another word, he turned, and sauntering down the tunnel. I followed, brown paper bag clamped in my jaws. From the track, I heard scritch-scratching as the other tunnel guard limped away before the next train made minced rat of him.

About half a mile down the track, around a curve from the last maintenance station, the rat butted his head against a metal plate. It rang hollow and a few seconds later slid aside. Another tunnel dweller stuck his head out, whiskers twitching.

"What you want, Shanks?" the door guard asked.

"Got someone to see the boss, Skeeve," Shanks said, tossing his head back at me. The other rat looked over Shanks's shoulder and grinned.

"How you be, Leo?" Skeeve asked.

"I be," I said. "When did they make you a door mouse?"

"While back," Skeeve said, shuffling aside. "Go on in, boss is in his usual spot."

I squeezed through the crack and found myself in an abandoned storeroom. Metal shelves were still bolted into the walls, and the heavy, steel fire door was bolted shut. A caged bulb burned, filling the room with low-wattage light. A dozen rats lounged on the upper decks, and twice their number lay spread across the floor. Some were big, some were small, and they came in all shades. Sitting in the back of the room, his piebald rump parked on a dusty, velvet cushion, was Reggie. The chittering stopped as I crossed the floor, and every head turned in my direction. I caught a whiff of fear and did my best to look friendly. One or two of them wouldn't be a problem, but the saying about cornered rats and how they fight wasn't a joke, and I was on their turf. I put the bag down on a half-broken cinderblock in front of Reggie and sat back on my haunches.

"Well, well, well," Reggie said, turning to look at me. One of his eyes was covered with a thick, milky cataract, but the other was dark, beady, and shrewd. "What has the cat dragged in?"

"You know me, Reggie, I never come without a present," I said.

Reggie jerked his head, and a rat nearly twice his size sauntered over. The underling unrolled the top of the bag. He tipped it toward Reggie, who sniffed at the contents and smiled, revealing a mouthful of too-big, too-yellow teeth.

"This what I think it is?" Reggie asked.

"Two park dogs with everything on 'em but the onions," I said.

"Always a pleasure to have you in my humble abode, Leo." His words had barely died away before the rest of the court started chattering among themselves again. The boss had given his blessing, and there was nothing more to see as far as they were concerned. "So, tell me, to what do I owe the providence of this visit?"

"I got an errand to take care of," I said. "But I need some help with it."

"Tell me about it," Reggie nodded.

I did. As I talked, two of Reggie's boys unwrapped one of the dogs. Still warm, the condiments dripped from the bun. Reggie squirmed forward and went to work. Though there wasn't much to the tale I told, he'd gorged himself on half of the first dog by the time I reached the end.

"So, what you want from me, is an idea of where to look for the happy couple?" Reggie asked, swiping a smear of mustard off his nose and depositing it in his mouth.

I swished my tail and shrugged. "If you can tell me where the girl is, that would be enough for me."

"I don't keep track of every feline in this great city of ours," Reggie said, taking another bite out of the dog. "But this Hunter ... him I know. Or, more precisely, I know of."

Reggie talked. I listened. By the time Reggie had told me everything a Sunday brunch bribe would buy, I'd shaped a pretty good plan.

—▫—

I followed Reggie's tip and found a spot across from some swanky digs on 67th. No one took any notice of me, and I hunkered in a shadow as the sun went down. There was a cold breeze, so I tucked my tail around me and got as comfortable as I could. It was half past dinner time when I spotted two cats, beating feet down the alley and coming my way. A splash of headlights from a passing cab revealed them. The smaller was a sweet, gray short hair with wide, gold eyes. And the other, unless I missed my guess, was Hunter.

The two bolted across the street and into the cover of the park. I stretched and followed. It wasn't hard. Hunter might have been a street stalker, but whoever the pretty kitty was, she was more accustomed to carpets and cuddles than keeping silent in the bush. I could have tracked them with my eyes closed if I wanted.

They skirted the edge of the Tavern on The Green, avoiding the pools of light and noise made by flocks of tourists. After slinking down a series of walking paths, they slowed when they hit the Sheep Meadow. I cut south, shadowing them, and hooked around near the transverse. The gray short hair paused, and Hunter padded next to her as she caught her breath. I drew closer, paws whispering over the manicured grass.

"Come on, Sheila, the hard part's over," Hunter said. He was a little winded himself, but he hid it well. "We can't stop now. We've got to get somewhere safe!"

"About that," I said, coming out of my crouch and drawing closer. "Gonna need words with you, friend."

Sheila's eyes went wide as half-dollars, and her ears laid flat to her head. She backed up, mewling and scared. Hunter whipped around hard, his tail and hackles raised. I gave him a sleepy smile and padded nearer.

"I ain't your friend," Hunter said, with as much menace as he could manage.

"Hunter, that hurts," I said, stopping a foot or so away from him. I saw the confusion in his face and followed up before he could get his balance. "Been looking for Princess. Folks tell me last time they saw her, you and she had gone strutting."

"Hunter," Sheila said. "Who is this? Who's Princess?"

The tiger stripe looked from me to his latest lady and back. I read it on his face just before he turned and ran, heading for the freedom of the open meadow. I moved half a second before he did, kicking up a divot as I launched myself after him. Hunter was sleek, and he was scared, but I had a longer stride. He tried to swerve, when he chanced a look back over his shoulder at me and tripped, tumbling ass over tail, yowling as he went.

Before he could get up to run again, I was on him. He tried to claw my neck, but my ruff was too thick to get any purchase. He kicked, and I grunted as he dragged foot razors over my stomach. It wasn't deep, but it was enough to make me mad. I raked my claws across his face, leaving bloody gouges on his nose. He hissed, but when I raked him again, his hiss turned to a howl. He fought to get away, and that was when I put my teeth around his throat. He struggled, but I'd cut my teeth on raccoons, and he just wasn't up to snuff. I squeezed, until he gave up. He wheezed, trying to breathe past my hold. Finally, he rolled onto his back, and showed me his belly. I let him catch a breath, but I kept my teeth close enough to make him nervous.

"I can't tell you where Princess is," Hunter wheezed.

"You can't?" I asked, skimming his already bloody neck with my teeth. "Or you won't?"

"If I tell you, he'll kill me!" Hunter mewled.

"If you don't tell me, he'll never get the chance," I said. "Because I'll tear you into pieces and leave a little scavenger hunt for the groundskeepers before I go on my merry way."

I put my paw on Hunter's stomach, in the same spot where he'd tried to spill my guts. I could feel his heart pounding. I flexed and gave him a hard prick of my claws. He pissed himself, steam rising from the urine before it soaked into the ground.

"The Persian," Hunter moaned. "I took her to the Persian!"

I backed off to look at his face but left my claws where they were. "That's good. Now tell me the rest."

Hunter nervously licked his chops, breath snuffling through his nasal cavity. "He has a spot, just off the beach. He tells me to bring him uptown pussies who've had all their shots, but who haven't been fixed yet. I bring him the goods when I get 'em, and he gives me something for my trouble."

"What does he do with them?" I asked.

"I don't know," Hunter said, shaking his head. "I bring them in, and he puts them in a room. I never asked!"

I nodded and added a hint of pressure with my sharps. "How much muscle does he have?"

"I don't know," Hunter hissed. "He's usually got a pair of manx with him. They do the spitting and snarling. And a big black angora. I didn't catch his name, but he's got one blue eye and one gold."

"All right, Hunter, last question," I said, leaning in close enough to smell the blood running down his muzzle. "And you better get this one right. Where is this place?"

Hunter gave me an address on the waterfront. I stood, slowly taking my paw off his belly. He lay there in the dirt for a moment, covered in his own blood and piss, before shakily getting to his feet, head down, and tail tucked.

"This had better check out," I said, turning away. "I can find you again, if I have to. And I won't be in a forgiving mood if you make me come looking."

Sheila was sitting right where I'd left her. Her ears went down as I approached. She pressed herself into the lawn like she thought I might not see her if she crouched low enough. I looked down at her and sighed.

"Go home, kitten," I said. "Get back inside, curl up with whoever, and be happy you didn't go where he was taking you."

I walked away and didn't turn to see if the gray lady was taking my advice. I headed east, cutting through the paths where I could and keeping to the concrete where I couldn't. When I came out on the other side of the park, I made my way toward a subway station. I could have kept walking, but I didn't have all night, and I didn't want to be huffing and puffing by the time I got where I was going. I dodged through the half-drunk, late-night crowd, and managed to sneak under a train seat where one of the lights had gone out and avoid the worst of the passengers. I reached my stop without being groped, shouted at, or spit on, which I chose to take as a good omen.

Back above ground, I found myself a world away from the glitz and glamour of Central Park's hangers-on. Chain-link fences clanked in the wind, the barbed wire on top showing they still had some teeth. Halogen lights burned into the night, making the shadows even darker. Freighters and tugs chugged along the waterway, pissing oil in their wake. All I could smell was old fish, rotting garbage, and hopelessness. I was in the right place.

The spot Hunter had told me about didn't look like much from the outside. Short and long, it was just a self-storage place. The kind with rusty "Do Not Enter" signs on the fence and blind cameras whose only job was to keep the junkies and door sleepers moving along. Even accounting for the foreclosure sign on the gate, the place felt off. The way you knew the guy on the corner had something under his Mack, and you hoped you could get past him before he decided to show you.

I padded around the perimeter, my ears on a swivel. I didn't hear anything though. Didn't see much, either. Still, if I was gonna check the place out, it was worth giving it the full treatment. So, I squeezed through the gap in the front gate and slunk my way up to the building's west side. I hopped on an old barrel, jumped onto an abandoned dumpster, and crawled along a small ledge near a rear window. A little moonlight trickled through, and I peered inside. All I saw was an old desk with a broken chair, a door, and a hallway. What wasn't visible, though, was any dust. With a firm paw I pushed against the window; it creaked open. I sniffed. The place was nowhere near as abandoned as it looked. Maybe Hunter had played it straight with me after all.

"Pah, what was that?" a thick voice asked from somewhere inside. "Claudio, go check on the girl!"

I winced and pulled back. The window dropped shut, and I flattened myself against the ledge. Below, a shadow moved through the darkened room. From my angle, I couldn't tell much about it, but it was big. It slunk down the hallway and was gone for maybe half a minute before returning the way it had come. Then it ducked behind a curtain I hadn't noticed and was gone again.

I waited, not moving a muscle. A minute passed, then another. After several minutes, and nothing moved inside, I pushed on the window slowly again, hoping it wouldn't make a noise. When it was high enough to wriggle through, I stopped and listened. No voices sounded the alarm. With one deep breath, I let myself fall.

I hit the floor like a whisper, paws spread wide, legs bent. I crouched there in the shadows and listened. Nothing. The skin between my shoulders was tight, and my ruff puffed out. One step at a time, I eased my way toward the hall. I hadn't noticed from above that all the doors along the hall had slots at the bottom, big enough to fit a food tray. The sort of doors I'd seen when I was doing shelter time. I hunkered down near door one and sniffed. I didn't smell anything, so I pushed on the slot. It swung open on smooth hinges, and I saw a small room with the floor and walls covered in thick pads. Unless it held a chorus of Cheshires, you could howl your head off in one of these things without anyone noticing. This first one was empty. So was the second and the third. The one at the end of the hall wasn't.

In the dim light leaking from the rooftop windows, I could just make her out. She was smooth and slender, with the same colors as her big sister. Her eyes were green, and her socks weren't quite as tall, but I could see the resemblance. She stared at me, tail twitching nervously.

"What do you want?" she asked. Her voice was still a little haughty, but there was an under-tremble that she couldn't cover.

"Here to take you home, Princess," I said. "Your big sister sent me."

Her eyes sparkled, and she sucked in a deep breath. Then her excitement turned to horror.

"Look out!" she hissed.

I dropped and flopped, rolling to my right. Something big and furry crashed into the wall where I'd been. It turned, and a pair of mismatched eyes stared at me. One was gold, the other was blue, and both were cold as December rain. Princess scrabbled at the slot, doing her best to hold it open, one eye peering out at us.

"Don't suppose you're going to let us just walk out of here?" I asked the big angora.

He rushed me, teeth first. I managed to get my shoulder up, but he bit and bit hard. I returned the favor, jabbing my top row into his upper back. I tasted blood, but if he felt the bite, I couldn't tell. He shook his head, trying to dislodge me, and I let him. It threw him off-guard, and I tumbled back against the wall. My shoulder hurt, but when I put weight on it, my front leg held.

"All right then, that's how you want it," I said, shaking my head. "Let's do it."

The angora didn't rush me this time. He'd played that card, and he didn't like how I'd raised him. Instead, he looked for an opening. I didn't give him one. I followed him with my eyes and willed my muscles to relax. When he came, I'd be ready.

He did, and I was. He tried to bull in on my injured side, going low instead of high. I let him get right under me and then jumped up and landed on his back. With my teeth sunk into his scruff, my claws dug deep grooves along his ribs. He hissed, but no other sounds passed his flaps as he tried to shake me off. I held as long as I could but took fur with me when I went. The big enforcer stumbled away, blood oozing down his sides. He stared at me with the same, chilly gaze, then leaned down, coughed once, and squared up again.

"Stop," the thick, heavy voice I'd heard earlier called out. The angora froze, and I raised my head to see over his shoulder.

At the doorway stood an unlikely trio. A pair of manx flanked it, their ragged ears and scarred noses announcing loud and clear that they weren't shy about throwing down. Between them stood the Persian. He was taller than I thought he'd be, with big bones under his soft rolls, and long, dirty-white fur. The fur stood up in a dozen places, and I had a sneaking suspicion he'd been sleeping before the fracas woke him. He wobbled when he walked, but there was nothing comical about the anger in his hard, yellow eyes as he stared me down.

"What is the meaning of this?" The Persian demanded, waddling closer.

"Was just minding my business, when your bruiser decided to pounce me," I said.

"Indeed," the Persian scoffed, standing next to the angora. "And what was the business you were minding, here in *my* home?"

"There's a kitten in that room," I said, nodding my head toward the door without taking my eyes off the crew in front of me. "She isn't gonna be any use to you, so I figured I'd take her home."

"Well, that's generous of you," the Persian said with a rolling, chuckling purr. "Pray tell me, why would she be of no use to me?"

"I had words with Hunter earlier tonight," I said. "He told me about your little arrangement."

"Did he?" the Persian asked.

"He didn't want to," I said. "But I was insistent. Which is

why I know he sold you a bill of goods with this one."

"Speak plainly," the Persian said, licking his paw and pushing some of his fur back into place. "You are quickly reaching the end of my patience. When I run out of patience, I am more inclined to let my boys have their fun."

"Girl's got a sister, name of Duchess," I said. "She told me she and the little one both got tranqued and fixed. Princess here wasn't straight with Hunter, because if she had been, she knew he would have walked away without her."

That got the Persian's attention. He kept his poker face, but I could see the wheels turning. He glanced at the little slot where Princess was now trapped half-in and half-out. The longhair looked back at me.

"She lied to him?" the Persian asked.

"About that, yeah," I said. "Thing she didn't know to lie about was that trinket around her neck."

"And why should her adornment concern me?"

"She lives with a pair of yuppies over in Manhattan," I said. "The vet wanted to tag them both, but the couple thought skin trackers were cruel and unusual. So, they put those rubber baubles around their necks. They can pick them up with their phones if they get close enough, and it's just a matter of time before someone in animal control cruises by and notices a blip on his screen. Then it's all door busters, neck snares, and a one-way trip to a cage downtown."

No one said anything for a long minute. The manx glanced at each other from the corners of their eyes before peering at the rubber diamond hanging around Princess's neck. The angora stood like a statue, if statues could bleed. The Persian narrowed his eyes at me and nodded. He kept nodding to a rhythm only he could hear.

"You have a name, soldier?" the Persian asked.

"Leo," I told him.

"I think you're a liar, Leo," the Persian said. "But I don't know if you're lying about the kit's fix, her tracker, Hunter, all of it, or none of it. Experience has taught me not to bet when I'm not certain of the outcome. So, I will give you the kitty and let you both walk out of here. In exchange, some day in the future, I will ask you to come do me a favor. A rather large one."

"And, just out of curiosity, what happens if I say no?" I asked.

"Then I will have Claudio tear you apart, and I will let Barn and Dag fight over what's left."

I glanced over at the other three. Barn and Dag were already hunkering, just in case their boss gave the word. Claudio didn't appear to even notice the Persian had spoken. It was my turn to nod.

"All right," I said. "I can live with that."

The Persian turned on his heel and left the way he'd come. The manx trotted after him, never more than a few paces from his rear end. "Claudio, show them out."

I pushed up the slot lid, and Princess wriggled through. The angora stirred, turned, and walked down the hall. Just past the desk he shouldered open a side door a few inches. I noticed the strike plate was broken, and the privacy chain had been the only thing holding it closed. He waited. Princess slunk past him, head down, and darted into the night. I pushed my whiskers against the opening, and once I was sure I'd fit, I glanced over at the silent enforcer with his mismatched eyes.

"No hard feelings, big guy?" I asked. Claudio stared at me. I nodded. That was about what I expected.

I managed to squeeze my way through the door before Claudio shoved it closed and found Princess waiting for me. She'd crouched in the gravel and weeds, out of the lamplight, but the sheen in her eyes gave her away. I butted her with my head as I walked past.

"Come on, kit, your sister's waiting," I said.

For a minute, I didn't think she was going to follow. But just then the building's half-broken shutter slapped closed in the wind, and Princess bolted after me. She stayed close enough that I could tell where she was, but she didn't say anything until we'd gone a dozen blocks. I was scoping out the stairs to a different station than the one I'd used earlier.

"Why did you lie to him like that?" Princess asked.

"Long as he thought you'd give him a litter, you were valuable," I said, crouching into the shadows as a guy in a heavy winter coat shuffled past. "If he had reason to doubt that, you wouldn't be worth the trouble he'd be buying."

"Did my sister really send you?"

"Nobody sends me anywhere," I said, watching as the station attendant pulled out his phone and stopped doing his job. "She asked me to find you. So, I did."

"Just like that?" she asked.

"I owed somebody," I said, jerking my head down the stairs. I walked close to the wall, slid around the corner, and ducked under the turnstiles. Princess came with. She wasn't all that good at stalking, but she followed close in my footsteps.

"And now you owe somebody else," Princess said, crouching under one of the wall benches. It smelled like a basement toilet under there, but it was quiet, and nobody bothered us.

"Yeah," I said, as a train came in. "That's the way of the world."

We didn't talk more as we made our way back to my little corner of the city. There weren't any track delays, and most of the riders were either exhausted from being out all night or tired from having just gotten up. Other than a Yorkie in a shoulder bag, and a black lab who was on eyes duty, no one even noticed us. The sun was yawning its way over the skyline by the time we topped the stairs, and I wanted nothing more than to lie down in my crate and sleep for a week.

Duchess was waiting for us, up and pacing on the deli's back stoop. At the sight of her sister, she purred so loud that I was worried she'd strain something. Princess seemed embarrassed, but she leaned into her sister and closed her eyes.

"Please don't say I told you so," Princess said. "I don't think I could take that on top of everything else."

"I'm just glad you're back," Duchess pressed her forehead to

Princess's. "Nothing else matters right now."

I made it most of the way to my little shelf before Duchess turned her attention on me. With less enthusiasm than when she'd greeted Princess, she stepped close and rubbed her cheek against mine. I tried not to wince as her whiskers raked the spot where Claudio had clawed the side of my neck.

"Thank you, Leo," she said, tears in her voice. "Thank you so much! I don't know what I can do to repay you."

"Get her fixed," I said, grunting as I made my way up into my crate. I flopped down with all the grace I could muster, one paw sticking out. "And be careful. If you don't know the way back, just pop down in the station and find a rat. Tell them you're a friend of Reggie's, and they'll get you where you need to be."

I watched as the two sisters made their way back onto the street and out of my life. I tried to get comfortable, ignoring the aches in my shoulders, and the stings from my cuts. I did my best not to think about what the Persian would want from me if he ever minced his way to my door. I closed my eyes, took a deep breath of my fragrant little alley, and counted favors instead of sheep. In the city, your life is only as good as your word, and favors were bought and paid for.

Neal F. Litherland

Neal F. Litherland, author and gamer, writes primarily science fiction, fantasy, and horror. He began his writing career in 2008 as a freelancer and ghostwriter. Since that time, his short stories have been published in multiple anthologies, including *Noir Carnival* ("The Price of Admission"), *Slaughter House* ("The Harlequin and the Hatchetmen"), and *Ghosts Revenge* ("The Legend of Black Jack Guilotine").

Neal earned his bachelor's degree in criminal justice from Indiana University. He lives in Valparaiso, Indiana, and when he's not writing, enjoys sword fights and acts as a guide to realms fantastical.

Blogsite: http://nealflitherland.blogspot.com/
Facebook: @nealflitherland
For Amazon and Goodreads, search: Neal F. Litherland

SAVANNAH AND SAVANNAH

You don't meet a cat with your name every day. Perhaps that's why Savannah Smith found herself so captivated by my bushy tail and twitching ears as she knelt beside me in the garden.

"Where did you come from, puss?" she asked.

I purred and licked my paw.

"I'm Savannah Smith, just like you. That's a funny coincidence, isn't it?" she said, looking again at the name on my collar and then tickling the back of my head. "Or perhaps you're supposed to be for me, is that it?"

I mewed, and the girl's eyes lit up; she wanted to believe I really *was* a gift for her; that much was plain to see.

They always do.

"Oh, you are so very lovely. And so soft, too," she said, running her fingers through my sandy blonde fur. "I've always wanted a cat just like you, but Mum and Dad won't let me have one. I'm sure they'd change their minds if they saw how beautiful you are, though, wouldn't they?"

I licked her fingers, my purrs growing louder.

The girl held her breath. I could almost see her mind at work behind her eyes, see her thinking up the excuses she'd give to her parents as she crumbled to temptation.

"Would you like to come inside with me, puss?" Savannah asked, exhaling at last.

I mewed again and leapt to my feet, circling around her. The girl smiled wide.

"Come on then," she said, jumping up and skipping towards the backdoor. I slunk after her, waiting patiently as she pulled it wide and held it open for me.

A big mistake, not that she could have known. *Never* invite a cat that has your name into your home.

I sauntered past her and into the house.

—◻—

"We've told you before, Savannah. No pets."

"But Dad, look at her! She's so beautiful and soft and lovely and nice and can we please keep her? Please, please, pleaeeeeeese?"

I stretched out in front of the roaring fireplace, my fluffy fur bristling in the heat. It's always best to let conversations like these play out around you until the time is right to intervene.

"We can't keep some random cat, my darling. Who knows where it's been?"

"But she's not random! Look, she's called Savannah Smith too; it's meant to be!"

"That *is* odd, isn't it, Pete? But still, it must belong to someone else...."

"Exactly, Laura. Exactly."

"But she's sooooo pretty!"

"It's a nice cat, yes, but that's hardly the point...."

My chance had arrived. I hopped onto the sofa and pressed myself into her father's leg. My purring grew louder, laced with layers of tantalising promise and hidden meaning that humans can often sense but rarely understand. Her mother reached over to tickle behind my ear—never my favourite interaction but something I was willing to play up to given the circumstances. I rolled onto my back and licked her hand.

"Oh ...," her father said.

"Oh ...," her mother agreed.

"Ohhhhhh?" Savannah asked, fidgeting on the floor.

"Well ... all right, let's keep her here for a day or two," her father said, tickling my belly.

"Yes!" Savannah shouted. She leapt to her feet and danced around for a moment before picking me up from her father's lap and then cuddling me tightly.

"Just until its owner turns up, understand?"

That's what they all say at first. Pay it no heed.

Once you're in, you're in.

—▫—

We were feared once, as all creatures with sharp teeth and sharper minds should be. Parents warned their young to watch where they stepped when we were close, lest we lure them away with wicked secrets and false promises. But with the passage of time, such warnings all too often turn into mere stories, stories become folklore, folklore becomes forgotten myth.

Lucky for us.

Savannah had little reason to be fearful as I stalked through the living room, examining my new home.

I pressed my paws into a plush, comfy cushion and purred contentedly.

—▫—

The girl promised her parents that she would look after me, that they wouldn't have to lift a finger. And she kept that promise well ... at first. She would prepare my tea, carefully mashing up tin after tin of jellied cat food each evening, her eyes fixed on me as I ate it up. She would vacuum my fur from the living room carpet, happily taking on the extra job despite her usual aversion to housework. And she would even clean out my litter tray, never complaining about the smell.

"Funny to see her pulling her weight for once," her mother said one evening, sipping from a glass of white wine. I was drowsing on the windowsill, soaking up the dry warmth of the radiator below me, watching as Savannah walked around the room with a basket, picking up my scattered toys and putting them away one by one.

Her father chuckled. "At this rate we won't need to clean this place ourselves ever again!"

But over time, the shine wore off. Things that Savannah had at first found fun turned into chores: brushing my fur became boring, sorting my food and litter tray became stinky inconveniences. Bit by bit, the girl avoided her duties, until she had ceased looking after me at all. Her parents stepped in to take care of me instead, begrudgingly at first but soon enough happy to wait on my every desire.

It couldn't have been more perfect had I planned it — which I had.

None of them referenced the broken promise directly. It was only a tiny promise, after all, one made by a little girl desperate for a pet cat to call her own. But it was a promise all the same, one that had been broken, abandoned, cast out. Without malice or intent, Savannah's promise had transformed into a lie.

And nothing tastes more delicious to a cat than a lie.

—◻—

In time, you become less and less of a stranger, until you're considered part of the family. Loved, cherished, trusted.

That's when the real fun begins.

"Savannah! Can you come in here please?"

I followed the girl as she walked into the kitchen. Her parents stood around a pile of ceramic rubble. "Look at this, just look at it!" her mother said, tears welling in her eyes. "You know this was your Grandma's vase, look at it now!"

"I didn't do it," the girl said. "It must have been the cat."

"Come on now, Savannah," her father said as I brushed myself up against his ankles. "You can't blame everything on the cat. Look, your bloody yo-yo is right here amongst the fragments!"

"But — but —"

"But nothing! You know how much that vase meant to your mum. Say you're sorry."

"No! It wasn't me, it really wasn't!" The girl glanced at me and I back at her, unblinking.

Are the first hints of doubt sneaking into her mind? I wondered.

"Go to your room, Savannah," her mother said, eyes fixed

on the remains of her vase.

"But—"

"Go to your room, now!"

The girl stormed out and up the stairs. I followed in her shadow, mimicking her steps as she slammed the door behind us and dived onto her bed. "I haven't done anything, nothing at all!" she shouted, face buried in her pillows. "It must have been...."

She turned to look at the foot of the bed where I sat watching her.

"You."

I didn't respond. Why would I? Always best to keep your cards close to your chest.

—◻—

Clever cats become bolder as time passes. Flicking out a claw to tear a cushion cover, biting into a roast chicken on the kitchen counter, pushing a fresh cup of coffee onto the carpet—all safe territory, if you're careful.

I would do such things whenever the girl found herself in the wrong place at the wrong time, and only ever when her parent's backs were turned. Savannah often caught me up to mischief and would shout out in protest, point her fingers in my direction, but her parents were already coming under my spell; she would always get the blame if I played my cards right.

And I always did.

"I'm on to you, cat," she whispered one evening. Her mother had just finished chastising her for ripping up a newspaper, leaving her to clean the mess she'd left strewn across the living room floor. "You're a menace, nothing but trouble. They'll catch you in the act soon, just you wait."

I considered her for a moment before turning my attention back to the bay window. In the garden, a fat grey squirrel was gobbling up seed from the family's bird table.

There was no cause for concern; the girl's fate was already

sealed, whether she knew it or not.

—◻—

It's natural to look back sometimes and wonder when everything started to fall apart. Relationships cool, people drift apart, lives shift. Sometimes family ties are the quickest to snap, already straining from the tensions and squabbles that lie just beneath the surface—it can happen without you noticing in the slightest.

Until it's too late, that is.

"Mum, have you seen my school bag? Mum?"

"Hmm?" Savannah's mother replied. I yawned from head to toe before curling up in her lap.

"My school bag. I thought I'd left it in the kitchen, but I can't find it anywhere."

"Oh, it's probably...." She tailed off, rubbing my belly.

"Probably where?"

The mother remained silent.

"... Mum?"

Silence.

Savannah appeared to become smaller in the doorway, shadows overwhelming her as she backed out of the room.

The school bag wasn't even the start. The changes had come bit by bit: carefully considered packed lunches became leftovers, leftovers became empty Tupperware tubs. Savannah's regular Saturday walks with her father became less frequent, then non-existent. Where her parents had once tucked her into a comfy, clean bed, she now pulled weeks-old sheets up to her chin, whispering goodnight to the shadows as she did so.

It's not nice to feel like you're being replaced. That doesn't mean it won't happen to you, though, if you fail to tread carefully, fail to pay attention to the little details.

Let your guard down long enough and who knows how your life might change?

—▢—

She notices the whiskers first, though the signs were already as clear as day if she'd looked close enough.

Savannah's voice had taken on a purred tone, vowels vibrating into one another in a constant murmur. Her arms were becoming fuzzier, fluffier, softer. Her fingernails were curving and becoming sharper at the ends, catching on her sleeves as she dressed herself each morning. All clear signs; all so easy to overlook.

Whiskers, though, are harder to miss.

I knew realisation had finally dawned when I heard a crash from the bathroom, followed by a strangled screech as Savannah looked at herself in the mirror. Three fine, sturdy hairs protruded from each side of her face just below her nose. Which was, now she studied it, becoming flatter, upturned at the end.

Catlike.

She swung around towards the bathroom doorway, where I sat cleaning my long, slender legs. "This is your fault, isn't it?" she hissed, her sharp teeth glinting under the harsh bathroom light. "Why are you doing this to me?"

I observed her for a moment, staring into her slit-like pupils. Then I returned to my work, licking my belly.

The girl screamed, swinging back to the mirror. She began pulling out the whiskers one by one, grimacing as each came loose from her skin.

But it was too late for that. Far too late.

—▢—

Savannah's parents paid less and less attention to her as time wore on, preoccupied by their jobs, the TV, friends, and each other.

And me, of course.

I caught the girl staring at me in the wardrobe mirror. My eyes lingered on hers for a moment before I returned my gaze to my reflection, admiring what I was becoming—my sandy blonde hair, my soft skin, my bright blue eyes.

"You can't do this to me; you can't do this!" the girl cried, pacing back and forth through her room.

Somewhere downstairs a muffled voice called out, "Will you shut that bloody cat up!"

Savannah looked at me, eyes wide, trembling from anger and fear alike. "Please," she whispered, "please make this stop. I'll do anything you want me to, anything!"

I smirked; the idea that *she* had anything left to offer *me*.

The girl cried out again. "This is my house, cat. My house, not yours!" she sobbed, her regrown whiskers twitching.

Perhaps she believed that or perhaps she already knew the truth, deep down.

She was wrong, either way—it had been my house since the day she invited me in.

—❑—

Desperation is a funny thing. So many people only jump into action once it kicks in. Had they been better prepared in the first place perhaps they might never have reached such dire straits.

Prepare, prepare and prepare again—why do you think cats always land on their feet?

Savannah tried her best to turn things around, I'll give her that. She did everything she could to win back her parents attention: following them from room to room, pulling at their trouser legs, whimpering. "Help me, please!" she might have been trying to say, feline eyes glinting with tears she could no longer shed.

But they couldn't hear her, not anymore. All they heard was mewing, hissing, screeching.

All they heard was the cat.

—❑—

What was running through the girl's mind as the end grew near, I wonder? Did she question all her tantrums, the times she snapped at her parents, the days she said she'd rather not go with them to visit her grandparents? Did she wish she'd cherished her old life whilst it was still hers? Did she regret letting her guard down, regret letting me in?

It's funny, really; all these years, all these lives, and I've never once cared enough to ask.

—□—

I had a pet cat and its name was Savannah.

She was a moody cat, a mean cat, a mopey cat. She spent her days prowling through the house, never able to settle in any one place for long. Try to stroke her and she would scratch and bite and hiss, so we mostly came to leave her alone, staying at a safe distance. She would only approach us at dinner time, albeit reluctantly, and even then, she would keep one eye trained on me as she ate, hungrily wolfing down bite after bite of tinned cat food whilst I gorged myself on chocolate treats. It was almost as if she were envious of me, of my life of luxury, of how my parents loved me so.

As if she wished it were all hers.

We kept her well though, regardless of her quirks. But then, one sunny morning, Father burnt his toast; bitter smoke poured from the grill and filled the kitchen. He opened the back door to let it escape without thinking—the cat made a dash for it, bursting through the gap and out from the house. I got up, thinking I should give chase, before lounging back onto the sofa. *Probably best to let her go*, I thought to myself.

Mother and Father never wanted a pet in the first place.

—□—

Summer has returned. I walk through my garden, enjoying the heat of the sun on my smooth skin. I stretch out my arms and arch my back—for a fleeting moment the outline of some distant memory takes shape at the edge of my thoughts, one where I'm stretching out by the fireside and not a girl but something else entirely. I shake my head and the memory is gone, just like that.

I spot a cat at the bottom of the garden. I've always wanted a pet, but Mum and Dad have never liked the idea. I draw closer to the cat, expecting it to flee. But it stays in place, almost like it's waiting for me. I bend down onto my knees and tickle it behind the ears. I look at its collar—"Savannah Smith." A funny coincidence, I think. Or perhaps it's a sign?

"Would you like to come inside with me, puss?" I ask, as the cat swishes its tail in the warm summer air. The cat mews and jumps to its feet. That settles it, I think. It's meant to be.

You don't meet a cat with your name every day, do you?

"Come on then," I say, jumping to my feet and skipping towards the house. I look back at the cat, which follows me at a distance. Then waiting patiently by the back door, almost as if it had used it in the past.

I turn the handle and open the door wide for the cat. She looks up at me, ears twitching, before slowly getting to her feet. I can hear her purr as she moves to take her first steps into the house.

I slam the door hard and then grabbed the cat by the scruff of its neck. I bring my face close to the cat's, look deep into its pale blue eyes. "You can't fool me, girl," I hiss.

It swipes a claw at me, but I hold it at a safe distance; it's no danger to me, not anymore. It stays still after that, the fight having all but abandoned it.

I toss the shocked, trembling creature back into the bushes at the bottom of the garden, nestled amongst catmint and crocuses. I think I can hear it mewing as I walk back to the door, as if it's desperate to regain my attention. As if it still wants to come back into the house with me, even now.

Little chance of that. Never invite a cat that has your name into your home.

Tom Antony Davies

Tom Antony Davies writes speculative fiction. Most recently, his short story, "Bonne Femme," was published in *Firewords Magazine* (*Firewords* 9). He lives in Manchester, United Kingdom.

Blogsite: http://www.tomantonydavies.com/
Twitter: @TomAntonyDavies

THE REAL THING

Every autumn, Charlie Sikes emptied the machines at North Shore. He could still recall that first year driving the lake road through flaming trees, listening to the World Series on the radio, the sun warm on his left arm and Drysdale setting them down in order. Some men would envy him, he remembered thinking.

A lot had changed in forty years. They played the Series at night now, for one. For another, the resort they'd planned for North Shore never really panned out. The ski lift and lodge hung on a few years, but the real skiing was two hours north where the resorts knew how to play the game. It seemed to Charlie that the effort to change had taken a toll on North Shore. More places went broke than broke even, and the locals had the hangdog look of the snookered. Too bad for them, Charlie snorted. A year from now he'd be in Tampa and North Shore would be someone else's problem.

One more year; the blink of an eye.

—□—

The machine at Pike's Chicken Shack was of the new style: weatherproof, graffiti proof, lots of jazzy colors. He'd brought it up himself two summers ago to replace the round-shouldered box that had been there since God knows when. Pike's hadn't changed much: still family-style, still socking enough away each summer to shut down after Labor Day. When old Pike died, his kids made a go at year-round, but the hunters and the truckers proved more trouble than they were worth. As he pulled into the gravel lot, Charlie saw the awnings had been removed and the windows shuttered.

It was done in a minute. He unplugged the machine, taped the coin slot, and loaded the bottles onto the truck. Mindful of the significance, Charlie took in the breeze and the rustle of leaves. Not likely he'd be up this way again soon. So intent was he on marking the occasion, he didn't see the cat slink around the corner, poke his nose along the open Coke machine door, and slip inside. Had anyone been watching, they might have called over, maybe shared in a laugh at a cat's lack of sense. But no one was watching, no one called, and Charlie shut the door with a resounding thunk.

"Well," he said out loud, feeling slightly foolish. "I guess that about does it."

He stepped up into the cab and sat filling out the inventory report. Drysdale won that long-ago game he suddenly recalled. He'd listened to the last out right here in this parking lot, joking with the Pikes and sneaking a beer in celebration. Hadn't given it a thought since the day it happened. How many guys put in forty years humping a delivery truck? Not too many, he suspected.

Paperwork finished, Charlie lit the cigar he'd saved for the occasion and took a long last look around. It was still pretty country up here but too far for commuters and not far enough for a weekend toot.

"Luck of the draw," Charlie whispered to himself then circled the lot and took off down the road. Two kids trailed after him on bikes. A stone truck thundered past. A pair of crows swooped and squabbled.

—□—

Inside the Coke machine, the young cat crouched in the delivery chute. The door had stunned him and the mouse he'd been chasing was lost to the darkness. If he were human, he would have seen the hopelessness of his situation. With no way out, panic would have seized him. But he was a cat, and his thoughts were of the darkness, total and absolute. In the time it would take him to die or be rescued, his eyes would be of little use. His senses reduced to sound and the smell of molded plastic, gear oil, the stone trucks, and the mice. The cat stood up, circled once, and sat staring. The darkness gave him nothing. He washed one arm and the back of an ear then circled back and settled on his haunches. The wind signaled the change in seasons. His mind went blank, and he fell asleep.

The smell of water woke him, and he sniffed out a puddle in the lip of the frame. He lapped away then stretched as best he could. Turning around, he tried to force his head past the delivery flap, but the slot was too narrow. He reached a front leg between the chute and the door, but it wouldn't fit. He lapped at the water. He tried to reach his leg through once more, but nothing had changed so he slept again.

Through the night, he alternately stretched, turned, fit his leg through the gap, and slept. He missed the nightly dollop of cat food and the table scraps the woman gave him, and the crumbs of TV snacks and puddles of ice cream at the bottom of the bowl. His was an easy life. He wanted for nothing and nothing was asked of him. Had he killed the mouse he wouldn't have bothered to eat him.

He'd eat him now.

—▫—

The cat's home was through the woods behind the Chicken Shack. He didn't come to Pike's for the garbage. He was a hunter not a scavenger, though he made an exception on Crab Cake nights. He came for the mice, stalking, pouncing. The first time he saw one, something clicked, his raison d'être right there gnawing a French fry.

Mice were so easy he sometimes signaled his presence to give them a head start. He liked when they hid beneath the Coke machine, the waiting game they couldn't win. Too frightened to freeze they'd make a mad dash. That's when he'd get them. Always he would get them ... except this once.

The next day his stomach churned, and he howled in frustration. The mouse he'd followed in had managed to escape;

Leon could tell from the absence of smell. Most of the time it was quiet—if you can call birds in the morning, locust and stone trucks all day long, and tree frogs and crickets into the wee hours, quiet. He knew the cycle instinctively, but only the birds held any interest. He'd caught his share, but their wings were an advantage. If it was a young bird he was after, the others would gang up, and more than once he'd taken a hit. The blue jays were the worst with their screeching and dive-bombing. All things considered, he preferred mice.

—▯—

"Leee – on! Here kitty-kitty. Here Leee – on!"

The cat yowled once then mewed pitifully. She'd named him Leon after a character in one of her children's books. The little girl loved Leon with all her heart. He loved her too, but what he missed most was the man of the house, football double headers, pizza, and lunchmeat. The man would rub Leon's stomach obsessively, pausing only to hoot and holler. It wasn't affection, more like ritual and nerves, the closer the game the more the man rubbed. His motivation didn't matter to Leon. Hoots and hollers were a small price to pay.

"Leee-on! Here boy!"

The calls came no closer. He whined a few times, but no one could hear. Soon the woman shouted something, and the calls stopped. Leon turned, stretched, and settled back down. Just before dusk, a sliver of sunlight seeped through a crack in the door seal. He rose to give it a sniff. In less than a minute the light was gone.

When Leon had to pee, he backed down the chute to give it some distance. For three days he resisted moving his bowels, but he'd always been regular, and on the fourth day he relented. It was humiliating. With no litter or grass to cover his business, he did the only thing he could. He reared up, braced himself, and kicked it past the delivery flap.

Leon stopped grooming to conserve moisture. He spent his

time sleeping, though positions were limited. Once he dreamt the little girl was feeding him ice cream. His tongue rounded the bottom of the spoon then shoveled it off the concave center — vanilla, his favorite. When he woke and realized he'd been fooled, he whined the night away.

At least he thought it was night. With no light except the brief sliver, he was fast losing track. He only knew it was high time to eat and drink. That was what he thought about when he wasn't sleeping. Not the pain of hunger but the act of eating; not thirst, but the sound of the faucet running. The little girl turned it on for him every night while she brushed her teeth. She was very thorough about brushing, which gave Leon time to drink his fill.

—□—

The mice knew something was up. They hadn't seen the cat in days, yet he was still here, the smell and sound of him. Mice may be skittish, but they have to eat, and before long a few ventured forth. Leon howled his presence, but when he didn't appear the mice grew bolder. The old dumpster had been a mouse haven for generations, serving up a smorgasbord of scraps. Now and then a cat would raid, but never for long and never like this one. This one never missed. They didn't know what he was doing in the box, but they soon figured out he couldn't touch them. In a matter of days, the dumpster was teeming.

—□—

What sounded like heavy fingers tapping turned out to be rain. At first, he thought the mice had gotten in, but the thunder rumbled, and he knew what it was. All the same to Leon, something new to listen to, so he listened to it. Before long the lip of the frame filled with water, and he drank to his heart's content. To the extent a cat can ruminate, the rain made things interesting. The mice were still out there. A little rain wouldn't put them off. When the wind kicked up, he could hear the leaves rattle and the old pines groan in the distance. Farther still a fawn bleated, and beyond that he heard the creek. After a while, the mice gave it up, the fawn fell silent, the wind died down, and he was left with the rain.

Since mice have to eat, they'll search out anything to find food, even a tiny crack in the Coke machine's frame. Leon could smell the foolish little mouse and the mouse could smell Leon. Getting in wasn't hard, but getting out in the dark, in a panic proved too much for him. Trapped and terrified, the mouse simply died of fright and after a struggle to reach him, Leon ate the poor thing, bones and all. A week later it happened again. Among mice word spread of the missing, and thereafter they stayed away.

Every so often someone stopped for a Coke. Leon tried to cry out but his croak would not project and the tape over the coin slot quickly sent them on their way.

—¤—

Shortly after Halloween, the weather turned cold. By then Leon's muscles were withered, and when he turned, which was seldom, he was frail and unsteady. His fur was greasy and his breath sour. He slept entire days away and didn't move his bowels for weeks at a time. Hunger no longer hounded him, only the cold. Positions were limited to a tight curl on his left or right side with his paws tucked and head curled under. Awake, his mind clouded with misery.

The cold held on into November, and a week before Thanksgiving it snowed a foot. Snowplows used the lot for dispatch. Motors rumbled, men milled about in the brittle morning light. Leon heard none of it. By now his life signs were dim and his breathing intermittent. But Leon wasn't dead. He'd lost all contact with the living world, but he was still a part of it.

—▭—

Life in North Shore blundered on. Two days after Leon's senses shut down, Audrey Lane spotted her neighbor at the roadside mailbox on her way home from the supermarket. She pulled her car to the shoulder to share a bit of gossip but misjudged the distance and ran her right over. The rumor spread that Audrey had a drinking problem, and in her remorse the rumor came true.

A week later, a flatbed trailer backed into a job site and made off with the county's new grader. Police rounded up the usual suspects, but the culprit came from out of state and the grader was never recovered. The rumor that the chief of police was involved eventually cost him his bid for reelection.

Over at the North Shore High, a new boy pulled a knife on the school bully and threatened to "cut his balls off." The new boy was sent to the juvenile center but returned in a month to a hero's welcome. The bully's father sued, but a dozen kids testified to their torment and the case was dismissed.

Just a stone's throw away from the Chicken Shack, a little girl awoke on her birthday to find a kitten wrestling with one of her slippers. She was a sentimental girl, and in memory of her first pet she named the kitten Leon.

—▭—

The rains returned soon after Christmas. For weeks the skies ran steely gray. Temperature hovered just above freezing, and the storms turned the North Shore lawns to lagoons. Basements flooded, roofs leaked, and housebound children drove their folks crazy. No one could remember a winter so wet. Inside the Coke machine water pooled on the coin box housing. More than enough to quench any cat's thirst, but Leon was lost in a dreamless void. In his suspended state, Leon registered nothing. But the spark of life still flickered, and now and then an ear would twitch or a muscle quiver. As the weeks turned to months his fur grew thicker and his claws curled over his toes. Any colder and he would have frozen, but the winter wore on as the warmest on record.

—□—

Most people would think it impossible. Nothing living could survive such a thing. But the cat is a confounding creature, and the myth of nine lives has some basis in fact. In free fall, a cat's limbs will billow. They've been known to fall ten stories and walk away. A cat would never think to chase a car or run into a burning building. Unless it's old, sick, or badly injured, a cat doesn't know how to die.

So Leon held on by a thread. Christmas came and went, and the old year passed into the new. By mid-January, the girls' basketball team was the hot topic, and further north ski lift operators cursed the snowless skies. Across the woods, the little girl tired of her kitten's bad behavior and banished him to sleep in the garage. She often pined for *her* Leon, but only the mice knew what had become of him.

Then one night, for reasons undetermined, the Chicken Shack gas line sprang a leak. And lacking Pike Senior's attention to detail, Junior had left a pilot light on. The blast lit up the North Shore sky and blew the Coke machine across the parking lot. The place was an inferno when the fire trucks got, there so they shut down the road and let it burn. In the smoking haze of daybreak, a pair of firemen sat on the toppled Coke machine. The younger one thought he heard a sound from inside. They listened for a moment then took a crowbar to it. Leon curled away from the light.

"Well I'll be damned," the older man shook his head in wonder. "How do you suppose he got in there?"

"Probably kids," the young one ran a hand over Leon's ribs. "Hardly nothing left of him."

"This place has been closed up for months," said another. "You don't think he's been in there all that time, do you?"

"I wouldn't put nothing passed a cat," the older man cackled. "My sister had one disappeared for over a year. One night she heard something at the back door and when she opened it there he was. Sumbitch had one eye missing and an ear chewed off, but other than that, he was good as new."

"Worthless goddamn animals," a fourth spit in disgust. "We ought to just toss him in the coals."

The older man rose to his feet. "You lay a hand on that cat and I'll toss *you* in the goddamn coals."

The young fireman lifted Leon out. His spine was bent, and his legs were drawn up, but his ears still swiveled, and they took this as a sign.

"It's okay, pal. We'll take care of you. You rest, and we'll have you back on your feet in no time."

And so they did. Someone brought a cat bed to the station. They covered Leon with blankets and watched over him like parents. At first, he could only swallow broth, but as his strength returned so did his appetite. Local cat lovers offered help, and kids ran a fund drive to cover expenses. The vet pronounced Leon blind and malnourished, but his organs still functioned, and his remaining senses were miraculously intact.

After a heated debate, the men named him "Sparky." North Shore's mayor alerted the press, and reporters covered the story. Overnight "Sparky" was front-page news. Donations poured in along with offers of adoption, but the firemen claimed the cat as their own, and, in a ceremony broadcast on the evening news, Sparky was named their official mascot.

Shortly after, the station house got another visitor. Flushed and breathless, the little girl pushed her way through and, at the sight of her Leon, she fell to pieces. The men were so touched, and the girl was so sweet, the whole town beamed at the happy ending.

Turned out it was just the beginning. Within days, the pair were featured on *Good Morning North Shore* and named grand marshals of the Memorial Day parade. Then the Internet got wind of it, and by mid-summer the world knew Leon's story.

Bloggers dubbed him the Coca-Cola Cat and his face graced the cover of *People Magazine*. The soft drink giant did their bit with a new fire truck and a scholarship fund for the little girl. In a summer of global tension and economic stress, a lost cat story was made to order.

—▢—

But feel-good stories have a short shelf life. By summer's end the buzz played out and the cat resumed life as a normal, if sightless, household pet—which was fine with Leon. He didn't mind being blind and had all but forgotten his four-month ordeal. Aside from a family ban on rearranging the furniture, his affliction had no lasting effects. To keep him from wandering off, the girl's dad fitted a tracking device to his collar. But the gizmo proved defective, and Leon soon managed to slip away. His recall of his former life was spotty, but one thing he could never forget. He used traffic sounds to gauge distance and kept to the shadows, so the birds wouldn't see. He cleared the trees at a jog and crossed the clearing to the parking lot. The site smelled of smoke, and lumber and paint from the Cola Cat Shack, (Junior's bid to cash in). Leon stopped to think things through. Without seeing, he knew that the dumpster was gone. He drew closer and sniffed along the network of nests and furrows, but there was no trace of mice. At the Shack, he checked the foundation, sorting through odors, none of them rodent. Then the smell of plastic struck a chord, and he bolted to the high ground. With the sun on his back and his face to the wind, Leon crouched and listened.

Before long, a truck pulled in carrying Pike Junior with a ladder and a Grand Opening sign. Had he been human and not blind, Leon might have laughed at his Cola Cat likeness. But cats have a rarefied sense of humor, and things like that don't strike them as funny.

Junior paced the length of the building, taking in his new sign from every angle. Then he sat in the car and looked at it some more. Leon closed his eyes and drifted in a doze, waking at the sound of Junior leaving. Seconds later a cloud settled over, exhaust, a bit of rot—

Leon's eyes snapped open and his ears swiveled right. By scanning scents, he tracked the location, zeroed in, and began to purr. The mouse would panic, nothing else left for it, just a matter of when and which way. Leon closed in slow and slower still, a pause for the pounce, then head first into Junior's new handicapped parking sign. More staggered than hurt, he circled off and faced the darkness, fixing their positions. The mouse was still there. Leon knew it, and the mouse knew he knew it. Down to this, the silence of time, deadly deep in the absence of man. The sun slipped behind a cloud. The mouse made his break. Leon stood, stretched, and turned for home.

Who knows why the mouse was spared? The signpost may have stung more than Leon's nose, or maybe the Coke machine finally spooked him. More likely it was age and who needs this, anyway? Some might say it was compassion, but they'd be wrong. Cats know nothing of compassion.

Tom Larsen

Tom Larsen was a journeyman printer for twenty-five years before scrapping it all for the writer's life. His work has appeared in *Newsday*, *New Millennium Writing*, *Philadelphia Stories Magazine*, *Best American Mystery Stories*, and the *LA Review*.

Tom and his wife, Andree, spent ten years in the Pennsport section of South Philadelphia, home to Mummers, Flyers, and that screw you slant that made the city great. The experience proved invaluable in crafting characters: "For a writer, Pennsport is a casting gold mine. No pretense, no rhetoric, just real people saying what they mean."

His novels *Flawed* and *Into the Fire* are available through Amazon.

THIRD EYE LIVING

"Your first life is for learning," my dam used to say as she nuzzled me and my littermates. "Learn to jump and run and hunt. Learn to be still and listen for your prey. Learn what it means to be a cat.

"Your second life, that is for feeling. Feel the wind in your fur, the sun on your back, the water between your toes. Feel what it means to be a cat. Feel the call of our people's song in the moonlight. Feel your body stretch and grow. And when you have grown and learned and felt, the rest of your lives are for living." Wise words from a wise dam.

I'd barely started living when my third eye opened. It isn't a physical eye, and not all cats have one. Some choose to close it as soon as it opens, too afraid of the larger view. A cat's third eye allows it to see far beyond the ordinary into the world of magic that intersects our own.

My man-human, David, stood over me, lecturing. I understood human speech, but he tended to be long-winded, and I tuned him out. Though I remained sitting upright in front of him, staring at his face, eyes wide, because it made him uncomfortable and it amused me.

I caught a shimmering form above his left shoulder as my third eye slowly opened for the first time. I flicked my ears and focused on this new thing. A fairy hovered next to David's head. It held a needle-sharp spear pointed straight at his ear and was grinning wickedly back at me.

I'd heard stories of fairies from my dam. Enemies of my people, the little flying demons existed only to wreak havoc on unsuspecting victims. If I let them roam my house and torment my humans, I'd end up a twitching, neurotic mess. I was young and powerful, and quite comfortable in my human home.

My tail twitched once. Twice. I gathered myself.

Then jumped.

David squealed when my claws bit into his shoulder. My jaws snapped shut on the fairy and I heard the crunch of his bones snapping. The taste of honey flooded my mouth. I swallowed the creature. Its magic landed in my belly like a warm fire.

As I pushed off David to the top of the china cabinet, he screeched and ducked, clutching at his shoulder. My claws are sharp, but I never meant to shred his flesh, only to catch the fairy before its poison spear infected him.

"Jeanne, your stupid cat's gone crazy," David shouted as I slid down the front of the cabinet, claws scraping against the glass. I twisted halfway and hit the floor feet-first. I'd learned my first life lesson well. As soon as paw touched floor, I ran. David grabbed for me, but it was child's play to evade him.

Jeanne caught me in the doorway. She'd always been kind. I didn't expect her tight grip or the humiliating way she dangled me from my scruff. "Mr. Fluffers, that was bad. *Bad kitty.* Did he scratch it?" She asked her mate as she carried me to the door.

"I'm bleeding, and you're worried about the cabinet?"

"Don't be a baby, David." She dumped me outside then slammed the door in my face.

I licked my fur to soothe the sudden itching of my skin. Outside was cold and damp. I preferred inside. I hunched down in the sphinx position on the back step. Lights flickered in the bushes across the yard, and I turned to study them.

I twitched my ears in irritation. The lights faded and then flickered again. Were they lightning bugs or was this my third eye seeing magic? The taste of fairy lingered in my mouth.

My nose told me there was more rain to come. The earlier downpour still puddled in spots. I picked my way across the lawn.

"He's coming."

My ears flicked at the whispery voices, like the rustle of wind over dry grass.

"Hide."

"Do you think he sees us?"

"Don't be daft. Of course, he sees us. He's a cat!"

I crouched into a hunting pose and crept closer to the bushes. My stomach rumbled at the thought of more honeyed fairies.

"He's getting closer. The Queen won't like this."

"*Hush.* And be ready."

I hesitated, one paw raised. Ready? For what? I lowered the paw. With a low growl I flexed my claws, preparing for battle. My dam had taught me about fairies. Her ears flattened, she'd hissed and warned us to watch for them. "Fairies bring nothing but trouble. They are the enemy." Her words slithered through my mind as I stalked closer.

How dare fairies invade my *home and threaten* my *people. I'll eat them all.*

I pounced at the rose bush, claws out.

And landed in a muddy puddle. Mocking laughter rang through the bushes as fairies flitted over me, wings trailing strands of magical light. I twisted for the attack. Something bit my hind leg, and I turned to defend my flank. A spear, smaller than a toothpick, dangled from my haunch. It tasted bitter when I pulled it free. Another tiny spear gouged my front shoulder. I yowled and swung a paw at the attackers, claws splayed. The first fairy darted away, and the second one yanked my tail. I spun around, but they were too quick. The second fairy, smaller than the first, held an armful of my ginger fur. The larger one smacked my ear, and they both flew upwards. I hissed and leapt after them.

And tangled myself in the rose bush. Thorns scraped tender skin. I bled from multiple gashes, some caused by fairy spears, but most from the roses. Panicked, I thrashed in the bush until I dropped free. Tufts of my fur clung to thorns like strange hairy rosebuds. With my tail tucked down, I ran for the safety of the back step. My head drooped in defeat.

I huddled next to the door, meowing. Maybe Jeanne or

David would hear me and let me inside where it was safe. Well, not safe anymore. The fairies knew how to enter. Somehow, I had to outsmart them. I meowed again.

When they finally let me in I hid under the sofa licking my wounds and considered a new strategy.

—□—

I awoke several times during the night. My third eye had opened my vision to new sounds as well. I twitched at each whisper and tiny wingbeat. They flitted through the dark house trailing mischief along with their magic light. I muffled a hiss when they came too close to my hiding spot.

When morning finally dawned, I was exhausted, but the fairies had flittered away. I dragged myself from under the sofa to curl up by the window where the early sun would warm me. Except, there was no sun. Rain dripped from a cold, gray sky.

I limped my way up the stairs to the sleeping cave of the humans and slipped warily through the door. David was up. I heard him in the water room and shuddered. Why humans chose to be in the rain was difficult for me to comprehend — even if the rain was warm. A good licking worked best for cleaning one's fur.

If he was up, Jeanne might allow me to curl beside her in the bed. I jumped lightly onto the soft fluffiness. David's side was still warm. Nestled in bed with my head resting on my paws, I felt safe. My eyes drooped. Jeanne murmured something drowsy as she rolled away from me, and I relaxed into sleep.

And woke abruptly as David grabbed me out of the bed.

"What is that dirty cat doing in my bed?" he shouted.

"He isn't dirty."

"Just look at him, Jeanne. He's covered in mud. What on Earth was he doing last night?"

"Fighting fairies to protect you," I answered. But he was only human and didn't understand cat. I twisted in his grip.

He tightened his hands. "You need a bath, mister."

That brought out the claws. But my heart wasn't in it. I still hurt from the rose bush and the fairy spears.

He carried me into the water room, shut the door, and dropped me on the floor while he ran a bath. Huddled in the farthest corner, I meowed pitifully for Jeanne to rescue me. When the door opened I dove for it, but she slipped inside and shut it before I could escape.

"Poor Mr. Fluffers. Were you fighting last night?" She caught me and gently carried me across the room and plunked me into the water.

I yowled at her betrayal, but she held me down while David poured more water on me. They laughed together as they talked over my pitiful cries for mercy. There was water in my fur. It dripped over my ears and into my eyes. I hated it.

Finally, they lifted me out and wrapped me in a towel. I suffered it, because it was warm, and Jeanne was gentle as she rubbed water from my fur.

"I saw a mouse in the kitchen again last night," she said as she fluffed my tail. "Did you set the traps?"

"Yeah, but they don't seem to be helping. There are mice everywhere this year." David rubbed at the mirror with a towel. He stroked his face to remove his whiskers. Stupid, if you ask me. Whiskers tell you much about the world if you know how to listen. He obviously hadn't learned the lessons of his first life yet. "It's time for Mr. Fluffers to start working for his kibble."

"Poor kitty. Did you fight mice last night?" Jeanne's hands stroked my fur much gentler than David's ever had. *She must be well into her second life. Do humans reach third lives and beyond?* I wondered.

"Mice beat him up good." David laughed.

"You humans are too stupid to reach a second life," I hissed at David. I would find a way to defeat the fairies and defend my humans. But only because I liked Jeanne. If it was just David, he could suffer fairy malice and I wouldn't lift a paw to save him.

—▢—

I sat in the windowsill licking the last of my fur into place. The rains tapered off around noon, and the late afternoon sun was a puddle of golden warmth. Across the street, the little black tuxedo cat watched me from her front porch. She yawned and stretched. I stopped mid-lick, my hind leg raised high in the air. She was older and experienced. Her home was clear of fairies. Perhaps she would help me.

I licked the inside of my thigh. She wasn't the friendliest of cats, and I must be polite. But first, I had to escape the house. With both my humans away for the day as usual, I was alone at least until the sunset. That's when the fairies would emerge to torment me and make mischief.

Unless I stopped them.

I prowled the house, testing doors and windows in each room. Somewhere one must be open. The downstairs rooms were shut tight. I headed up stairs to the sleeping cave. No luck there. I hissed at the door to the water room as I passed.

The last room was up more stairs. A spare room, it was full of unused things, boxes, and an old sofa where I cleaned my claws. This angered my humans. But the fabric was perfect for removing broken bits of claw and sharpening the rest. And the fluffy filling from its shredded arms was fun to chase.

The door looked closed but when I jumped against it, it creaked open a crack and I nosed my way inside. I sneezed and swatted at the dust floating in the air then stopped to hone my claws on the sofa. The small window on the back wall above the sofa pushed outward with a nudge of my paw, and I squeezed through. From there, it was kitten's play to jump down to the roof of the garage, then to the garbage bin and the street. I'd done it many times.

The tuxedo cat lounged on the porch railing of her house. I quickly scampered across the road, dodging the great beasts of cars that rushed by, and paused under a bush to lick my fur back into place. The tuxedo cat was, after all, an attractive female and as my elder, must be shown respect. Flicking my tail, my head down, I slowly approached the porch, stopping beneath the railing where she lounged with her front claws spread and her tail dangling. I flopped down on the grass, my ears twitched forward to acknowledge her dominance.

"What do you want, youngling?" She blinked emerald-green eyes.

"I need your advice." I swatted idly at a grasshopper that landed too close. "What do you know about fairies?"

"Enough to stay away from them. Nasty creatures." Her tail swished.

"They first appeared yesterday. One tried to stab my human's ear; I ate it. They taste like honey. They were plotting something in the roses." I slapped my paw onto the bug, but it jerked out from under it and hopped away. Its wings buzzed in the still heat of the afternoon.

"Fairies like to swarm this time of year. Best to find a new home."

I froze at her words. Leave my humans? Fend for myself? Yes, cats had done so for thousands of years and I was skilled, but I *liked* my humans. At least I liked the woman who treated me well and fed me tasty food.

"Isn't there a way to fight them?"

She lowered her chin to her white paws. "You *could* ... but fairies can be brutal. It's safer to avoid them. You might get your humans to plant different flowers. I dig up the ones that attract fairies, and my humans finally learned."

I studied the mounds of bright orange marigolds surrounding the porch. "Is that all it takes?" I could pick some to carry back home, but the taste would linger in my mouth for days.

She lashed her tail. "Stupid youngling, that's just one step. I can show you how to work wards to keep them out. But you must chase them away before you perform the spells." She jumped from the porch railing to the grass beside me. "Well? Are you coming?" Her tail was low and swished side to side with impatience, and a touch of irritation.

I hurried after her into the bushes at the side of the driveway where she showed me claw marks on their stems. I sniffed and tried to make my own marks. She cuffed me at each attempt until I got it right. We spent an hour working our way around her yard as she showed me the proper marks for each type of flower. I caught not even a flicker of wings. Her magic was strong.

We stopped at the edge of her lawn by the garbage cans. The smell was enticing, but I refrained. I had no desire for another bath.

"Be careful, youngling," she said with a final tail twitch. "Fairy magic has defeated cats much older and wiser than you." She turned and leapt to a garbage can, then onto the garage roof, and disappeared behind the roofline.

I walked slowly back to the road, pausing to study my home. From there, I could hear the buzz and flicker of fairy wings around every window and door. I lapped a drink from a puddle in the gutter. If I was going to mark all the wards, I needed a lot of urine.

I scurried across the street to my front lawn where the fairies were waiting to swarm me. One jabbed me with its spear. I yowled and twisted to swat it with a clawed paw. It flittered out of reach, its mocking laugh tinkling behind it. I hissed and crouched, muscles bunched to spring.

A bird whistled, high and shrill, and the fairies darted back into the bushes. I dove under the front porch as a shadow of wings swept over the lawn. Magpies on a hunt. Good to know the fairies feared them. But I also knew, if the birds grew bored enough, they'd have no problem taking on a full-grown tom like me.

A magpie landed on the grass, strutting and preening its black and white plumage. It gave me a shrewd look with one beady, black eye, then swept its wings wide. With a screech, it launched into the air.

My skin crawled, and I licked my fur to calm it. Had that been a warning or an offer of help? I knew little about the outside since my owners kept me in the house most of the time. To be fair, I preferred the comfort and pampering that came with being a house cat. Now I wondered how I could keep them safe if I had no idea who the players were in this dangerous game.

By the time my fur calmed, the sun was setting, and the fairies began to emerge once more. If fairies were nocturnal, were there night hunters I could beg for assistance? What night hunters ate fairies? Questions I should have asked the tuxedo cat.

I silently thanked her for what teaching I had received as I scurried through the bushes, setting wards and marking my territory. The fairies trailed behind me. After each spell I cast it seemed they strained harder to fly, as if their wings were coated in syrup that grew thicker with every mark I placed.

The last ward sealed the yard. I turned, expecting the fairies to be gone. But they stood in the center of the lawn, glaring at me. Their gossamer wings drooped down their skinny backs.

"You think you won, pussy cat?" The leader spoke in a voice like a mouse, high and squeaky. "The fight has just begun!"

A dozen fairies poked their spears into the air and shouted war cries.

My hackles rose; I hissed and showed my fangs. What had the tuxedo cat said? *You must chase them away first.* Stupid me. Trapped inside my own wards with a dozen angry fairies, I flexed my claws and hissed again. The streetlamp cast a macabre light across the scene.

Their leader darted forward but tripped and fell in the tall grass. I guessed he wasn't used to running on the ground. His wings drooped, unable to lift him. My tail lashed as I smacked him with a paw and pinned him to the ground. He squeaked, and the other fairies rushed to his aid. I swiped my free paw and sent them tumbling. Fairies weren't so scary when they couldn't fly. All it had taken was spreading one ward spell around the yard. Why had I made such a fuss? This was easy. I flexed my claws into the back of the leader. Only he wasn't under my paw anymore.

A sudden pain in my backside made me jump. I whirled around to face the new threat. Five fairies crouched with their spears aimed at my eyes. I swatted at them. They shifted beyond my reach. At another surge of pain along my tail up to my rump, I whirled again. A second group stood behind me poised for attack.

I leapt at them, growling. Tiny spears stabbed at my front legs. My tail lashed, knocking one fairy away. A lucky swipe downed another. It fell screaming under my claws. The rest scattered as I snapped the trapped one's neck.

Numbness crept up my hind legs from where they'd jabbed me. I stumbled to my feet, picking the dead fairy up in my mouth, and trundled across the lawn and up the steps to the front door. My legs were wood. They wobbled like David when he'd drunk too much. I placed the fairy on the welcome mat then crept into the darkest corner of the porch to lick my wounds. The fairies stood their ground in the middle of the lawn.

Glowing eyes like lamps swept over the porch as a beast rumbled into the driveway. It rolled to a stop; the growling died abruptly. The fairies scattered to the mounds of zinnias and alyssum in the flowerbeds along the porch. Doors slammed on the car and my humans emerged. They chattered as they approached, oblivious to the fairy menace hiding in their flowers. My wards didn't slow them, but wards are meant to keep fairies away, not humans.

I tucked my nose under my tail. When they saw the slain carcass of my enemy on the doormat, they would understand the danger. They'd help me fight the fairies. I squeezed my eyes shut in satisfaction. Though young, I'd been valiant in battle. I'd protected them and alerted them to the menace.

David emitted a high shriek when he caught sight of the dead fairy.

"What is it?"

"That stupid cat left a dead mouse right in front of the door."

The woman bent and picked up the fairy by its tail. She

dangled it and frowned.

Now they will understand and praise me for saving them. Jeanne will clearly see it is a fairy, not a mouse. If it had been a mouse I'd have eaten it.

"What's Mr. Fluffers doing outside? I thought we left him in. Did you leave a window open?" She turned to look at the yard then back at the body dangling from her pinched fingers. With a shudder she flung the corpse into the bushes. "Here kitty, kitty. Mr. Fluffers?"

"Maybe I left a window open. Stupid cat." He unlocked the door.

The woman followed him inside. "At least he's doing his job catching the mice before they get into the kitchen." The door shut behind her, muffling their bickering.

I stared for a long moment. *Mice? Really? She couldn't see the wings and the evil smirk on the dead fairy's face? And she just shut me out.* I stumbled to the door. My legs had stiffened more. I thumped on the door with a paw and meowed.

The fairies gathered in the dusky yard, eyes glinting as they caught the streetlamp's gleam.

I turned to face them and hissed. The fur on my back bushed up.

They flitted closer, their wings shimmering. As they advanced, they mumbled threats. But their wings, still weighted from my spell, rendered them unable to fly. They raised their spears and aimed them at my chest. The lead fairy grinned, displaying his pointed fangs. The spell erupted from their spear points in a cloud of purple glitter. It shot at me, roiling and rolling up the porch steps. I yowled and hopped backwards with my spine arched and my tail high. Tuxedo cat hadn't warned me fairies could cast spells as well. When the spell hit, it engulfed me with the cloying scent of petunias in full bloom. I sneezed. I'd overestimated my ability to deal with them.

The fairies laughed and continued to advance, one tiny step at a time through the grass.

I meowed as loud as I could, imbuing my pleas with the

feelings of a scared kitten. I was barely grown. I edged back until I pressed against the door. Their spell washed over me, draining my strength. I felt my own wards fading under the assault. The fairies' wings buzzed. The leader managed a nimble hop over a dandelion.

Without warning, the tuxedo cat slammed into the gang of fairies. She took out three with one mighty swipe of a paw and snapped another between her jaws. But she didn't eat it. She spit it into the grass like a hairball. The other fairies scattered into the flowers.

The tuxedo cat pinned me down with a ferocious glare. Her tail lashed. "Stupid kitten," she snarled. "Go repair your wards. And next time, do *not* eat them. The magic builds inside and weakens you."

I hung my head, my ears flat against my skull, and limped from the porch.

"Hurry," she urged with a sharp cuff to my ear.

I stumbled in pain to the first set of claw marks I'd made earlier. I raked my claws on the stem of the lilac that hung over one corner of the fence. My ward was fraying. I pulled it back together with each pass of my claw, tying it tightly to the bush, and then limped to the next one.

The fairies gathered under the streetlamp like a swarm of moths. Hundreds of fairies, their wings buzzing, hovered and darted, watching and waiting for me to fail. I hunched my shoulders and hissed. This was *my* home, *my* humans. I flicked urine over the rocks at the edge of the lawn, spraying my claim. *Mine.*

"Hurry, youngling!" Tuxedo cat's urgent yowl sent me running despite the stiffness in my legs.

I traced my steps. Claw here, spray there, to reinforce the failing wards around my home. I even dug a hole and buried waste at the back of the yard. Each mark, each bit of me I left behind, claimed this house, this yard, as *mine.*

My legs burned. I was down to the last few dribbles of urine when I rounded the house back to the front porch. Tuxedo cat sat hunched on the first step, her fur bristled. Four fairies had her pinned. She held a damaged paw to her chest where its blood stained the patch of white fur. I smelled her fear and determination.

With what strength remained, I made a flying leap at the fairies, claws spread wide.

"No!" Tuxedo cat lashed forward with her wounded paw. She smacked me hard.

I landed off-balance and rolled into the daisies.

The fairies screamed in anger, their shrill voices grating on my ears. Their spell detonated and sent Tuxedo cat flying across the lawn. She landed in an awkward heap.

Something popped in my back leg. I ignored the burning pain as I dragged myself upright again. I didn't yowl; the battle was beyond posturing. The fairies had attacked me, my humans, and a respected elder cat.

One painful step at a time, I stalked forward dragging a now useless hind leg. I ignored it as best I could. My shoulders wriggled, and my tail lashed.

The fairies backed away. They still wore evil grins, but I saw uncertainty creep across their faces.

I took another step forward.

The fairies drew together, spears wavering in my direction.

I took another step. My claws flexed as they landed, shredding the dandelion.

The fairies shouted defiance, but their voices were weak, afraid.

I growled, letting the low throbbing sound roll from me.

The fairies shivered.

I lashed my tail, once, twice.

Then pounced.

They flung a new spell at me. Time slowed as I floated through the air toward my enemies. I felt my way through their magic, shifting, using my third eye to avoid the sharp, stinging pricks of the spell. I felt what it was to be a cat. To mark one's claim, and to cast guardian wards. I knew who and what I was.

I was a full-fledged cat. I'd learned my lessons.

The first fairy's spine cracked. The second lay gutted and bleeding from my claws. The third splattered on the side of the porch. The last one whimpered as I crouched over its trembling form. One wing hung broken down its back, and the other twitched in a feeble attempt to fly away.

"Tell the others," I whispered, "tell them that this is *my* house. I will not tolerate your kind here. Go!"

I swatted the fairy with my paw. It sailed toward the glittering fairies swarming just outside my wards. But when it flew past the spell it dropped, screaming, and burst into flames, like a moth too close to a candle. I watched the purple sparks trail it to the sidewalk. When it hit, it bounced once, then lay still.

I posed like a lion, chest out, chin held high, and let loose a howl of triumph. The song of my people rang into the night.

Tuxedo cat sat hunched on the lawn. She nodded her head and flicked her tail in approval. "Don't get cocky."

I twitched an ear in acknowledgement.

The door opened behind me and golden light spilled onto the lawn.

Tuxedo cat hissed. She scurried across the road to her own porch.

"Mr. Fluffers?" Jeanne stood outlined in the light.

Mine, I howled to the fairies. The magic of the wards flowed through me, circling my home with a net of safety. My third eye perceived it as lines of light weaving through the bushes and flowers and over the house.

David joined Jeanne on the porch. "Love is in the air, apparently. We should have had him fixed last month."

Jeanne came out and scooped me up. "Has Fluffy-bumpkin been fighting that nasty neighbor cat?" She used her high squeaky voice that usually annoyed me.

I wriggled in her grip.

She snuggled me against her. "He's been fighting. Maybe it is time."

"He's bleeding. And he needs another bath."

I yowled and struggled. No more baths. I could clean my own wounds. But she held me tight, and I stopped fighting her. I hurt, and I was tired, and her warmth felt good. I settled against her and let the purring rumble forth.

The door closed behind us, shutting out the fairies. They were safely beyond my wards.

I let my third eye slide closed. Just for now. I'd have to stay vigilant and keep the wards strong. But for tonight, I would relax in the loving care of my humans.

And, though I would never admit it, the warm bath felt good.

ABOUT THE AUTHOR

Jaleta Clegg

Jaleta Clegg lives in Pasco, Washington. In addition to writing, her interests include such diverse activities as costuming, quilting, cooking, video games, and reading She's been a fan of classic sci-fi books and campy movies since time remembered. Her collection of bad sci-fi movies is only rivaled by her collection of eclectic CD's (break out the disco accordion polka folk music!). Jaleta wants to be either Han Solo or Ursula the Sea Witch when she grows up—if she ever does.

She loves teaching kids of all ages about stars, constellations, nuclear fusion, space travel, mythology, writing, and rocks. Jaleta volunteers with the Boy Scouts of America among other groups, and at one time, served on her local library board. She believes in teaching people to think for themselves and to be self-sufficient, which, for her, are self-serving undertakings since kids who know how to do housework, laundry, and cooking leave her more time for writing.

The *Fall of the Altairan Empire* space opera series starts with *Nexus Point*. All eleven books are available in e-book and print through Amazon and Smashwords.

Website: http://www.jaletac.com
Books & Blog: http://www.altairanempire.com
Facebook: @Jaleta
Twitter: @Jaleta_Clegg
On Amazon and Goodreads, search: Jaleta Clegg

CAT'S SCHRÖDINGER

Safe and warm within cardboard walls
a calico Felis curls up and ponders
whether her pet human is alive or dead
when he is unobserved.

More important is the theory
that Schrödinger's can opener
is immortal and can be mastered
without opposable thumbs.

ABOUT GUY ANTHONY DE MARCO

Guy Anthony De Marco is a speculative fiction author; a Graphic Novel Bram Stoker Award® finalist; winner of the HWA Silver Hammer Award; a disabled veteran, a prolific short story and flash fiction crafter; a novelist and poet; an invisible man with superhero powers; a game writer; and a coffee addict. One of these is false.

A writer since 1977, Guy Anthony De Marco is a member of the following organizations: SFWA, ITW, WWA, SFPA, IAMTW, ASCAP, RMFW, MWG, SWG, HWA. He hopes to collect the rest of the letters of the alphabet one day. He is almost done suffering through an MFA program and is on the road to recovery.

Additional information can be found at Wikipedia and GuyAnthonyDeMarco.com.

Facebook: @GuyAnthonyDeMarco
Facebook: @SpeculativeFictionAuthor
Twitter: @GuyADeMarc

THE STRAY

There is a meadow of wildflowers where the moles congregate. I sun myself under the cover of daffodils and observe their burrows for long hours. My eyes drink in the light, and I relish the hunt. I wait for the perfect ambush. It is important that my pounce is timed to the last possible second for a clean kill. Others play with their food, but I do not do this. I do not kill with the desire to cause suffering. I kill because if I do not, I do not eat and can only slink away with an empty belly and wounded pride. That is no way for a tomcat to live his eighth life. I am predatory because it is in my nature to be so. Claws and needle-sharp teeth are the weapons the world gave me. A cat has nothing of his own but those weapons and the fur on his hide. I'm forced to make due. I act from necessity, crunching and constricting my meals into bite-sized pieces.

The mole is coming now. Its blunt snout, with pinkened flesh covered in patchy gray fur and prominent, crooked yellow teeth, opens and closes. A sightless morsel of meat is all I see as I push off my haunches and leap. A swipe of my paw dislodges the mole from his burrow. A snapping deathblow from the second swipe breaks its spine. It contorts, a shattered thing, mouth speckled in blood droplets. I flip it over and open its belly like a paper sack, pushing my white chin into the sugary sweetness of the burrower's blood, and make a snack of its entrails. It twitches and spasms during the mutilation but is dead within seconds. It is long gone as I swallow the red pebble that is its heart.

I lick my paws clean of bits of blood, bone, and tissue. This evening, my hunger is satiated, my stomach full, and the predator can rest.

After, I stand for a long period near the spot of the kill. It is a tradition for me to mark this place and remember it. A hunting place; this is where I killed the mole. This small patch of earth holds meaning now, and I will not forget what was done here.

—□—

While bathing myself, I watch to make sure no others steal the second mole that I killed. That one is for the big cat with the shaved fur that cannot hunt. It is a gift for her. She lives across the meadow in a pink people place. There are others of my kind that live with humans, those that are fat and spoiled and forever stuck in kittenhood. It is hard to relate because I am not like that. I have never been. My relationship with the big shaved cat is built on respect. I see in her something I recognize.

She is a survivor. Like me, she is all alone in an unforgiving world. I am there for her when things get cold and empty, just like she has been there for me in times past. We take comfort in each other. I nuzzle against her frail little legs and do what I can to make her warm, and she scratches me behind the ears, paying close attention to the sweet spot that makes my eyes close and my throat purr. It is rare for me to allow such contact; it puts me in a vulnerable state, but I do not mind with her. She is kin. I am closed against all things, but for her. In our private moments, I open myself and give. For the briefest space, I cease to be aloof and standoffish, and unafraid to show her love. It is genuine. The feel of it throbbing between my ribs is special. It is not the same as when I see a female cat in heat.

This is different. It is like the love a mother has for a child, but I do not know if I am the mother and she is the child or the other way. Perhaps it doesn't matter. I know only that she is important to me. If not for her, I would be lost to my predatory behaviors. There would be no feelings, only the hunt, and the struggle for survival.

She makes things better. Though shaped like the gods that all animals call human, she is not one of them, but a cat, like me. I smell it on her. Her scent is of the dirt, the grass, and the untamed wild. That is all it takes to be feline. She walks with the grace of a cat, moving sinuous and quiet when she meets with me. She holds a skinny finger to her cracked lips and purrs a sound. The sound is "shh."

There is another reason I know she is a cat.

It is because she is kept in a cage.

I've seen the carriers and the cages. I have been in places where many cats are kept in cages, and some go with pink people to new places, and others go to sleep eternal. I have escaped these places. But the big shaved cat seems incapable of escaping her prison. It is much larger. There are great fences, blooms of barbwire, and chimneys that send up smoke that burns the nostrils.

There is only one place where I can visit her. A torn section of fence where the barbwire is bent and pulled back, allowing a small creature entry. The metal scrapes against my back when I slink through, but I do it for her. She is worth it. I like to hear her happy noises, and though her purr is strange and broken, she gives it to me all the same.

She is there now and so I go to her, mole in my mouth. I must cut through the forest, twining between the soaring pines that lord over all and cast deep shadows. To a cat the shadows are welcoming. There are towers along the fence, and men in uniforms live in these towers. They blow cold breath and hold tight to metal death tubes. I have seen the work of the tubes. Their flying knobs of shrapnel tear worse than tooth and claw. I have seen cats cut to ribbons in this way. It is a risk, but we meet between the towers at a place the men cannot see us.

She is waiting where the curve of earth is smooth beneath the ragged hole in the fence. She smiles big, and her smile is missing teeth. She is young; her baby teeth still fall out to make room for her big teeth. I think her fur was yellow once, but she told me the men in uniforms shave it down. She cannot tell me why, only that they want everyone to be the same in the great cage. No one can be different. There are no names in the great cage, only numbers. A number is scrawled on her small arm. It is carved into the furless flesh with black ink, and she said it hurt worse than anything. At times, the men in uniforms bark at her like dogs, and that makes me hate them. A dog is the primordial adversary. It is wrong for a cat to be in thrall to a dog, for all dogs are dullards in the end.

She is skinnier. Each time I come, her body seems to be lessened. It makes me sad and I try hard to hunt often for her, but some days there are no moles or small rabbits and I come with nothing. On those days, it feels like I have failed her.

Her eyes are green and large, and they glitter, and this is another way that I know she must be a cat. They are sunken into deep, dark hollows, and sometimes she stares off into the realm of forever before she sees me, and only then does a small glint of happiness come to her eyes.

"Hi, kitty."

I weave between her legs and drop the mole at her dirty feet. She quickly hides it away in tattered striped pants. Her little paw lowers and scratches me along the sweet spot, and I arch my back to show her how much it is appreciated.

"I missed you. Did you miss me?"

I purr, summoning a thunder from within, and give it all to her. Yes. I missed her.

She kneels, and I see that it pains her to do so. There are purple markings along her ankles, and one of her lower paws is squashed. She stretches her neck and nuzzles her head against mine, and it feels just right. There is heat in her though her environment is always cold. It radiates like the sun during the warm months.

"I have to leave soon," she tells me.

Her meow is strange and melodious, but the intent is clear. She is profoundly sad.

"They say we are going home. They say we can see our families again. I can't wait. I hate it here, Benjamin."

The title she has given me resonates, and my ears twitch at the familiar name. Cats need no names. We are shadows in the courtyard and eyes in the night, and a name seeks only to define the indefinable. For her, I will answer to it. The laws of the big shaved cat are much different, but she is still one of us.

She pauses, listening to the sound of a train whistle in the distance. The rumbling locomotive travels day and night, a great carrier of pink people. On the worst nights it stinks of urine and fear. Many cats have tried to cross those tracks and many cats have paid for it.

The big shaved cat furrows her brow, and quiet fear washes across her face. She is silent for a time, and then she seems to accept that the danger has passed.

I do not understand the purpose of this sprawling camp, but it is a bad place. The trains come, and the scared ones get off and then they are changed. Their fur is taken. Their belongings and baubles are removed. They are put in the striped cloth, each one of them looking the same. It is like pulling a house cat from the only life it knows and making it a stray. Perhaps that is the reason for a bad place like this.

It creates strays of all shapes and sizes, and I know from experience that the life of a stray is jagged and hard. That is how it feels here. The big shaved cat has meowed out the name for it before, and it is called Out-Wish. Out with the wishes because here the wishes die.

"Don't worry. I'll come back for you. I'll take you home and you'll live with me, Mommy, Daddy, and my big sister. You'll get fat and you'll never be cold again."

She presses her face against my side as she hugs me. I feel her blunt cat teeth stretched up in a smile.

I do not know what that will be like. I have never existed beneath the roof of a home. My home has been the field, the forest, and the small dark caves that most know nothing of. But I am getting older now and the fantasy sounds intriguing. A change. Something new. And I would be with her....

"We are leaving tomorrow. Come to the fence and I'll wave goodbye."

I will come. Though she doesn't like me to venture too far through the fence. It is not safe, and she says they will hurt me. I must remain on the outer rim to watch until she comes. Now she thrusts her face close, and her mouth finds the scruff of my neck, and it is a kiss she plants, wet and soft. It is there one moment, gone the next. And just like her kiss, she is gone too, limping off toward the bunkhouses.

—▫—

It is a restless night in the wild. I open and close lazy slit eyes as the hours crawl onward. The moon is high and lunar light touches me, but it's not warm like her. I drink from the creek and I look at myself in the water. A mauled ear, scars across the snout, and eyes that have lost the brightness of kittenhood. Each life I've lived has etched into this feline-flesh a lasting scar, but the big shaved cat does not mind. She accepts me as I am. She does not see an ugly thing to ignore as it slinks underfoot. She sees in me something I have long since stopped seeing in myself.

—▫—

It is morning and the air is crisp. I watch and wait at the tear in the fence, lying low to the ground, cleaning my paws with a rough tongue. The caged workers wander around in a daze, most of them looking hollow in their striped clothing. The men in uniform march about, baying like hounds, and each bark fills me with revulsion for them.

There is a squat building near the center of the camp, and acrid smoke billows from multiple chimneys. It lingers in the air. Something about it is cloying and wrong. Sometimes the cinders rain down on the shoulders of the prisoners, and wetness rolls across their filthy cheeks. I do not like to see fellow strays in these conditions. They are denied the freedom of the meadow, and that is a cruelty.

A line of the caged ones is being marched toward the building where the smoke pours and there in the middle is the big shaved cat. She moves forward on her wounded paw with great effort and sneaks a little wave at me from afar. One of the uniformed men pushes her hard with the butt of his death tube. She stumbles but keeps upright.

He shakes his head and barks before directing the line of strays through the threshold of the building. They are lost to the gloom within.

And so, I'm left to wait and watch.

The smoke pours up to blacken the sky, and for hours upon hours there is nothing. I do not like it. A deep instinct tugs at me—I cannot feel her now. Did the train take her home? Did she fall because of her wounded paw?

I rise and pad across the uneven earth toward the building. She has forbidden me to explore beyond the fence, but cats are mostly ignored, and none bother to notice me.

The building is a labyrinth. I pass signs with words I cannot read and little rooms full of cabinets and metal desks. The hallway snakes deeper, and I pass a horrible room. I do not know why it is horrible, but it is. It smells of almonds. The uniformed men, wearing masks, are wiping the floor with big mops. It feels wrong to linger because being near the door hurts my chest. Cats recognize the sour places of the world. Sometimes cats can hear the screams even after the screams have come and gone.

I keep padding through the labyrinth that is Out-Wish, and after a long trek, I catch her scent. There is a room at the end of the hall; orange firelight invites me inside. I do not want to go in, but I must. A uniformed man is there but his back is turned as he busies himself with something.

I venture in, my body low and quiet to escape the man's notice. He is tall and gaunt and overtop his uniform he wears a black apron. His arm bears the sigil of all the armed men in Out-Wish. He is distracted at the mouth of a large oven, pushing a pronged rod back and forth at something. It is only ash and bone bits, but the aroma of meat still lingers.

I stay away from the oven and the man. They do not interest me. My attention fixes on the mountain of clothes in the corner of the room. Its peak rivals the mountains beyond the meadow, and it is full of striped pajamas, dirty pants, and shirts torn to shreds. I circle the base of the mountain slowly, and then I find her. Not her, but a piece of her.

Her little leather clogs sit near the bottom, and a bright rosebud of blood from her wounded paw marks the sole of one. I sniff daintily and hurt comes to my heart. It is the hurt of knowing, and I do not care if the man hears. I give voice to it. A tortured shriek escapes my fanged maw and pierces through each alcove and crevice of Out-Wish. She is not here. She is gone, and when a cat is gone, its ninth life spent, there is no coming back.

The man turns from his oven. He snarls, and his words turn to mush in his mouth like a slobbery canine. I leap on the mountain of discarded clothes and claw my way to the top, gaining purchase against the wall with my powerful hindquarters. He is swinging his pronged rod at me, intent on inflicting hurt. It is the same kind of hurt that he gave to the big shaved cat. And for her I choose to give back.

I pounce across the distance between us and land on the man's gaping face. Claws unsheathed, I go to work, flaying flesh, puncturing gelatinous eyeballs, and raking sharpened nails against a blubbering mouth. I am an oven all my own for a man as repellent as this one, and I am full of fire reserved solely for him and his kind. This is my last fight, and I go into it proudly for her.

My jaw stretches open and I sink needle canines into those eyes—eyes that have witnessed far too many atrocities—and then I hear the clomping of boots and barking of other men. I am pulled from the man's ruined face and slung to the floor. But his sense of direction is skewed, and he pitches forward. His upper torso falls into the mouth of the oven and his screams reach a crescendo. It is a small justice and I hope that somewhere all the strays he put down can hear it.

Boots are falling upon me now. I feel my soft organs rupturing, and I am so far from myself that when my spine snaps, it is nothing to me but the breaking of a distant twig.

Streams of red leak past fangs that have closed on so many prey animals, and I close them once more, a predator at peace.

There is a meadow in my darkening mind.

She is there, her fur grown out again, and she runs instead of limps. Her arms are held open to an old, embattled tomcat. This place is not Out-Wish, because here, wishes can come true.

We are going home together.

JEREMY MEGARGEE

When Jeremy Megargee was a child, he picked up his first Goosebumps book by R. L. Stine and fell head over heels in love with all things horror. His love affair has grown stronger over the years and now borders on obsession with stories that explore the darkest recesses of the human imagination. Like Thorny Rose, he stalks those stories with the ability to invoke a creepy-crawly feeling deep in the marrow of his bones.

As he grew older, Jeremy discovered the works and inspirations of Stephen King, Edgar Allan Poe, H.P. Lovecraft, Clive Barker, and any author that sent him further down the path of the macabre. During his teen years he adopted the tradition of reading Stephen King's, *The Stand,* each summer to lose himself in the devastation of the superflu and to marvel at the sadistic magnetism of Randall Flagg.

His love of horror fiction and the great authors of the genre inspired him to write—to tell his own tales intending to terrify, to disturb, and to capture the morbid curiosity of a reader just as he was caught so early in life. Jeremy feels he accomplishes something a little magical when he inspires those same feelings in his readers. He believes there's still magic in the world, and it's most powerful when manifested in the form of words scrawled across blank pages. If the magic contained within his works is of the dark variety ... he wouldn't want it any other way.

Jeremy Megargee lives in Martinsburg, West Virginia with his pug, Cerberus. When he's not writing, he enjoys hiking mountain trails, weight training, getting tattooed, being a garden-variety introvert, and of course, reading.

Facebook: @JMHorrorFiction
Instagram: @xbadmoonrising

TIN OPENER

They killed my tin opener. The humans called her Margaret, but what do humans know? She was my tin opener.

More than that, she was a witch, and a good one. A crone for the village, a sharp mind, and a healer. She knew the best way to mend broken bones and how to scratch my ears so that I purred deep and long in her lap. I liked her, and they killed her. A poor choice. I knew she was dead when I saw her and felt her magic dissipate with the blood spilling on the floor. Hearing is the last sense to go; I trilled at her while I paced around the body. My tail swished and flicked. When I was certain, I dug into her purse for silver coins to place on her eyes. Then I curled against her chest as we waited for the reaper. The reaper was nice; I'd seen her before. But Margaret passed too soon.

"What do you want, Jasper?" came the death whisper as shadows converged into a tall form beside the body. Her face was only a skull this time, perhaps because of the short notice. She usually wore skin, at least.

"She was mine and they killed her."

"Indeed, she's dead—her soul waits." A pale hand held itself out for Margaret's ghost to take. She was a lovely ghost, pallid, but strong as her recent death allowed.

"I had another twenty years," the ghost grumbled. Her milky eyes glared at the reaper.

"You did, but they killed you. Complain to your familiar, not me."

"I failed you, tin opener," I mewed, standing high so she could pluck me up.

"You couldn't know; the signs weren't there. Which means it was deliberate. You must let the coven know, Jasper, so they can give me the rites and pursue those that did this."

"Yes, Margaret," I agreed, rubbing myself against her rough

chin and soft, wrinkled cheeks.

"And don't be sulking about it. Angela will see you're placed with someone else soon. You're too smart to be without a witch." She popped me down next to her abandoned body and took the hand of the reaper, folded into the shadows of her cloak, then winked from existence.

"She will go over peacefully. Do you require anything else?" she asked, her eyeless holes staring down at me.

"Yes. Can you open that jar of blood on the desk?" I tilted my head to the heavy work table, scarred, and burned from various potions.

"You don't drink blood," the reaper said, skeletal jaw askew.

"I know, but that's not why I asked. Can you?" She studied me a moment longer and went to the jar, her cloak chilling the swirling air as she passed. She unscrewed the lid and set the jar back on the counter.

"That is what you wanted?"

"Yes, thank you," I said, stretching myself long in supplication to her. Not an act we performed often, but death deserved a level of respect.

"You are a strange creature. You have never asked for such a thing with your other witches."

"My other witches were due to meet you. A cat has many minds." My tail danced, live as a snake. I caught it with a paw and stilled it.

"Make sure one of those minds doesn't get you killed, Jasper. You're not due for some time."

"Naturally, oh cold one." I stared her down. I knew my eyes glowed in what was left of the candle light, and she shook her skull at me. With a wry laugh she was gone, and I was alone in our cottage with the low flames and the body.

Not for long.

I leapt on the table and rooted through Margaret's supplies, sniffing and batting at the various items. Over time, familiars learn a thing or two about the magic our witches use, and I had seven generations of witches behind me. Not all the same type, of course. I had hedge witches, and coven leaders, and ladies who knew ancient secrets of the forests and could talk with the trees — and the things inside them.

My favourite witch had been Sayeeda, a young business woman with skin like ochre clay. Her magic was ages old, passed down from a time when rains cleared villages and the fires atop of mountains were warnings. I was with her for forty years, watched her raise a family, and saw them grown. Her death was natural; the reaper expected. I have no problem with death — those of us with many lives can't afford to be squeamish about it. But I have a problem with my charges being taken from me prematurely.

The circle was simple enough to make. A scratch to open the bag of ashes was nothing for my claws. The sigils were trickier though — the powder clogged my nose as I rubbed them into the carpet. Back on the table for an aerial view, it looked right. I jumped down and padded to Margaret's bedroom, slinking underneath her chest of drawers. I squeezed between the chest and the wall to the top drawer and pushed it out and then scattered its trinkets over the floor. She would have scolded me for the mess, but the coven could clear it up later.

I sniffed through the items and selected a silver brooch, an amber ring, and a gold chain. They were all genuine and worth a good amount, handed down to Margaret from family or grateful clients. She was a magpie with her precious things, hoarding them away in the drawer rather than wearing them as some did. These would do.

I ferried the items back into the living room and dropped them into the middle of the circle, and then checked it for gaps, smudging my paw prints to keep the integrity of the lines. It was as good as it could be. Back on the table, I sniffed at the blood to check for pureness and then pushed the bottle off the edge. The blood splashed over the circle and the jewellery lying within.

Flames leapt from the circle of ashes, the livid purple of old juniper berries. They flew around and around like a cat chasing its tail. The jewellery floated level with the table and then higher still, and a man popped into existence in the centre of the circle. He was tall, taller than Margaret had been, with long, black hair that reflected the flames, tousled and buffeted by the heat. He frowned in the dim light and waved his hand. The candles scattered about the room flamed brighter.

The man started when he spotted the body on the floor. "What in the earthen world?" He glanced about, finally settling on me. His lovely turquoise eyes narrowed to slits. "Great, I'm stuck with a cat and a crone that killed herself in a summoning. How long must I wait for the circle to break and I can leave?"

"Excuse me," I said, from the edge of the table top. "She was far too good a witch to die in a basic summoning, and you were easy to find. Just because you hide out of the way in uninhabited places doesn't make you special. Just try finding some of the elder things," I nodded toward Margaret, "she could have them dancing on a pin."

His dark red lips formed a wide *oh*. "You talk?" A blush crept over his tawny skin.

"No, I'm just a very good puppet. *Of course*, I talk, idiot. It can't be her speaking. Honestly, you can't tell her soul has gone?"

"Well yes, that's why I was confused. What are you?"

"I was her familiar; my calling for generations."

"You're a familiar?" His eyebrow hiked, and he studied me anew.

"You must have met a familiar before."

"Sure, but you're ... well ... you're ginger."

"And?" I asked, my tail flicking like a metronome.

"Aren't familiars usually black? Black cats, black dogs, bats?"

"Much as it may surprise you, fire man, we can be whatever colour we're born with. I happen to be ginger, and my witches have been fine with that. At least, none expressed a need to roll me in soot. You're the best form of vengeance the universe has to offer? For a djinn, you don't seem that smart."

"No need to be rude—whatever your name is—"

"Jasper."

"Okay, *Jasper*. Odd name for a cat that."

"I'm an odd cat. Can we get down to business?" I asked, closing my eyes against his glare.

"Business?"

"Yes, I summoned you for a reason."

"Wait, you summoned me?"

"Well, the corpse didn't do it."

"How did you cast a circle?"

"I'm resourceful. I want you to do something for me."

"Hold on, I don't bargain with cats."

"Well, you *are* standing in a summoning circle. My offering is fair — an even trade. What's the problem?"

"*You're a cat.* Perhaps a magical cat, but still a cat."

"And you're a jumped-up fire spirit, what's your point?"

"Frankly, I don't know if we can do this," he said, looking about the room again as if someone was listening in.

"Why not? The jewellery is mine to give; I inherit what was my witch's. Again, I've offered fair trade, and the circle is obviously adequate, since you're standing in it."

He paused seeming to consider my words, and then plucked up the jewellery that'd fallen to the floor and weighed it in his hand. "These are real."

"Of course, I'm not in the habit of summoning without proper payment. What do you take me for?"

"Honestly, ginger —"

"Jasper."

"Right. Honestly, Jasper I have no idea how to proceed."

"Simple. You've been paid, and now you do as I ask. If you keep dicking around, the corpse will start to smell. I can be very patient." The djinn looked at me, brows arched again, then glanced back to Margaret's body.

"The old lady meant that much to you?"

"She was my charge, yes. She cared for me and fed me, and they stole the time remaining to her."

"Okay. What is it you want?"

"I want you to track down the ones who did this and kill them."

"You're summoning a murder?"

"Think of it as a 'rebalancing.' This was not meant to happen—it wasn't Margaret's time. We're just putting the clock right."

"You're not intending to bring her back, are you? 'Cause that's off in the cards. We don't do that."

"I've been around long enough to know necromancy is never a good idea, fire man. What is *your* name, anyway?"

"I am Aziz, Jasper the cat. And if all we're talking about is balance, I can assist you."

"Good, I was beginning to think I'd have to send you away and call a demon instead."

"You know a demon would eat you, right?"

I looked at him for a silent moment, fighting the urge to roll my eyes. "I know it could try."

"You're confident for a cat."

"A familiar."

"A smart cat."

"A magical bloody being, you absolute oaf!" I hissed, hackles up, tail straight as a rod. "And one who could easily send you to the top of mount Snowdon."

"What's that?"

"It's a very cold mountain in Wales. Now, will you deal or not?"

"Yes, all right, let's get to it. I find your murderer, I kill him, you give me these items." He held the jewellery up; the gold glinted in the flames. The amber shone like trapped sunlight, bright enough to equal the life of the reprobate who killed my Margaret.

"And two books," he said, nodding to the shelf beside the dying hearth.

I considered his request. "Not her book of shadows or the older grimoires, but you can choose two of the others for your collection."

"Then we have a deal. Do you want me to report back once it's done?"

"Like hell, I'm going with you." I dropped from the table and opened the circle with a clean swipe of one paw. "If circumstances allow, I mean to scratch the killer's eyes out."

"You're crazy," he sighed, and then bent to pick me up. He was warm, like lying in the bank of a dying fire, and he smelled of crisp, clean air and peach blossoms. I nestled into the crook of his neck and purred.

"No crazier than a djinn who just dealt with a cat," I murmured, sinking my claws into his waistcoat for a good hold.

We appeared in the graveyard, amongst the old stones and wisps of old ghosts.

"Really?" I asked, disappointed by the worn cliché. I sniffed the air as we stood in the shade of the crypts.

"They're in the church," he said, scratching behind my ear.

"More than one?"

"Three of them. All young idiots playing with powers they don't understand."

"They understood enough to murder Margaret."

"That they did, ginger. That they did. Now do you want to claw their eyes out?"

"Let's see what they're like first," I said, still curled in the crook of his arm. I pressed against his chest and he headed for the church, silent as a cat on the frosted grass. With me in his arms, we passed through the locked door as easy as smoke.

The inside was dark, lit only by the stubs of candles. Left to burn too long, they hissed and spit in the gloom. In the shadows, we watched as three men milled about, spilling salt as they fashioned a crude circle on the floor of the cavernous room. Items were dotted around the circle's edge—a dead raven, rich, red wine, and incense far too strong to be any use.

"Do you know what they're doing?" Aziz asked in a low murmur.

I shook my head, eyes scanning their faces. I recognized the blond one; a man from the village who'd shadowed Margaret before, learning how to heal. From healing to this? My ears flattened against my skull and I glared at him. The other two were strangers. The fattest resembled the blond, maybe a brother or a cousin.

"The fair-haired one is local, I don't know about the others," I whispered to Aziz.

"I think they're making a summoning circle for a demon. Incorrectly, which is probably why you don't recognise it. They needed hags blood for the ritual. Your lady wasn't a hag though, she was a crone. They're not smart enough to realise that."

"This could be entertaining," I said, watching them scurry around. "Why are they summoning a demon?"

"The usual reasons: money, power, wealth. All irritating and predictable. Humans are so fixated on the material. None of it matters, in the end they return to the stars only to be shoved back into the flesh."

"That's a miserable way to look at reincarnation, fire man."

"Without memories, it's a waste." He shrugged, pushing me into the crook of his neck as he did so.

"My tin opener could recall previous cycles. She knew what she had been and what she was seeking to be. She would have kept working at it too."

"Tin opener?" he asked, leaning his head back so he could look at my eyes.

"My name for her. It's a great honour to be the giver of food. I could hunt on my own, but I trusted her to feed me."

"So, allowing her to serve you food was your way of honouring her?"

"Yes, precisely," I said, pleased he could grasp the basics. He shrugged again, brows high, but asked no further questions.

"How do you want to do this?" He nodded back to the men. They were ready to start their bastardised ritual now. One person stood at each point of a large triangle they'd drawn within the circle, the variety of odd items within hands' reach. Horrendous amateurs, they were all standing inside their own circle!

"Isn't it about time for you to show up?" I asked, looking at the smaller, central circle. It was no good, it couldn't possibly hold, but they didn't know that.

"Playing with your food, *billi*?"

"Mice have more sense."

"As you wish." He set me down and I stalked closer, slinking just beyond the candle light.

"We summon thee, old unclean one," called one man, an olive-skinned squirt with a tattoo of an ankh—unearned I was sure—on the side of his neck. "We offer death and vice, blood and wickedness to guide your way." The bird was thrown into the circle, the wine poured over it. A cup of blood went in next followed by a stained knife that I knew belonged to the blond one. It was Margaret's blood. I felt a growl curl low in my chest and bit it back, flattening myself as low as I could so I wouldn't bolt forward.

"We call upon you now at this darkest hour. Heed our call and appear," the blond beckoned, raising his hands above his head. I quietly considered praying for lightning to strike them but was cheered when a bloom of turquoise flame shot up from the inner circle, flooding the chamber with light.

"Who seeks to disturb my eternal contemplation?" boomed Aziz, his skin now dark as ink and his eyes glowing from the fire that shrouded him.

"Y-you're Thobarabau?" the fat one warbled, flinching.

"Shut up, Findlay," hissed the blond.

"Fuck you, Arthur, he's huge," Findlay shot back.

"Yes, I am," Aziz said, peering above them, "Am I not what you expected?"

"You're dark skinned. I thought demons were pale," said the tattooed idiot.

"Don't be racist to the fucking demon, Jamie," The blond, Arthur, sighed, his hands going to his temples. Well at least he knew he was a disaster.

"If you looked in the grimoire for my name, you will see my association with Mesopotamia. You call it Syria now, but we don't care for such paltry labels. Why did you summon me?" Aziz continued, nostrils flaring as thin trails of smoke emerged.

"We want to bargain," said Arthur, grasping control from the jaws of inadequacy.

"What do you offer?"

"Murder, sacrifice, lives for your cause," said Jamie, surging forward to the edge of the circle. "We will shed blood in your name."

"And what do you seek?" Aziz voice reverberated throughout the church, the promise of condemnation and judgement lurking in his words.

"Power. Influence over those around us to bend them to our will," Arthur said, the scratch of desire threaded through his voice. I wondered who he had in mind for that desire and worried for the women of the village.

"Power is a two-pointed tool; it pierces those who wield it. Are you sure this is what you want?" Aziz asked, his hair rising behind him in an intricate braid that twisted and brushed like my tail when I'm agitated.

"Yes, we are willing to pay the price," Jamie assured him, looking at the other two. Findlay looked fit to run for it, but Arthur stood his ground, rod straight.

"As you wish. Jamie," Aziz nodded at the tattooed one, "take up the knife from under my feet and stab fatty there through the throat." Aziz' tone was casual, his illusion wavered as he floated above the circle.

"What?" squeaked Findlay.

"No, we've offered you blood already, hag's blood to desecrate the holy ground," Arthur said, eyes wide.

"I'm sure that would have impressed Thobarabau, but you spelled his name wrong and your circle is flawed," Aziz said, shrugging as he dropped gently to the floor. He stepped aside to allow Jamie to scoop up the knife.

"Who are you?" Arthur asked.

"I'm someone who's not so dumb as to give my name to a summoned spirit," Aziz laughed, flashing teeth sharp enough to match mine.

"I banish thee," Arthur spat, slipping a vial from his pocket and flinging it at Aziz's torso. It burst, spilling over his clothes and evaporating into a puff of steam.

"Was that meant to do something?" Aziz asked, taking a step closer to the man. He loomed over him.

"But that was holy water, why are you still here?"

"You really should have done your research, Arthur. Stabbing the witch was a big mistake." Aziz sighed, letting fire spill from his eyes and down over his arms as he leaned closer. "I'm a fire creature, not a demon. All holy water does is provide me a good steam cleaning." He enfolded Arthur in a fiery hug. The flames surged upward enveloping them both in a cocoon of peacock heat. Arthur fought to pull away, but Aziz lifted him off the floor; the man's harmless kicks to Aziz' legs cast blue sparks around them.

A dreadful, squealing shriek rent the air, and I tore my eyes from the flaming pillar that was Aziz and Arthur. Jamie had fat Findlay pinned against one wall and was stabbing him in the chest and throat. I stood to get a better view just as Jamie delivered the fatal stab through Findlay's thigh.

"Good work, Jamie. Now come here and stab yourself in the chest," Aziz called, still holding onto the twitching form of what was once Arthur. There was no odour of burning flesh, only the metallic smell of Findlay's blood pooling on the church floor beneath his dangling feet, for which I was grateful. I could live the rest of my lives ignorant of the smell of burning humans.

Jamie did as bid. He walked to the centre of the circle and buried the blade deep under his diaphragm and then fell to the floor. Aziz dropped the smouldering remains of Arthur next to the bloody mess that was Jamie and cast flames over their bodies.

"Tidying up?" I asked, emerging from the shadows to sit beside him.

"They're not worth funeral rights."

"A touch brutal for your kind, no?"

"We only honour those who deserve it. These were nothing more than greedy, undeserving degenerates and murderers."

"You seem a bit hostile toward them."

"Says the cat that bartered for their deaths?" He raised an eyebrow at me and I rubbed against his legs, hinting to be picked up. He did, plonking me against his chest where I purred, contented.

"I'm just saying your methods were irregular."

"They deserved a lot worse. Your lady trusted the blond and he turned on her. I don't hold patience for those who act without honour. I may trick the unwary, but I do not lie or exploit. All the worlds could do with less treachery."

"Amen to that," I murmured and nuzzled his neck.

"Let's return to your cottage and finish our transaction."

—◻—

Peaks of light crept through the windows of the cottage, tinting the walls pink and orange. Aziz stood at the bookshelf, perusing the titles.

"You must have many of those already," I said. "Your lot saved most of the Library of Alexandria, after all." I sat beside Margaret's body watching him.

"We did, but modern knowledge is more interesting." He pulled a copy of Computers for Dummies and a volume of Oscar Wilde's collective works from the shelves. "These will do."

"Whatever you like," I said, watching him tuck the books into a pocket of his bag.

"It's been an experience doing business with you, Jasper of many witches. I hope when we meet again it's under better circumstances. I am pleased your charge made her way over peacefully."

I nodded and flicked my tail. "Enjoy your reading."

He smiled and was gone in a blink, only a faint curl of blue smoke lingered. I stood, stretched, and padding to Margaret's summoning mirror.

"Show me Angela," I commanded, and its surface rippled like water. Angela's image displayed bleary-eyed in the early morning light.

"Jasper, is that you?" she asked, squinting down at me.

"Afraid so, Angela. You need to come; Margaret's been killed. The reaper has arrived and gone, but there's still the burial rites."

"Oh goddess—on my way," she said, her image fading to black. A good head witch, she'd be here in ten minutes.

I made my way into the kitchen. On the washing board sat an old-fashioned tin opener, its handles spread wide. I hopped up on the counter and, taking it in my mouth, returned to Margaret, placing it on her chest. Then I curled beside her, purring in the glow of morning, and waited for Angela.

I would make sure they buried her with it.

Charlotte Platt

Charlotte Platt started life in Lancashire, grew up in the Orkney Islands and now lives in Caithness, Scotland. When she's not writing, she enjoys walking in the forest and near rivers, dark comedy and pugs.

Her recent work, "Meet the Family," published in *EconoClash Review: Quality Cheap Thrills #1*, and her story, "Black Building Session," featured in *Twilight Madhouse Vol 3*, are available on Amazon. Charlotte placed second in the British Fantasy Society's 2017 Short Story Competition and was short listed in the 2017 Write to End Violence Against Women Awards. She prefers writing horror and urban fantasy but will generally run with any good idea.

Twitter: @Chazzaroo
Amazon: *EconoClash Review #One*
On Goodreads, search: Charlotte Platt

CATS ARE PATIENT

Commander Hegel's whiskers twitched. So did his white-tipped tail.

"Pffft. We are talking about six thousand years of work, Cleo. Six thousand years! The most protracted invasion in the history of the galaxy, all about to be negated, flushed away, because somehow, you permitted a human in your sector to catch on. Inexcusable. Totally inexcusable!"

The spaceship's carpet-lined control center, deserted but for the two of them, seemed claustrophobic all the same to Cleopatra, who was accustomed to open spaces. Her long, calico fur stood slightly on end reflecting her discomfort.

"I didn't 'permit' him," she answered defensively. "There was nothing I could do. He's a sensitive."

"Mmm. You mean he's psychic?"

"No. Allergic. Can't get within ten feet of one of us without sneezing."

"Hmpf." Hegel, whose black and white coat bore a remarkable resemblance to a human military uniform, flexed his claws in frustration. "I fffail to ssee," he said, stretching, "what allergies have to do with it, other than perhaps generating a predisposition to distrust us. This human.... What did you say his name was?"

"Hayden. Michael Hayden."

"One way or another, he *must* be dealt with. And it's your responsibility, Cleo. We've worked far too long and hard to let one over-smart human fffoul things up for us now. Ailurian High Command would have my head and yours if the operation had to be scrapped this late in the game. I'm depending on you to handle the problem. How you do it is none of my concern so long as it's done. Understood?"

Cleo wasn't at all sure she understood. In the long history of the Ailurian invasion, they had never once, to her knowledge, been forced to dispose of a human being.

"You mean," she said hesitantly, "that I ... well that is ... are you saying we'll have to ... er ... eliminate him?"

"I sssuppose that would effectively shut him up, now wouldn't it?"

"But.... How can I eliminate one human without arousing the suspicions of the rest?"

"That," Hegel sniffed, "is your problem."

"But—"

"Your territory; your problem. Do whatever you have to but sssee to it he shuts up! Now get out of here. I'll expect a fffull report within three days."

"But—"

"Thhhree days, Cleo. Now get lost, will you? It's time for my afternoon nap."

"Yes, sir."

Three days! Not much time to accomplish what no cat in invasion history had ever done before.

Cleo teleported home to bask on a garden bench in the afternoon sunlight of her human host's back yard and contemplate how to deal with the dilemma. She dozed as the sun moved several degrees west and bees buzzed in the potted hyacinths and honeysuckle nearby. The sounds of claws on the wooden fence and a collar bell tinkling roused her. She opened her eyes to find Vladimir, the spotted, orange tabby from next door, gazing down at her.

"Problems, Cleopatra?"

Cleo yawned, stretched, and sat up before replying. "Yes. How did you know?"

He cocked his head to one side, regarding her with yellow-gold eyes. "When you're upset, you flip the tip of your tail, even when you're sleeping. Did you know that?"

She hadn't known it, but Cleo was loath to admit it, so she demurred by paying him a compliment. "You're very observant.

Ever hear of a human named Michael Hayden?"

"Mmmmmm, can't say as I have." Vlad extended his left front leg to give his paw a thorough tongue washing. "Why?" he asked when he'd lowered his foot again. "What's he done?"

"Not much. Just figured out that we're conquering the planet, that's all."

Vlad interrupted his ablutions on the right front foot to blink at her in disbelief. "What?"

"It was really Chandra's doing," Cleo growled. "She's the reason he first got suspicious!"

"Chandra. You mean the little black short-hair with the human who owns the Dreamquest Book Store? That Chandra?"

"That's the one. Pffft. The little idiot. She knew very well he was one of the sensitives, allergic to us all, but she got some sort of perverse kick out of deliberately following him around when he came into the store, rubbing his legs, and trying to crawl in his lap. No wonder he grew suspicious!"

Vlad hissed. "Ssssso, if it's true, and he's caught on to the invasion.... This is unprecedented! The first time in six thousand years a human has discerned the truth about us. Commander Hegel must be livid."

"He is. And it's happened in my sector, so I have to ... well...." She still had trouble saying it, but Vlad clearly understood all the same.

"Eliminate the human?" His eyes narrowed to slits, contemplating that also-unprecedented action. "Really? Hegel ordered that? He can't be sssssserious!"

"Oh, he is. I have no idea how to do this, Vlad. The whole mess is just horrible!"

"But then again, it's not as though we've *never* been found out, is it? Just the first time a human has done it. Terran dogs have known about us for centuries."

"Yessss, but they're far too stupid to communicate the information to their masters."

"Fortunately for us," Vlad said. "Not that humans are all that terribly bright on the whole, either. All you usually have to do to win one over is purr and rub your head on its hand, then maybe give it a few fawning licks and mrrrrow — it's all yours."

"Maybe so, but you shouldn't underestimate a human either. Now and then they demonstrate surprising insight. Take Mike Hayden, for example...."

"Hmmm. You're sure he knows?"

"I'm sure. He visited my humans last week. I heard him say it. 'I'm telling you, they're aliens,' he said. 'Furry little aliens plotting to take over the entire planet. And they're succeeding! Look at them. They're everywhere. They own the Internet. They're printed on bed sheets and pillow cases, cookie jars, calendars, posters, wall clocks, pot holders — you name it, there's a cat on it. Did you know the only three books by the same author ever to make the New York Times best-seller list at the same time were three *Garfield* comic collections? Every year some loaded dowager leaves her entire fortune to a cat. And did you know that Morris and Grumpy Cat each make three — count 'em — three million bucks a year? They're winning. They're taking over the whole darn world and we don't even realize it. We're not doing one thing about it!' He knows, Vlad. He knows!"

"Hmmm," Vlad said again. "Ssssticky sssituation for us, then. How do we ... er ... how do you...?" Apparently, he couldn't say it either.

"I don't know," Cleo said. "But I have to find a way."

Sensitives had always given the Ailurians problems. But somehow Cleo expected that any real trouble would come from the human ailurokedics and phobics, many of whom had attained substantial prominence over the planet's long history. It was said that an aide was once summoned to the Emperor Napoleon's bed chamber to discover the great conqueror of Europe cringing in terror before a tiny, mewling kitten. Ailurophobia. Johannes Brahms, on the other hand, had supposedly kept a hunting bow near his bedroom window, and shot any cats that had the misfortune to wander into his garden. Ailurokedos.

These, though, were exceptions to the rule. Mike Hayden was something else entirely.

Vlad paced on the other end of Cleo's bench. "Do you think your humans believed him?" he asked.

"They didn't. But then, they're already cat converts. If Hayden's theory were to reach the ears of the world's cat-haters, it could mean trouble. Big trouble. Six thousand years of subtle, methodical planning down the drain."

"Hm. Possssssibly. But the truth wouldn't be easy for him to prove."

"I know. But Commander Hegel thinks we simply can't afford the risk. Mike Hayden must be dealt with. My problem is how."

Vlad stopped pacing and sat down again. "All right. Let's consider methods, sssshall we? Sssssome are obvious. There's running under foot to trip him on his way through a plate glass door; surrounding him with so many shedding long-haired cats that he sssneezes himself to death; or, maybe just sneaking in to sleep on his face one night."

Cleo found none of those means particularly appealing and said so.

"Okay. We could always ask for Ailurian volunteers to wait by a roadside and rush in front of his car until one results in a fatal accident."

Cleo cringed. "No. Aside from the danger that would pose to the feline volunteers, the glaring flaw in that plan is that Mike Hayden, unlike the majority of California's humans, doesn't own a car."

"Oh. What else is there?" Vlad scratched his neck with a rear leg, making the bell on his green collar jingle again. "Blowing out a pilot light and turning on the gas in his kitchen?"

"Nope. He lives in an apartment with two roommates. I suppose it's possible, under the circumstances, that Hegel would consider them expendable, but somehow I doubt it."

"How about luring him into what the humans call a *ménage à trois*, and then arrange to have him done in by a jealous lover?"

"Nah. Too complicated."

"You could ask the High Command to provide you with a virus sample or two that are guaranteed fatal to humans."

"Might have possibilities. But.... Vlad, this isn't going to be easy!"

"And I can't ssssay I envy you the task." Vlad stood on all fours once more, his ears perking up. "But I'll leave you to your ruminations. I hear my human opening a fresh can of tuna. Time for lunch!"

He leapt from the bench and was over the fence before Cleo could reply. Not that she'd expected much help from him, anyway. No, she'd just have to consider her options a while longer.

Often, the obvious occurs to you only after you've pondered the unobvious for uncountable hours. With the sunlight gone, Cleo prowled and mulled over the possibilities until dawn. Then, exhausted, she entered the house through the cat door and napped for a few hours on the foot of her humans' bed. After breakfast she thought some more as she perched on the back of the sofa and surveyed the traffic going by on the street. It was raining, and a lousy day outside for cat or human.

She was administering her noontime tongue bath when the solution occurred to her. Hegel, she hoped, would approve. It was the perfect way to silence Mike Hayden.

The hardest part, of course, was catching him alone. The guy was almost always with somebody, except on rare occasions at home when both his roommates were out. Then there was the problem of getting into the place. There, Cleo let the rain be her ally. Under the umbrella of a protective shrub, she watched the apartment and was encouraged when one of the roommates came down the stairs, tramped through rain puddles to the carport and drove away. One down. Carefully, she crept up to the landing and hid in the shadow of an oversized flower pot containing a long-dead geranium. Eventually, the door opened again. She was in luck—the departing human was the second roommate. Poised, she waited until he turned his back to her and fumbled with his black umbrella. It was all the time she needed to slip behind him through the still-open door.

You could tell, she noted as the door clicked shut and the roommate's footsteps clattered down the concrete stairs, that three bachelors lived here. The place was a mess. Hayden was nowhere in evidence. But she'd seen him arrive that afternoon and was certain he hadn't gone out again. So now he was home.

Noiseless, she padded down the carpeted hall, pleased to see light flowing from a room at the end of the hallway. The door stood ajar. Perfect.

She looked inside to see Hayden lying supine on the bed, immersed in an *X-Men* comic book. Perfect again. She could walk in completely unnoticed.

After twenty seconds of silence, a comic book page turned.

"Hello, Michael Hayden."

X-Men flew three feet in the air and fluttered to the floor. "Huh?" Startled, Hayden sat up, searching the room for a human that wasn't there.

Cleo jumped onto the desk, sauntering over a *Dungeons & Dragons* chart to an open laptop. The computer's screen flashed from sleep mode and began bleeping at her in electronic outrage. Error messages with exclamation points in yellow triangles popped up in little white boxes across the awakened screen.

Meanwhile, Hayden was bellowing at the top of his lungs. "All right, who let this stupid cat in here?!"

"I did," said Cleo.

When he could close his mouth, the human stared at her in shock. "I knew I was over my limit with three beers," he muttered.

"What's the matter, Hayden? Surprised?"

"Are you for real? Geez, this has got to be a dream. I'm asleep, right? And this is a dream?" He began pinching the furless flesh of one arm repeatedly; an action entirely lost on Cleo, but then, humans had a number of unfathomable eccentricities.

In the interest of expediting things, Cleo sat down on the

dungeon-in-progress, lifted a back foot and furiously scratched her flank, sending a healthy supply of dislodged fur flying out into the room. Right on cue, Hayden sneezed.

"I'm not dreaming," he concluded brilliantly.

"Sssso far, so good. Now, how much of the rest have you guessed?"

"Rest? What rest? I don't believe this. I'm talking to a cat. A cat, for God's sake!"

"Oh, can it Hayden. Let's not play dumb, hmmm? You told my humans we were taking over the Earth, remember? I was there. I heard you."

Hayden inched backward on the unmade bed. "But ... but that was a joke," he stammered. "I didn't mean it. Honest! It was a joke!"

"Mmmm. Not sssuch a funny joke, all told, since it's true."

Hayden sneezed again, straining to focus on her through allergy-teared eyes. "I don' belieb dis," he mumbled, sniffling. "Id' ... id's imbossible. Id can' be habbening...."

"Oh, it's 'habbening' all right. I wish it weren't. You and your theories are jeopardizing sixty centuries of effort. Over those generations, humans have taken us into their hearts and homes — some have even worshipped us — and not once did they ever suspect a thing. Until you came along. All of a ssudden, Hayden, you've become an exceedingly bad risk."

From some place or other, the human produced a rumpled white handkerchief and honked into it noisily. "You can't be serious," he said, with a somewhat more intelligible speech pattern. "Cats taking over the world? I mean I said it, but I never believed it. You couldn't. You'd never get away with it!"

Cleo winced at the cliché. Humans were so incredibly unoriginal. "In point of fact," she told him, "we're about to begin the final phase of the operation. It should only take another thousand years or so."

Dumbly, the human echoed her words. "A thousand years...."

"That's right. Cats are patient. Very patient."

All the way back against the wall now, he was trying to say something else but sneezed again instead.

"I'm sure you can ssee," Cleo went on, "why we can't have you running around loose, jeopardizing everything we've worked for. You see that, don't you?"

"No!" Hayden managed to say between sneezes.

Cleo noted he'd bunched a large part of the bed covers into one hand. In a moment the blanket came sailing across the room at her. She dodged the fuzzy missile with ease though it sent the dungeon map and several D&D figures flying when it hit the desk. The diversion was sufficient to allow Mike Hayden to escape the room.

Unconcerned, (cats, after all, are never overtly concerned with the actions of human beings) she followed his hurried footsteps into the hall, back across the cluttered living room, and out the front door, which he'd left standing open.

Taking refuge once again behind the flower pot, Cleo watched Hayden head rapidly down the stairs. He nearly bowled over the first of his returning roommates halfway down.

"Scott!" he yelled and grabbed the other human so hard that they both nearly fell. "There's a cat! In the apartment! It ... it.... I swear to God, Scott, it *talked* to me! It said —"

"Calm down, will ya?" Scott took Hayden by the arm, and, with the second roommate, Dan, close behind, led him back up the stairs and through the apartment door. "We'll find it and chase it out, dose you with some of your antihistamines, and you'll be fine."

Cleo peeked around the flower pot and through the open door to see Scott sitting a protesting Hayden down on the sofa while Dan searched room-to-room for a cat he wouldn't find.

"I'm telling you, it *talked* to me, damn it!" a near-hysterical Hayden insisted. "It told me I was right about cats being aliens and taking over the planet and ... and ... oh, God, we've gotta call someone, the FBI, the CIA, *someone!*"

"Holy crap, he's high!" Dan had returned from his fruitless cat hunt. "Can antihistamines cause hallucinations?"

"No! It's true!" Hayden's voice cracked, becoming a near-sob. "We've gotta warn the government! For God's sake, guys, help me!"

"Okay, okay, just relax." Scott fished his cell phone from a jacket pocket. "I'm calling, okay? I'm calling."

Dan shot Scott a knowing look. "Nine-one-one?" he mouthed.

Scott nodded.

—▢—

"Sssso, the Hayden matter is finally dealt with?" Tail high and paws extended, Commander Hegel stretched out on the flight couch, kneading the cushions with his finely-honed claws. "Good." Stretch concluded, he resumed a seated command position and turned expectant green eyes on Cleo. "He's dead, then?"

"Not at all." Cleo failed to prevent her fur from bristling just a bit. "Not necessary. I simply told him the truth and let things progress naturally from there."

"Pffffft!" Hegel hissed his stunned disapproval. "The truth? You told him the *truth?*"

"I did." Cleo preened a little; couldn't help it. "And I've discovered another truth. Humans are psychologically incapable of handling the truth about us." She paused to flex her own claws in the short-napped flight deck carpet. "At the urging of his friends and his physician, Michael Hayden self-committed himself to a two-week stint at a mental health clinic. He's out now, on anti-psychotic meds, and is fully convinced that his entire encounter and conversation with me was a hallucination."

"Mrrrrr." Hegel's half-purr, half-growl sounded less than convinced. "You're certain of that?"

"Mmmmmmm, yes," Cleo purred in her own rite. "But I've put certain safeguards in place, just in case."

"Sssssee that you do. I'll expect periodic reports."

"Yes, sir."

The abrupt arrival of Hegel's seal point Siamese first officer through the bridge's oval cat flap signaled the end of their briefing session. Hegel turned to him at once and began talking about some technicality of the ship's geosynchronous orbit. Apparently dismissed, Cleo took her leave through the same hatch, reflecting as she navigated the corridors back to the teleport chamber, that she really deserved more credit than this for her brilliant resolution to the Hayden problem. The commander hadn't even asked about her safeguards. She'd implemented them just this morning, and they were, of course, brilliant too.

Planetside again, she set out to make sure the plan was working. She stationed herself on a short block wall outside Hayden's apartment and indulged in another tongue bath while she waited.

Hayden should be biking his way home from work (that was Xena's post) and arriving any minute now. Along his route, Chester and Katrina would watch him. When he went to Dreamhaven Books again, Chandra pulled duty. (Call it penance.) Vlad, Pumpkin, Albert, Sasha, Vicky, and a dozen others rounded out the tag team for every possible location this human might visit.

Bath complete, Cleo studied the clouds for a while, deciding that they probably wouldn't drop any more rain. She heard Mike Hayden's bicycle coming before he rounded the corner, but she stayed put as he approached, prepared to remain in full view as she studied him.

He noticed her only after he'd parked the bike, chained it, and taken off his helmet and rain poncho.

Double take.

She met his gaze with wide gold eyes, said nothing, waited, and was rewarded as he glanced nervously in every direction, looking for more of those feline eyes that he'd glimpsed peering at him from behind the trees and planters along his route home.

Excellent. He'd spotted them. And for the rest of his natural life, he'd continue to see them, vigilantly watching his every move.

Safeguard successfully established.

They locked gazes one last time before Cleo jumped to the ground and primly trotted away. She heard Hayden clatter up the stairs, enter the apartment, and slam the door. He'd never know for sure if the Watchers were real or illusory. But if ever he tried to expose the Ailurian invasion again, Cleo's team and their descendants after them would make certain that his sanity would be once more called into question. No one would believe him.

A brilliant solution, Cleo thought, and one that should keep the humans convinced that they still ran the planet, if only for that one last crucial millennium. After that ... well ... after that, they would all know.

The feline overlords, meanwhile, would wait as they'd been waiting for over six thousand years.

Cats are patient.

Jean Graham

Jean Graham's short stories have appeared in over seventeen anthologies and magazines, including *Memento Mori*, *Misunderstood*, *Dying to Live*, and *Time of the Vampires*. She is a frequent convention speaker and am a member of both Science Fiction Writers of America and Horror Writers of America. Jean lives in San Diego, CA with 5000 books, six cats, innumerable dust bunnies, and one husband!

Website: http://jeangraham.20m.com/
Facebook: @JeanGrahamShortStories
On Amazon, search: Jean Graham

MANDY BURKHEAD

LONGING

The cat sits before the window
staring longingly at the yard outside.
It watches the birds flitter from branch to branch,
the squirrels chasing each other around and around tree trunks.
It sees the people pass by on the sidewalk
and lifts its rump in expectation of a good scratching.
It blinks at the bright sunlight streaming through the clouds
and jumps nervously at a car zooming by on the street.
With a sigh, it leaps from its perch on the window
and makes its way to a box full of sand
on the bathroom floor,
the only real dirt its feet will ever sink into,
and it cries to itself because
all it ever wanted was to shit outside.

ABOUT MANDY BURKHEAD

Mandy Burkhead, author/poet is also a freelance copyeditor for her publishing company, Burkshelf Press. She and her husband, D.G. Burkhead, co-authored and published their first full-length fantasy novel, *The Black Lily*, in August 2017. The couple now lives in Nashville with their cat, Luna, and their dog, Zoe.

Mandy earned her Bachelor of Arts in English from Lindenwood University, St. Charles, Missouri, and her Master of Library and Information Science from Valdosta State University, Atlanta, Georgia.

When not working, Mandy enjoys reading, video games, cosplay, attending sci-fi and fantasy conventions, and just generally *nerding* out.

Website: www.burkshelf.com
Facebook: @burkshelf
Twitter: @burkshelf
For Amazon and Goodreads, search: Mandy Burkhead
The Black Lily is available on Amazon, Smashwords, Barnes & Noble, and iBooks.

EDITOR'S NOTE

I hope you enjoyed *From a Cat's View*; thank you for reading. Please consider leaving a review on Amazon and support our talented contributing authors by sharing which stories are your favorites.

If you'd like to be notified when the second volume of *From a Cat's View* is published, please subscribe for updates at Post-To-Print.com and follow our Facebook page, @FromACatsView.

—Robin Praytor

Printed in Poland
by Amazon Fulfillment
Poland Sp. z o.o., Wrocław